Tremor in the Hills

CRISTINA MATTA

Publishing Assistance Provided by:

Michelle Morrow www.chellreads.com

I dedicate this book to the inspirations for
Tamara:
Celeste, Claire and Tamoshka Garcia Garrido.

And to everyone who has suffered through an earthquake.

Contents

TREMOR IN THE HILLS

Chapter 1

Drip. Drip. Drip.

Water dripped from the kitchen faucet. Dust lingered in the air. The bleeding man on the floor reached his hand out. His finger, shaking weakly, scratched into the pool of his blood. A gurgling sound came from his throat, and the finger went limp. The dripping continued.

A mile away at the same time, I stood sulking. I didn't want to be back in Peru. I had no idea what disaster was coming for me. I was still living the previous one.

I hated my life.

""Tamara," K'antu screeched my name. "Tamara!"

Her voice brought me out of my trance. I was standing on the lawn of my aunt's house in Manchay, Perú, gripping the grass with my bare toes as if that would secure me to the ground. My friend gave me a glass of pineapple juice. The nightmares came even when I was awake. K'antu understood.

Walking from under the canopy, I flung the pineapple juice at one of the bushes by the swimming pool. K'antu's hand touched my shoulder. I shrank back, a surge of fear coursing through my veins. Since the earthquake, I could not stand the touch of other human beings back home in the U.S. I would lie on the floor for hours next to my old black Labrador Retriever and feel her body as she breathed. I hadn't let my mom hug me since last year. K'antu's hand was bony. It was the same hand that had reached out a year ago to save me from a falling wall, only more skeletal. She had lost a lot of weight since last summer. And I had gone a little crazier.

"Come on, Tamara," she said, dropping her hand. "I know it is hard being back here. I don't want to be here either, and I live here. But nothing bad is going to happen this year."

I turned away.

K'antu said, "Hey, let's go out on the dune buggies tomorrow. Want to? Or we could take out the weapons and get you back in shape."

K'antu was a trained warrior in the art of Incan weaponry. The knowledge had been passed down through her father and so on back to their pre-Spanish ancestors. Not only skills, but an impressive collection of weapons: *Macanas, ayllos, huaracas,* a beautiful copper helmet, and K'antu's favorite, a knife known as *Tumi,* the shaft of which was carved to look like a warrior, and the blade a sharp half-moon.

I looked past her at the party. It was late afternoon and getting dark. The scent of Perú, freshly cut wood mixed with sand, dust, and a little salt air from the ocean wafted over us. Afro-Peruvian music thumped rhythmically from the DJ's station in a far corner. I wanted to feel like I had before the earthquake. I wanted to dance and laugh and stuff myself with food. Instead, it all made me want to claw at my eyes and ears. Every detail was a memory that sucked me back to the events of last year when, in August, an earthquake of 8.1 magnitude had torn the town apart. I had almost died. Many people had. Those dead people were the zombie-like creatures of my worst nightmares.

K'antu was trying to distract me. As her friend, I should have reciprocated and talked to her, but I could not focus on her right now. Goosebumps appeared on my arms, and I shivered.

"You can't be sure it won't happen again. Hasn't it been happening all year?"

Yes, but..." K'antu began coughing.

I looked at her, again. There was something wrong with her. She had lost a lot of weight and looked ill. I had not noticed it at first, when I had arrived two days ago. I was wrapped up in my own stuff. She was going through something awful right now. *Why couldn't I ask her about it?* I knew why. I was afraid her problems would remind me of the earthquake. And I couldn't bring myself to say anything, even to help her. No matter how small or insignificant, every mention of it felt like it was all happening again.

"The aftershocks? Well, yeah..." K'antu pursed her lips. "But they are getting more infrequent now, and they were never as strong as the first one. I am sure nothing bad will happen while you are here. And... well, if there is another earthquake, Laura's house is different from your Aunt Ada's. It won't come crashing down on you as Ada's house did."

"Please, K'antu." I covered my ears and bent over. I could

almost feel the ground rumbling, getting ready to explode. My stomach hurt.

I come to Perú to visit family every summer. My mom and dad used to come with me, but they own a dance studio in Chicago, and for the last few years, they have been too busy. So, they stick me on a plane and send me here. I used to be okay with coming, but this year I fought them. Hard. I lost.

"Tamara, what happened last year? It can't possibly happen again."

"I don't want to talk about it." Tears rolled down my cheeks. And then I talked about it anyway. "If I hadn't been in the living room –"

"But you were. And you survived."

For the people of Manchay, it was survival. Anything more was extra.

"You don't get it, K'antu. I have nightmares. Constantly. And nobody gets it. No one understands."

What a bitch I am. I had gone back to earthquake-free Chicago. *Why was I complaining?*

Like a true friend, K'antu didn't point that out, "Your aunt Laura understands. She is letting you stay here the whole time instead of you going to spend half the time with Ada, right?"

Have you ever heard anyone say "pshaw"? I had only seen it in books. Until I heard it come out of my mouth. "As if I could stay with Ada anymore. She doesn't have a house."

The houses in the lower-income areas of Manchay were all slapped up with adobe bricks. No building code regulations existed, so whenever a family felt like it or had a little money, they would stick a second or third floor above the already creaky original one. In a strong natural disaster, these turn into asthma-inducing rubble.

My voice cracked. I stopped and began the breathing techniques one of my therapists had given me to recover from my nightmares. When I felt I could talk again, I hissed, "And this party – it makes it worse."

"How?" K'antu looked surprised.

"Look at the cake," I told her. It was a three-tier, red, black, and white Alice-in-Wonderland-looking confection, probably costing a hundred dollars. "Ada couldn't buy one of those before her house crumbled, and much less now. Why spend that kind of money?"

K'antu's face looked more haggard than it had a moment ago. Instantly I regretted pointing out the economic difference between my two aunts. My friend was probably poorer than my aunt Ada. I stared at her for a minute.

"I am sorry, K'antu." I stammered.

She smiled at me, quick to forgive. "You are right, Tamara. It's not fair. But speaking of cake, it's here, and it needs to be eaten. Let's go get a piece?"

"I don't want to go over there."

"Come on…"

"No. I don't want cake, and I don't want to talk to anyone. Except you."

K'antu frowned, finally getting impatient with me. "Tamara, I get that you're nervous, but another earthquake is not what the people here are worried about now, and you shouldn't be either."

"None of us are safe if another one hits," I said, ignoring her.

"Even here – that earthquake probably loosened the foundation of this house."

"Oh Tamara," K'antu laughed, "That's ridiculous. Hey, come on, for now, forget about it. Let's have some fun, courtesy of the people who make all the money."

I narrowed my eyes. She sounded like my aunt Laura. If I lived here, I would be in constant fear –like I was now. I was sure I would have a heart attack every time a truck so much as honked or the wind blew sideways. I was walking away from her when I heard someone call my name

"Tamara, there you are. I have been looking for you. You remember Rodolfo Alvarez, don't you?"

It was my Aunt Laura, hand in hand with two men, dragging them both behind her. As she got closer, she let go and kissed me on the cheek. She waved a hand at the man standing to her left, Rodolfo. He was a tall and stocky man with dark hair streaked with grey. His face was not traditionally handsome, but he had an air of confidence tinged with the arrogance which made men seem attractive. His family owned the second most successful vineyard in town. My mother's family owned the first, run by Laura. Even though Rodolfo and my aunt were in direct competition, they were also good friends. I remembered being afraid of him when I was a child, but I could never pin down exactly why.

He smiled at me and ignored K'antu.

It wasn't entirely his fault. My aunt had not bothered to point her out. K'antu was only my aunt's maid, after all. Manchay still worked under a strict but unacknowledged class system.

"And this is Tomás Romero. I don't believe you have ever met him. He is our esteemed magistrate here in Manchay," Laura continued, pointing at the short man with heavily lidded eyes and a politician's smile.

He was standing on the other side of Rodolfo. I had not met him, but I had heard a few things about him from my cousin Elías. For instance, after the earthquake, while people struggled to rebuild, his house had been rebuilt larger and more luxurious than before.

I stared at the man.

My cousin was bitter about the situation he was in, and I didn't blame him. But my cousin worried me. I had been in contact with him every week since I had gone back to Chicago. In the weeks before I came back, he told me he was involved in organizing a group fighting for better solutions to the devastation caused by the earthquake. He didn't say what they were planning.

Both men kissed me on the cheek.

"How beautiful you have become, Tamara," Rodolfo said, seeing a girl with an unruly crop of curly hair the color of horse chestnuts and hazel eyes with long, curly black eyelashes.

Tomás leered.

"And I am sure you both know my friend K'antu," I ignored the compliment. "*Tía*, you forgot to introduce her. I know she's the help, but that's still rude."

"Don't be silly," my aunt's tinkling laughter filled the air.

She was an excellent politician, always sociable. She annoyed me a lot. "K'antu isn't here. But if she were, I would have been happy to greet her. Such a delightful girl, gentlemen. She is my assistant, as well as helping in the house. She did all the work on this lovely party."

I spun around.

My aunt was right. K'antu wasn't there. I swallowed hard. I started to go find her, but Laura grabbed my arm and squeezed it. Hard.

"*Cariño*, Rodolfo has wonderful news," she said to me. "His son Mario is here in Manchay. Or rather, he left for three days, but he'll be back tomorrow. And he can't wait to see you. Isn't that great?"

My memory conjured up a chubby boy with overly large glasses and short, thick black hair with a cowlick right at his temple. I remembered when we were both seven, we had gotten into my aunt's makeup, snuck into the vineyard, found a worker taking a siesta, and decorated his face like an Incan warrior as he slept. The worker took it good-naturedly when he woke up, but my aunt had been livid. Mario and I had laughed so hard that day. But we had to spend the rest of it indoors. If the man hadn't drunk so much of the wine he picked grapes for, he might have woken up during the painting session and stopped us. So as far as we were concerned, it was his fault.

I had not seen Mario for years. One year he had disappeared from Manchay. No one had ever explained to me why, but once, I had overheard the servants talking. His mother had absconded to Spain with one of the vineyard's best-looking customers and had taken Mario with her. I had not understood what that meant at the time. Soon after, I had met K'antu, and I put him out of my mind.

Until now.

"Yeah, sure," I yanked my arm from her grip, not sharing her enthusiasm for a boy I barely knew. I would never have reacted like that to her before. Many things had changed since last year. She didn't try to hold me again but hovered near me. She wasn't going to let me out of her sight, so I took the opportunity to focus my attention on the little man whose responsibility it was to run the town. "Señor Romero, since you are here, maybe you wouldn't mind. I'd like to know when my Aunt Ada can rebuild her house. Isn't she supposed to be receiving money from your government?"

"Not at my party, Tamara," Laura said between her teeth. She beamed at the two men.

"What do you mean, *Tía*? Why shouldn't I ask him now? Señor Romero will be going back to his house to sleep tonight, right? It is probably a beautiful house isn't it, no cracks or collapsed walls? It isn't a tent-like where my aunt Ada and cousin sleep? Maybe he can explain how he feels about his people living in tents a year after –"

"You are right, Tamara," Tomás smiled, showing his crooked teeth. "I will be going home. I will sleep in my beautiful bedroom. And if I'm not mistaken, it is very much like the room you will be sleeping in tonight."

We locked eyes. There was a flash of triumph in his. I looked away. He had hit a nerve. I felt guilty I had not gone to stay with my Aunt Ada – and didn't plan to on this trip. Never mind that my visit was mainly because of Laura's birthday party. There was no way in hell I was going back to Ada's shell of a house with a tent plopped inside of it. Short of inviting her to Laura's, I didn't see how I would see her at all this visit. I never wanted to go to the center of Manchay again. Ever.

An aid organization called People Help had donated a bunch of tents right after the earthquake. Ada and Elías had set up theirs in what had been their bedroom. According to my cousin, none of Manchay had improved much in the last year. Piles of rubble lined the streets or lay right in the middle of them, and dust still floated in the air. I had told my mom and dad I would be staying exclusively with Laura on this trip. I hadn't talked to my Aunt Ada yet because I did not want to allow her to offer what was left of her house to me.

I grit my teeth and addressed Tomás again, "Yeah, you are right, I will be sleeping in a nice place. I... I can't sleep at Ada's house. It isn't livable. Why is it taking so long for anyone to help her?"

Getting answers from him might help alleviate the guilt I felt. Perhaps I could call Ada with good news. But he went on to crush my tiny glimmer of optimism.

"Naturally you are concerned about your family," he said. His eyes disappeared under the hooded lids. "It does you credit, my dear. But you don't understand. These things take time. My administration and I have been working closely with People Help, the aid organization that has come to help us. Also, my deputy or I go to Lima every week to raise money. Believe me, Tamara, we are doing all we can. Your family should have patience. Good things are coming, I promise."

He patted me on the arm and turned to Laura, babbling something about dinner.

"I wonder if you'd have patience if you had to live in a tent, you pompous pig," I muttered under my breath.

"It does take a while to raise money to help these people, Tamara," a voice behind me said.

A lump of fear caught in my throat, and the hair on my arms stood on end. I swiveled and faced Rodolfo. He had probably been behind me for a while, but I hadn't noticed him.

"We are all doing what we can to rebuild. That is what my son Mario is doing here–"

This was useless. He kept talking, but I tuned him out and scanned the room, hoping to find K'antu. Years ago, the first weeks after I had met K'antu, my aunt Laura had tried to keep me away from her. Laura had insisted K'antu was an employee, and so I should find another friend –K'antu had work to do anyway and didn't have time for me. But trying to keep me from K'antu had made me want to befriend her more. I had insisted on K'antu spending all her free time with me, and over the years, what had started as kind of a forced friendship based on principle had turned into something tangible. My aunt accepted it reluctantly.

Instead of finding my friend somewhere in the crowd, my Aunt Laura had walked off. I wish I had noticed earlier; I could have gotten away. She was talking to a tall man with 1970's style eyeglasses – large, roundish, and slightly shaded. She listened to him. She looked around, her face pale. She caught my eye and waved at me to come to her.

I forced my feet to move in her direction. I wanted to run because I sensed something was wrong, but I needed to know what it was. Laura was trembling, her body stiff. She reached for me, so I gave her my hand. Her hand was as cold as ice.

"You are Tamara?" The man's glasses reflected lights from the roof of the canopy when he looked at me. "I was asking your aunt about you. You are friends with K'antu, right? Where is she?"

"Yes, I am friends with K'antu. But I don't know where she is. What is going on?"

"I need you to find her for me. Now."

"But – why?"

"Do it." he paused, "Please."

I looked at my aunt, who said in a quiet voice, "Please, Tamara, go. Try to find her. Her husband has been murdered."

Chapter 2

The next morning, I sat at the dining room table picking at scrambled eggs with my fork. One of my legs twitched. I had Restless Leg Syndrome, and it was worse in Perú. Before I had gotten up this morning, I had looked out the window to see the man from the night before standing outside talking to Laura. Men scoured the property, and several headed toward the hills behind the house. I had tried to find K'antu the night before, but she was gone. Or at least, she was not on my aunt's property. Laura had not allowed me to go far, despite her plea for my help.

My mind was all over the place. K'antu's husband had been murdered. I had not had the chance to ask her about him. No, that was a lie. I had not cared enough to ask her about him. My mind was consumed with fears of another earthquake. I wanted to go home to Chicago. But also, I wanted to look for K'antu. I was a mass of conflicting fears. Afraid of this place, but afraid to leave my friend.

K'antu was seventeen years old, like me. Why the hell was she married? Why hadn't she told me? I mean, yeah, I hadn't asked, but she could have told me. Why had she left the party? And why wasn't she coming forward now that this husband of hers was dead? Did she know he had been murdered? Worse, did she do it?

I shook my head, trying to erase that awful thought. No, she didn't. Someone had killed him, but I was sure it wasn't K'antu. I stood, planning to go out – further this time – and find her myself. She would explain what was going on when I got to her.

Before I could go anywhere, Daniela, one of the maids, walked into the dining room carrying a pot of coffee. She looked at me and stumbled, spilling steaming coffee on her white apron. She wiped at it with a napkin. "Tamara, *cariño*, I did not know you were down already. Your Aunt Ada is in the living room waiting for la Señora Laura. Should I –"

But I was already on my feet and running to the living room. Ada was my other, poorer aunt. I liked her a lot better than Aunt Laura. Flying through the door, I ran into her arms, and she enveloped me in a giant bear hug. "*Tía*, I am so happy to see you. Crazy things are happening here. K'antu left, and no one can find her. Her husband was killed, and I didn't know she had a husband, and he was killed, and now he's dead, and K'antu must be in danger because she disappeared..."

I burst into tears.

"Tamara, *cariño*, sit down. Daniela told me Laura is busy right now, so we have time to talk." She led me to one of the sofas. "So K'antu had not told you anything regarding this past year?"

"No, we uh... we mostly talked about... stuff... the... the party and... you know." I stopped talking and avoided her gaze.

Ada clicked her tongue and shook her head. She had not been at the party. I wasn't sure if she had been invited. She and Laura got along for my parents' sake, but they do not socialize much.

"I am sorry, *Tía*." I felt so guilty. It wasn't my fault she hadn't been to the party, but I hadn't called her and didn't want to go to her house.

"Sorry for what *cariño*? Tamara do not feel bad. I could have come to the party, but I had other things to do."

"Other things –"

"Never mind. Listen, it has been a hard year for all of us, but especially for K'antu. As you know, she lived with her grandparents because her parents were killed in an accident when she was a baby. Her grandfather died a month after the earthquake."

K'antu's grandfather had been everything to her; her parent, her teacher, and her hero. With his death, she must have suffered a lot. Why hadn't she told me?

My aunt patted me on the knee. "After the funeral, K'antu came to Laura and told her she had gotten married to Eduardo, a childhood friend of hers from Patabamba, where she grew up. Soon after, K'antu stopped coming to work. Laura waited a week, and then she came to me. She told me she was concerned about K'antu, that she had not come back to work and had not sent notice. Laura wanted to tell her she still had her job if she wanted it. She would give her more responsibilities and a raise."

"So, you found K'antu, she came back, and Laura promoted her to party planner. That's a good thing, isn't it?" I said .

"Party planner and general secretary of all Laura's events. It was good, yes. But let me finish. Laura and I went to Patabamba because I suspected that is where K'antu went with Eduardo. We found her there all right. But we did not like what we saw."

She stopped talking.

"Why? What did you see?" I braced myself. I wanted to know but also didn't want to know.

"K'antu had lost a lot of weight. But worse than that, she had several cuts and bruises on her arms and one large, faded bruise on her face. We asked her, and she told us she had fallen on the hillside." Ada's face was blank, as if she were deliberately trying not to let me read her thoughts.

Bruises. A brick. Falling. A brick falling in the darkness. My face. Bruised. Bloody. Darkness. Greenish light. The ground rolling under me. Where...

"Tamara!" My aunt's voice brought me back.

Sweat dripped down my forehead. I wiped it with the back of my shaking hand. I had to be normal. Had to. With a considerable effort, I said, "You can indeed slip pretty badly if you walk wrong on the terrain."

Ada shook her head.

"So, you did not believe her?"

"We didn't. Laura was arguing with K'antu about returning to work when Eduardo came in. We started asking him questions like why they had left Manchay. He refused to answer her and kicked us out. We left Patabamba more worried than ever. Laura told me to go home, and I had things I had to do, so I did. I don't know exactly what happened next, but K'antu was back at work a few days later. And, as you said, she wasn't only a maid anymore. But still, she would disappear every so often, and every time she came back, it looked like she had fallen down a hill again. She –"

Before Ada could continue, Laura came in, followed by the man from last night. We stood.

"Good morning Ada, good to see you," Laura said. "Tamara, good morning. This is the chief inspector of the Manchay police, Joaquín Sanhuesa."

He looked to be in his mid-twenties, young for such a high-ranking officer. His hair was curly but cut short. Whorls of black locks clung to his head. He had a strong jaw and triangular torso, like a swimmer. Something fizzled inside me. I laughed inwardly at myself. He wasn't my type. Yeah, he was attractive, except for the pair of coke-bottle glasses sitting on his thin, straight nose. And he lived here. I would never date anyone from Manchay. Now that Laura's party was over, all I had to do was help K'antu, and I could go home and hug my dog. And it would be a long time before they saw me again.

"Tamara." He said, nodding also at my Aunt Ada.

"Have you found K'antu yet?" I asked. "Do you know what happened to her husband – what is his name again?"

"Eduardo," both of my aunts said in unison. Laura told us all to sit down. She sat next to me on one of the sofas and gave me a quick hug. Ada sat on the other side of me, an aunt sandwich. The chief inspector faced us. Daniela came in with the coffee urn – the kind you would see in a dusty antique shop in the States, but everyone had in this town. Probably the same one I had seen her with a few minutes ago. I hoped the coffee was still hot. Laura thanked her and told her we would serve ourselves.

"No. We have not found K'antu yet."

A look was exchanged between him and my Aunt Laura.

"What? What is it?" I asked.

"Tamara, Eduardo was found in the small house he shared with K'antu in the center of Manchay. He was lying face down in a pool of his blood. His throat had been slit."

The inspector stopped. He was looking at me. I must have had a sick look on my face because Ada dumped several cubes of sugar in a cup of coffee and pressed it into my hands. I pushed it away. "Oh my God."

"Eduardo had been drinking. There was a mostly empty bottle of *Pisco* on the table and a broken glass near his left hand. There were some strange scratches in the blood that the crime lab is analyzing now." The inspector looked at my Aunt Laura, who nodded. "The main reason I am telling you all of this, Tamara, is because Laura thinks you may be able to help. K'antu trusts you."

Did she? I had thought so but doubted it now. "Help do what?"

"A *Tumi* was lying in the blood next to him. In the blood were three perpendicular lines. It looked like Eduardo was trying to draw a K in his blood before he died." He said.

My heart skipped a beat and my scalp shriveled.

Chapter 3

"Tamara, you look like you are about to faint. Here. Drink water."

"Did you remember something? Do you know where to find her?"

My aunt Laura and the chief inspector spoke at the same time. My aunt passed me a glass of water.

"No. Nothing. It's nothing. I'm fine. And no, I don't know where she is." Had Laura told this guy about K'antu's collection and her training with weapons? Was she now their main suspect? Were they hoping I would remember details K'antu had said to me that would lead the police to her? But I didn't. We had not talked as much as the adults seemed to think we did. She had kept a great deal from me. Probably because I had been so vocal about my fears. I could have kicked myself for being so self-centered.

"Try to remember, *cariño,*" Laura said.

"I don't know." She had not said anything to me. And even if I did know, I would not give them information until I confronted K'antu myself. I had had enough. I had to get out of there. I stood and ran from the room. I could smell *Chupe de Camarones* cooking in the kitchen.

My family's vineyard, *La Bodega Colibrí,* had been passed down through generations. Laura ran it by herself because my mom lived in the U.S. The large white house with red, curved tile roofs faced sprawling green lawns and a lush garden with a variety of hummingbird-attracting flowers. The vineyards lay beyond, spiny rows of vines in a desert. Incongruous and successful. At the back of the house, close to one of the paths up the hills was a garage completely open on one side. It had room enough for Laura's two cars and two dune buggies.

I ran past all of that and was crossing a bridge over one of the creeks when to my horror, it began to shake. My knees buckled, and I fell forward on the smooth rock surface. I couldn't breathe, so I couldn't scream for help. I froze. I closed my eyes and lay there feeling the world spinning. A moment later, I felt strong, calloused hands pull me up.

"Señorita Tamara, are you all right? You fell." The man said. He helped me to my feet and made sure I could stand before letting go of me.

"I... I'm fine. I ... was that... was it...?" The movement had stopped, but I felt faint. I swayed and almost fell again. He grabbed onto my arms to stop me.

"*Temblor?* No, do not worry. It was not that. This bridge is so close to the highway that sometimes when trucks pass, it shakes." He muttered angrily about reckless drivers.

"Really? A truck? Well, that's a relief." I grasped the railing, swallowing hard, the wave of panic subsiding. "Thank you so much, Señor, for helping me. I am fine now. I guess I overreacted…"

"Not at all. I know how you feel. You were here last year. It was awful. We all remember. Now, if you are sure you will be all right, I must get back to work." He looked at me anxiously.

This man was treating my fears with respect. Not like my family. I smiled widely at him. "I am sure. Thank you again."

He walked off. I stepped off the bridge and stood still, earthquakes on my mind. I thought back to the previous year, to the small front room of Ada's house. I could still hear laughter and the happy sound of glasses clinking as people came in to see me and say what a shame my visit was over. I remembered the exact moment K'antu had appeared at the door. It was as if she had brought the disaster with her. The sudden rolling motion of the ground below me, the side-to-side shaking, the pitch-darkness when the electricity went out, the roaring in my ears, the cracking of the wall behind me… At three and a half minutes long and 8.1 on the Richter scale, it was the most destructive earthquake Manchay had seen in over a hundred years.

Many people perished that night. K'antu had pulled me from under the rubble and dragged me outside right before the entire wall had collapsed. I had gone back to Chicago with nightmares and a temporary asthma-like condition from breathing in fine particles of rubble released into the air. I suffered, but I was safe. Safe – but guilt-ridden for deserting the people who had lost so much –especially the friend who had saved my life.

Taking a deep breath, I shook the memories out of my head and looked at the green, grassy lawn was dotted with grazing llamas. Here in Manchay, in the undamaged area of my family's property, I remembered things I had tried to forget for the past year. I shivered. I had planned to take a walk under the shade of the grapevines and schmooze the workers. Maybe one of them knew where K'antu was. But I changed my mind. I walked as quickly as I could over the bridge again, turned, and walked past the house toward the garage. I would take one of the dune buggies and go looking for her. I had never gone far on my own, but I didn't stop to think about it. I needed to find my friend, and that I see her before they did. I was convinced of one thing: the girl who had risked her life to save mine was no murderer. And I was going to do everything I could to prove it.

Chapter 4

As I got closer to the open-air garage, I smelled the strong scent of cologne. I wrinkled my nose and went to the Sand Sniper 150, a bright blue two-seater. There was a clanking noise coming from the front of the vehicle by the engine.

"Hello?"

A boy my age walked around the buggy. We stood face to face. He was four inches taller than me, with thick, wavy hair the color of chocolate.

"Who are you?" I was not pleased to find anyone fiddling with the vehicle I wanted to use.

He wiped his hands on a cloth and extended one out to me.

"I'm not surprised you don't remember. I am Mario. And you must be Tamara. I have been waiting to meet you again. Wow, you're cute. I did not remember – I was thinking... but never mind. You're cute." He repeated, grinning.

"Oh, you are Rodolfo's son. Well, Rodolfo's son, what exactly are you doing with that dune buggy? I am going to take it." I wasn't sure exactly why I felt so antagonistic. Maybe because he was screwing with my plans. If I stopped for any reason, I might get cold feet and not find K'antu, which would be a disaster. If the police found her and put her in jail, I would lose my chance to make it up to her for ignoring her situation.

Mario's eyes opened wide, "You mean this dune buggy? I don't think so. It is not going anywhere anytime soon."

"Why not?"

"It's not working."

That wasn't possible. Laura always had her vehicles serviced and ready. I came closer and peered at it. "Not working?"

"Yes, you see, the engine is completely inoperable, and I was about to take it all apart to fix it."

"Don't be ridiculous. You're taking the float out to clean the carburetor."

I always learned a lot on my visits to Perú: the right way to peel a mango, adobe houses don't hold up in earthquakes, and how to fix a dune buggy. I also knew how to chop off the head of a straw dummy with a *Tumi* knife... Oh my God, I pushed that thought out of my mind. Yeah, it was one of K'antu's skills. She had taught me. She had enjoyed it. It doesn't mean she did it on a real person.

Mario's eyes opened wide. "How did you –"

Laura had insisted I learn about the dune buggy engines, just in case. But there was no way I was going to enlighten him. "So, hurry up and finish. I need it in five minutes. I'll wait."

He lifted one eyebrow at me.

"No, forget it. I don't want to wait... I guess I will just take the Power Buggy."

I went to the little safe built into a small concrete block on the ground in the corner of the structure, turned the combination, and got the key. Both of Laura's dune buggies were by BMS Motors. The Power Buggy was larger, which was why I had been planning to take the other one, but no matter.

"So, you are planning to take the Power Buggy? I don't know if I would do that if I were you..." he said.

"Don't mess with me, Rodolfo's son. I have places to be." I climbed in and was about to turn it on when I felt a hand grasp my arm. I turned.

"Why do you keep calling me 'Rodolfo's son'? I have a name, you know."

"Why do you assume you can lie to me about the engine? I have a brain, you know."

He let go of my arm and laughed, showing his straight white teeth.

"Okay. You win. I was messing with you. Your curls distracted me. What do you say we start over, Tamara?" he said.

I had to go. I put my foot on the gas and backed out a little faster than I should have.

The Peruvian coast looks alternatively like a giant pile of sand and a clump of tan rocks with occasional dottings of *huarango* trees. The area outside of *La Bodega Colibrí* was sandy. Up in the foothills, especially along the rivers, the geography got rockier.

Higher up, paths led to villages in the mountains. This was where I was headed when another engine approached. I stopped the Power Buggy and turned. Mario's hair blew in the wind like a male model in one of those overdone deodorant commercials. But when he pulled the Sand Sniper beside me, not a hair was out of place. It was infuriating.

Running my fingers through my unruly mop of hair, I said, "Why are you following me? Also, I thought you said the Sniper was incapacitated."

"Nah, I was almost finished," he said, "I thought I'd come and remind you. You aren't supposed to be going that way."

He pointed an oil-stained finger toward the path I was headed for.

"Oh yeah? How do you know I am not supposed to go there?"

"Because of this. It was on the wall. Maybe you didn't see it?" he handed me a piece of paper. It was a sign. It had my name on it and a reminder of the rules of the dune buggies. It was signed by Laura.

I could feel my face reddening. I snatched the paper from him and threw it on the ground.

"Hey, Tamara, don't be mad. Seriously, you shouldn't go there by yourself."

"That is none of your business." Never mind the thought of going there, not knowing what I would find, made dark, horrible feelings of apprehension swirl in my belly. I wasn't going to tell him that. I put the buggy in gear.

"Tamara, wait."

"For what?" I pressed the gas.

"At least let me go with you," He shouted. I slammed on the brakes and turned the buggy off.

"I don't want you to."

"But you can't go up there by yourself."

"You need to get off my back. I'm going there to find my friend K'antu."

"That's not a good idea."

"Actually," I said, not exactly telling the truth, "I was told to by the police, so I am just following orders. Do you want to help me do that?"

"No..."

"Then leave me alone." He was unbelievable. I turned to go.

"I mean no, you don't have to find her." His voice was so quiet I almost didn't hear.

What the hell did he mean? Of course, I had to find her. Standing with my back to him, I thought about what I was doing. I glanced up at the arid hills. Did I want to go there by myself? I had been part of the way with my aunt before – but never to Patabamba. You couldn't see the town from where we were standing. The path leading to it first passed a small oasis with a pond surrounded by trees on a small, flat piece of land, an area as far as I had ever gone. A few miles beyond the oasis was Patabamba but between the oasis and the village was absolutely nothing as far as I knew. It would be a spooky drive. And once I got to the town, I was not sure if anyone would welcome me. I had never been there. Unwillingly, I began to feel relieved that he had come to a stop me.

"I know where she is," he whispered. I jumped. He had come up behind me. "She's not there."

"How do you know?" I turned to face him. He was close. I tried to back up, but I couldn't. I was already pressed against the bars of the buggy.

"I just know. Believe me."

"Believe you? The liar who said these weren't running. I pointed at the vehicles. "Why should I?"

"Because of my pretty face."

I stared at him. Now I remembered. He never took anything seriously as a kid. He hadn't grown up yet. "I don't care what you say, I need to find her, and I'm guessing she would have gone to her hometown."

"I am telling you she didn't. Although I am not so sure she would want me to be telling you. But since I'm a nice guy, I don't want you going there by yourself."

"Not so sure she would want... me..." I sputtered, "This is a waste of time. K'antu needs me, and I am going to find her – in Patabamba."

He shrugged, "It'll be a wasted trip."

Taking a deep breath, I tried to ignore the doubts creeping into my mind. What if he was right? It didn't matter. All of this was distracting me from my goal: finding K'antu and figuring out what was going on. "Go away and leave me alone."

"Are you so sure you want to get involved in her problems?" He asked, staring intently at me.

"How can you ask? Never mind, I guess I shouldn't be surprised. For your information, K'antu has done a lot for me, so now it is my turn to help her."

Sun glinted in his eyes, making them greener. "So, you are determined?"

"Didn't I just say that?"

"You'd do anything for her?"

"She's my friend. I want to help."

"Come back with me. I will take you to her."

I frowned. "How do you know where she is if no one else does?"

"It'sa long story, Tamara. Would you trust me for now? Please? I promise I will take you to her. Let's put these away." He pointed to the buggies.

"So, she is not in Patabamba?"

Mario walked back to the Sniper. He sat in the passenger seat and stared at me. I gave in. I stomped over to the Power Buggy and turned the key in the engine.

"You'd better not be messing with me, Rodolfo's son."

His lips pressed together, "Believe me, this is nothing to mess around with."

True. Looking back, if I had known everything that was going to happen, the girl I was at that moment would have taken off back to Chicago and never looked back. Well, except in my nightmares.

After we parked the buggies, he said, "Go tell Laura you are with me. Tell her I am going to take you to Rodolfo's for lunch."

"Oh, so now you are telling me what to do?"

"Do you want to see K'antu or not?"

"Fine." I stormed inside to find Laura.

∞

Mario drove us off the property, my first time since arriving in Manchay. We headed towards Rodolfo's house, as far as I could tell. It was all I could do to unclench my fists and wipe the sweat off on my pants as we got closer to the center of last year's disaster. We passed a small shack behind a crude wooden "Fresh Figs" sign on the side of the highway that looked exactly as it had after the earthquake. I turned my head away and breathed deeply. *In and out. In and out. In through the nose and out through the mouth.*

Mario turned his head. "Is everything okay?"

"Yeah, fine." Why should I let him see how nervous I was? I looked out the window, and my eyes bulged. We were heading closer to the center of Manchay. Why hadn't I thought to ask him exactly where we were going?

"Are you sure you are all right, Tamara?"

"Where are we going?"

"I told you. To see K'antu. Are you changing your mind?"

"Yes. No. I, uh, I mean..." Oh God. If finding K'antu meant returning to the scene of devastation, did I want to go through with it? I should tell him to take me back. After all, what made me think I should get involved? The police are good at this kind of thing, right? They had no right to enlist me as the K'antu-finder. Joaquín, the detective, could do it. And when he did, Laura would make sure she was not blamed for Eduardo's murder. I was about to tell Mario to turn the car around when he started talking.

"Because if you are, then it is no problem. They will find her eventually and put her away. Probably the women's prison in Lima. It's not a bad place, I hear if you don't mind rats – the rodent kind, and the humankind."

"What are you talking about, Mario? She did not kill her husband. I am sure they just want to ask her some questions. They must have an idea of who did it. This town is not that big –"

"Yeah. They have an idea. And their idea is K'antu killed him."

"But that's ridiculous... wait, how do you know?"

His eyes were on the road, and the knuckles on his hands were white from gripping the steering wheel.

"I just know, okay?"

"You say you know, but you don't know anything. You can't. You don't live here. You are like me, clueless."

"You are wrong. I do know a few things. And the situation is more complicated and serious than you think, Tamara."

He loosened his fingers on the steering wheel and muttered. "Maybe I'm making a mistake. Yeah, this is probably too much for you, Tamara."

He pulled to the left and slowed down, looking over his shoulder like he was going to make a U-turn.

"What are you doing? You can't make U-turns on the highway."

"I am taking you back to Laura's house. I'll tell her you were going to Patabamba."

"You have a lot of nerve, Rodolfo's son. Do not turn this car around," I said, temporarily pushing my fear of Manchay out of my mind. He hesitated, so I raised my voice and glanced behind me to see if anyone was about to slam into us.

"Keep going Mario, I mean it."

So, he did. We drove in silence for a minute before I said, "You are wrong. This has nothing to do with K'antu."

"Tamara…"

"Take me to her. We will find her and bring her back to Laura's house. My aunt will know what to do, and everything will be alright."

He slammed his hands on the steering wheel. "I overheard a

conversation my father was having on the phone this morning, okay? It was about getting K'antu so they could lock her up."

My stomach sank. "Your father? He thinks she did it?"

Mario's lips pressed together again. He stopped the car and got out, walking to another fig vendor. This one's shack was shabby but intact. When he got back in the car, he handed a bag of fruit to me and sat staring out at the panorama. I grabbed it and bit down hard on a fig.

"Did Laura ever tell you why I left Manchay years ago?" He asked.

"No." I wiped fig juice from my mouth on the back of my hand.

"My mother was born in Patabamba."

"Uh-huh," I mumbled, taking another bite. The fig was delicious. So, his mother was born in the same place as K'antu. So?

Mario ground his teeth. He said, "She was my father's maid."

I froze. That was weird. But maybe it was the reason why she ran away from Rodolfo. What did all this have to do with K'antu?

He went on, "Because of her low social standing, my mother was treated badly. Rodolfo never married her. He let us live there, and she continued to work for him. Eventually, my mother took me and ran away with one of the vendors who came to buy wine from my father. I hated Rodolfo for years, but I came back this year to see who he is. Now I know he is a good man who lived by the reality of his circumstances. Overall, here in Manchay, things haven't changed much. K'antu comes from the lower class, so people like my father – and your Aunt Laura – will simply assume she did it, and they won't look any further."

"You are wrong. Laura will protect K'antu."

His face showed no emotion. Doubt crept into my mind. Was he right, or was I? We sat for a moment. Laura would do anything for K'antu... right? I thought about this morning. In my mind's eye, I saw Laura exchange meaningful glances at Joaquín. What had those been about? She had wanted him to tell me about Eduardo's murder – details he should not have told me. Why? Were they hoping I would lead them to my friend? If Laura wanted to protect her, would she have encouraged me to find her, or would she have openly defended her to Joaquín?

"I see you are beginning to wonder." Mario shook his head. "I'm sorry."

"Don't be," I said curtly, "it won't be an issue once K'antu tells me what is going on. I will make sure of it. Let's go."

He started driving again. I concentrated on my breathing relaxation techniques as we drove through the narrow streets littered with piles of rubble. Some houses were hidden by walls of cardboard or adobe brick. Others sat behind wrought iron fences. None of them were without damage. We bumped along. Not much of the road's surface was flat and smooth. There were either tire-flattening potholes or piles of rubble of varying heights. Mario was a good driver, but the tires still tipped on the edge of a few potholes.

"We are in my Aunt Ada's neighborhood," I said.

"Yes," he responded.

"Are you taking me to her house?"

"No. We are going to K'antu's house."

I was confused. "She lives here?"

"Four houses from Ada. It's not technically her house. She

and Eduardo set up camp in it when they got married. The family let K'antu stay for practically nothing."

That wasn't the huge favor it sounded like. The fact that it was a house near my aunt's meant it had likely sustained quite a bit of damage in the earthquake.

"Terrific," I said and chewed my lip. It was all I could manage not to get out of the car and run screaming until I got to the airport in Lima and into a homebound plane.

Mario slowed to navigate a large hole in the road. I looked around. On one side of the street, there was a long wall painted with a mural of Machu Picchu, the Incan city magnificently hidden in the mountains from Europeans for centuries.

"That's pretty..." I said, trying hard to stifle panic. I was in a familiar place, but it did not look like it had when I was young . It looked like a war zone. At least we would be with K'antu soon. I could drag her back to Laura's house and avoid spending a great deal of time here.

"Do you know what that is called?" Mario asked.

"Uh, a wall?" I said. Sarcasm is a great way to hide fear.

"The wall with the painting. The people call it '*un muro de la verguenza*'."

"A wall of shame? Why?"

"After the earthquake, lots of money started coming into Manchay from different sources: aid agencies, governments, private donors. But despite all the money, things have not improved."

"Obviously."

"I came back to Manchay to work with People Help, an aid agency working in disaster zones."

Aunt Laura hadn't told me that. I studied his face. He was doing something good for the people here. A slight feeling crept into my consciousness. Envy? I would have hated doing what he was. Or would I?

He must have sensed my scrutiny. He smiled. "I am studying to become a forensic pathologist. I thought it would be good for me to join the organization and come back to my country to help out. Good for many reasons…"

"Yeah?"

"Yeah. Anyway, People Help has doctors here, but they also do other stuff, like distribute tents and other supplies. When we first got here, things were bad, and during the year, we realized no improvements were being made to ordinary people's homes. We started talking to people – the people who live in houses like this. Many of them told us all they had received was a $500 stipend. And the worst part is they were told that is all they would receive for the time being."

"Five hundred dollars? That's all?"

"Yes. We did a lot of research and interviewed a bunch of people. We crunched the numbers. We concluded most of the aid money that was supposed to be coming in wasn't reaching the people it was meant for. But we weren't sure exactly what was happening, so people went to Lima and complained to the central government. A few weeks after, people from the local government started building these walls. What's behind the walls is in the same condition as the day after the earthquake: broken homes and rubble. But the walls look pretty, they were cheap to build, and they distract people from the reality."

"But that's horrible."

"Yep," Mario screeched to a halt in front of a wall made of what looked like woven reeds. No one had bothered to paint this one. He took the keys out of the ignition. "Come on. K'antu is inside."

The last time I was in this area, I had almost died. I stepped out of the car and stood rooted to the spot. There was a vein pumping in my eye as I stared at the house in front of me as if it were a prison. Instead of a wall, there was a high fence in front of it. The house looked pretty normal, through the fence, except for the pile of bricks in the front yard. This house, K'antu's apparently, was a mish-mash of construction styles; a result of few, if any, town regulations, and one of the reasons why the slapped-together houses of this area had sustained so much destruction. The gate of the fence had yellow crime scene tape wrapped around it. I took an involuntary step back, my hackles raised. The nerve pulsated behind my eye again so strongly. I could hardly see, and my breath came in staccato bursts. Mario made his way to the house next to K'antu's. He was about to knock on the door of the wall when it was flung open, and something flew out, slamming into him.

Chapter 5

He fell against me, and I would have fallen too, but the flying object caught me. "Tamara?"

It was my cousin, Elías. His eyes protruded frog-like, body shaking.

"It is me, Elías.

What's wrong with you? Why are you in such a hurry? Are you okay?"

"No, I mean yes. I am sorry." He glanced behind himself, and for a moment, it looked like he would start running again, but he took a deep breath and calmed down. "I was not paying attention to where I was going. I am so glad to see you, *prima*. You had not called me yet, so I wasn't sure if you would."

He wrapped his arms around me in an awkward hug and held out his hand to Mario, who slapped him on the back as he took his hand.

"Of course, I was going to call." I stammered.

But he did not seem to notice my discomfort. He looked back toward the other side of the wall. "Listen, *prima*, I want to spend time with you, but I am on my way to work. What are you guys doing here? Why don't you go to my house? Mom is there. She will be so excited to see you."

He put out his arms and tried to maneuver us away from the door.

"No, I, we –" I said as Joaquín, the chief inspector, came out of the house Elías had emerged from.

My cousin saw him and started to walk away fast, "Call me later, Tamara."

The inspector looked after him with a thoughtful expression on his face. He turned to us. "Tamara, Mario, what are you two doing here?"

I stepped closer to Mario. "We are looking for K'antu."

"Visiting," Mario said at the same time.

"She is not here. And you should not be looking for her. We will take care of it. Go home. If K'antu contacts you, have Laura call me right away. Mario, take her back to Laura's house."

"But you asked me about her," I stammered, "You –"

Joaquín walked to a rusty red moped, hopped on, and drove away.

Watching him leave, I made fists with both my hands and fumed. "That arrogant –"

But Mario cut me off. "Never mind him. She must not be here since he didn't take her away, but let's go inside anyway. Maybe they'll tell us something they did not tell him."

We stepped into a small courtyard. Dusty fruit trees hung on for dear life, and a small, inactive fountain – the ghosts of a courtyard past. We got to the door, and Mario rang the doorbell. We waited. Something shuffled closer. A small figure appeared in the doorway. Mario spoke to it, and the door opened wider.

"Come on, Tamara," Mario said.

I hesitated. The house looked like it was about to keel over. I did not want to go in, kind of like people don't want to lose their footing off a two-hundred-foot cliff. But Mario breathed in like he was going to yell at me, so I forced myself to go inside. K'antu was more important than my fears about earthquakes and shaky houses collapsing. Once inside, I looked around. We were in a front room. In the dim light, cracks in all four walls looked wide enough for a small child to hide in. There was an old sofa of faded brocade in the middle of the room and an old china cabinet bursting with broken plates and yellowed pieces of old wine glasses by the far wall. The smells of mothballs and cooking rice hung in the air.

Our was an old woman, four feet eight inches in height, but stooped over with osteoporosis, making her look even shorter. She had a babushka on her head that had once been red but now was as dusty as her skin. Not an inch of her looked like it had been bathed in the last ten years. She grinned at me, showing a gap in her upper row of teeth.

"This is Tamara, maybe you remember her –" Mario talked to her in Spanish.

She spoke to him. Her tongue was thick, and she slurred when talking. I did not understand what she was saying. She and Mario had a short conversation, and then she disappeared.

"Did you ask her about K'antu?" I asked.

He waved his hand at me.

A second later, a skinny young man came out of the darkness of the hallway.

"Hi Tamara," he said, shaking my hand. "I don't know if you remember me. My name is Miguelito. Elías' dad is my mother's brother."

"Miguelito?" I vaguely remembered a Miguelito, but not this one. The one I remembered had been healthy. "What happened to you?"

Mario elbowed me in the ribs.

"Stop," I hissed at him, rubbing my side. "Miguelito?" I wanted to know.

"Do I look bad, Tamara?" he tried to smile.

"Well, uh, kind of." It wasn't my most diplomatic moment. But it was shocking to see the change in him. If this was the same Miguelito I had played with when I visited my cousin, something was seriously wrong.

"Miguelito, we are looking for K'antu," Mario got us back on track, "Can you help us find her?"

The boy flung his arms in a gesture of fear. He looked toward the back of the house and put his finger to his mouth to indicate we should be quiet.

"Please," he said in a low voice, "Do not talk of her right now. La Señora Guerra is here."

"Who?" I asked.

Mario took me by the arm and whispered in my ear. "Lorena Guerra. Tomás Romero's deputy. She also works with me at People Help."

"The deputy magistrate?" I asked.

He nodded. "Miguelito, why is she here?"

"She is explaining our "benefits" to my great-grandmother. I mean, she is explaining why we don't get any more benefits." He ended in a cracked whisper, and a tear fell from his eye. He looked at a spot on the floor.

My eyes followed his gaze. There was a thin mattress by the wall. Two small children lay on it. They both had large eyes set in narrow faces. One of them was clutching a cheap carnival bear with had shredded newspaper stuffing spilling from a hole in his side. The other child shivered under a stiff, thin blanket. The child with the bear began to cough. Blood dribbled down her chin. The ground beneath me spun.

Mario grabbed me. His face was grim. "Calm down, Tamara."

"But the room is moving."

"Stop." He whispered. "Nothing is moving except you."

He was right. The gore on the girl's face made me feel sick. "The girl –"

"There is nothing you can do for her. Leave it alone."

"Leave it alone?" His words made me so angry I forgot my queasiness. Instead, I felt sick for the little girl. For her illness and her vulnerability. That wall behind her could come down at any moment and squash those two little scarecrows. Mario's hands were still on my arms. I was about to shove him away when Miguelito started talking.

"This used to be our living room. Last year in the earthquake, the rest of our house collapsed. Now we use this as our bedroom."

He waved at us to follow and walked toward the back of the house. I glanced at the children. The girl had stopped coughing. They stared back at me, silent.

"Come on," Miguelito was calling. I pried my eyes away from the two tiny forms on the mattress and followed him into the next room. It had four corners of adobe columns, but the walls were missing. In the middle was a large, square canvas tent, the words "People Help" on all four sides of it.

"This used to be our bedroom. But we cannot sleep here now. It gets too cold at night. Plus, we had to sell the beds for money to buy food, so now we sleep on the mattress in the front room."

"We?" I began. Mario shushed me by squeezing my arm.

As I stood there trying to process what I was seeing and what the boy was saying, a surge of wind blew through the canvas. My skin turned to ice, and I uttered a stifled scream. Mario squeezed my arm and pulled me a little closer to him. It was the wind folding back the side of the tent opposite the front room.

"Don't worry, the stakes are strong," the boy assured me as if that was what worried me.

"Why is this still here? It has been a year. Shouldn't this room be rebuilt already?" I knew the answer. I had asked the same question to the magistrate yesterday regarding Ada's house. But yesterday, my reasons for asking had been because of an abstract notion of fairness. Now, standing in the grim reality, I couldn't believe no one had come to help them rebuild this house – or help the sick children who lived in it.

Miguelito turned abruptly away. His voice cracked. "It should, but nobody cares. They have left us here to die."

I was stunned. I couldn't move, and I could barely breathe. As I gasped in the air, behind me came the raspy sound of unhealthy lungs. One of the girls was coughing again. The boy took a deep breath, stretching his rib cage to the limit. I looked at his wasted body and figured I could breathe after all – much easier than any of them, at least.

"Let's go into the kitchen. Lorena is waiting," Miguelito said.

"What about your sisters?" I asked.

But he had already gone past the tent.

"Come on, Tamara," Mario said. "There's no use getting upset over something you can't do anything about."

At that moment, I hated Mario. I wanted to lash out at him. How could he be so callous? And yet, I wished he had not brought me here to face this kind of reality. I was in this house of horrors, forced to confront my selfish and hypocritical thoughts. My year-long battle with anxiety over what had happened to me in the earthquake was a joke compared to what was happening here in this house.

"Let's go," he said, oblivious of my feelings. He pulled me, and we moved.

We went through the tent. The last room was not a room at all. There was only one complete wall of adobe bricks with another half wall at a right angle. These two connected walls held a rough brick oven with a metal stove on top. The wizened old lady who had opened the door to us was fussing with a teapot. Sitting at a rickety table was another woman. For a split second, I thought it might be K'antu. But it wasn't. Mario had lied. K'antu wasn't here. I needed to leave so I could continue looking for her. When all of this was over, and I was on my way to the airport, I could mention these people to Laura and tell her something must be done for them. There, I was already rationalizing my way out of doing anything helpful.

"Please sit," Miguelito said. Mario pushed me toward a chair, eradicating any hope I had; he would say no, we needed to leave.

Mario and I sat down on hard, metal chairs. The old woman brought us hot, weak tea in chipped cups.

"Señora Guerra, you know Mario. And this is Tamara, Laura's niece. I'm sorry about the cups," Miguelito said, "but everything was damaged in the earthquake."

"Ada's niece also," I said to the woman, feeling like I should acknowledge the connection to this part of town. "You know Ada, surely? The woman four houses from you with the collapsed second and third floors?"

"Tamara. Of course. I have heard so much about you from Laura and Ada both. I know her. Yes, it is a shame about her house. Sadly, there are too many of those, too many," Lorena shook her head.

"A shame? Aren't you in a position to –"

"Tamara," Mario said. I looked at him. His hand made a slight movement toward Miguelito, who was looking paler than before.

How my asking these questions would hurt these people was not something I understood, but I breathed deeply and merely said, "Yes, it is a terrible situation. Please, Miguelito, do not worry about anything. These cups, this is all fine. The tea smells wonderful. But we have to go."

"I am also leaving," Lorena said, standing, "Mario, will you be at the People Help office tomorrow? I need to bring you the latest figures. They are not good, I'm afraid. I feel most distressed, especially when I must give such news to families like these."

"Yes, I will be there." Mario pressed his lips together. He did that a lot.

Lorena left.

"Let's go, Mario," I said. How could he be calmly discussing work while my friend was out there somewhere, alone and afraid, being hunted by the police as a killer while she mourned her husband's death? "We don't have time for this. We need to find K'antu –"

"No." A little voice came from the opening of the tent. "You can't. You won't. You cannot discover where she is. You would give her to the police. We will never tell you –"

It was one of Miguelito's sisters. She was holding herself up on the edge of the tent. But before anyone could go help her, a voice rang out from behind her.

"So, you do know where she is." It was Joaquín. He had come back. He grabbed the little girl by her skinny wrists. Miguelito's sister made a strange sound – a combination of hacking and gasping. Miguelito rushed over and pummeled his fists on Joaquín's chest, screaming at him to let his sister go. Mario was about to interfere, but before he could, Joaquín scooped up the girl and disappeared into the tent. He soothed her, and she was quiet. I went in to see. She was back on her mattress, staring at him. He wiped her forehead with his handkerchief, and she closed her eyes. He stood.

"You lied to me, Miguelito. Now tell me where K'antu is."

"No. My sister does not know what she is saying. I do not know where K'antu is. I swear."

"Why can't you leave this family alone? Can't you see they have enough to deal with?" I said to Joaquín.

"Tamara, didn't I tell you to go home?" he said. But he wasn't looking at me. He was staring at Miguelito. A cell phone was

53

making noises in Miguelito's pocket. The contrasts of towns like Manchay in Peru were not easy to explain to someone from the outside: satellite dishes on the roof of a half-destroyed house or cellphones inside a pocket sewn several dozen times to hold worn fabric together. It wasn't sacrificed for luxury items exactly. It was more like a necessary prioritizing not accurately judged by someone from a rich country.

"Answer it." The room's dimness made it impossible to see the chief inspector's eyes behind his thick glasses.

"I…" Miguelito stuttered.

Joaquín went and took the phone from the boy's pocket. He glanced at it. Then he took his phone and called someone. "Get up to Patabamba. Now. Juan is on the move. K'antu is probably there with him."

"Who is Juan?" I said to no one in particular. Miguelito swayed and bumped into me. He was sweating.

"Tamara, get out. Now. If you don't go home to Laura's, I will put you in a cell at the police station." Joaquín took my arm and moved toward the front door. "Mario, you too. Go home."

I wrenched my arm away from him. "Mario? Who is Juan? What does he have to do with K'antu? Is she in danger? What does he mean Juan is on the move? What is going on?"

I was hysterical. Mario put his arm around my shoulders and tried to calm me down as he guided me to the front of the house.

When the three of us got to the street, Joaquín turned to me, "Tamara, I know K'antu was your friend, but you have no idea what you are doing by trying to find her. I am warning you, leave it alone."

He got back on his crappy little vehicle and went away.

"Who is Juan?" I sobbed in frustration.

Mario ran a hand through his hair, the tousled waves flopping right back into place. "He is Eduardo's brother."

I hiccupped and took a deep breath. "What was he doing contacting Miguelito?"

Mario looked away.

"It has something to do with K'antu, doesn't it? And you know what it is," I said.

"Let's go. I will take you back to Laura's house now."

"No. I am not going anywhere until you tell me what you know," I had gotten nowhere by following Mario. I should have gone to Patabamba.

"I am afraid you are, Tamara. And you will stay out of it from now on." The voice was coming from behind me. I turned. It was Rodolfo.

"Señor Alvarez? What are you doing here?"

"Joaquín called me. You two need to stop looking for K'antu. The police will take care of it. Now let's go. Mario, you can go directly home. I will take Tamara to Laura's house."

His car was parked behind Mario's. There was nothing for me to do but go back – for now. I got in and slammed the door without saying anything to Mario, who stalked over to his car. As Rodolfo drove away, I looked back and saw the pitiful figure of Miguelito in the flimsy doorway of the wall of shame.

Chapter 6

"I don't need you to babysit me," I drummed my fingers on the worktable. The morning sun shone through the open courtyard. I was in a sizeable three-walled building on Rodolfo's property. It was set up as Elías' workshop. My cousin was a glassblower. Before the earthquake, he had worked in town as an assistant to a shop owner. Both the shop and the man had been crushed in the disaster.

"I'm not babysitting you, Tamara," he said. He was busy cleaning the marver, the flat slab of metal where he rolled hot glass, with a dry towel, "we are waiting for Laura to come back."

"You mean you are watching me, so I won't go anywhere until she comes back."

"Yes. That's right," He gave up, admitting the obvious, "You should not be going off on your own. It's dangerous."

I shrugged. I had plans for later. He could stop me temporarily, but not forever. "Elías?"

"Yeah?"

He had dust in his hair, making the light brown color look blonde. His white shirt was open, displaying his tan pectoral muscles. There was a large bandage pasted to his side right under his ribs on the left side.

"What were you doing at Miguelito's house yesterday?"

Wincing, he folded the towel and laid it on the worktop. He stood hunched over, his eyes closed. "Visiting."

"Is your side hurting you? Do you want me to call a doctor?"

"No. I am fine."

He didn't look fine.

"Don't lie. I can see you are hurting. Let me go find –"

"No. No doctors. Don't go anywhere. There is a first aid kit in the cabinet. Please get it. All I need is a new bandage and aspirin." He pointed to a large wooden trunk in the corner.

"What happened to you anyway?" I went to the trunk and brought back an old metal first aid box.

"I... I burned myself. No big deal, it happens. Part of the job." He avoided my eyes and tore off his bandage.

I looked. It was no burn. I didn't know anything about injuries, but it looked a lot like a cut from a sharp object.

"Elías! That is not a burn."

"I don't want to talk about it, Tamara, and neither do you." He spoke through his teeth.

"But –"

He turned toward the back of the room, a wall of brick with three square holes. The three holes were furnaces. The first one melted raw material to make glass and was typically heated to 2,400 degrees Fahrenheit. The next furnace was cooler, used to remold the glass as it cooled. The last chamber was used to finish the cooling process. The finished piece would have to cool at a slow rate, or it would crack.

"Don't wish for danger, for it will come to you," he muttered.

"What does that mean, *primo*?"

"It means bad things happen."

"What bad things? What has happened to you?"

"Not to me, to Eduardo. I – he – now he's dead and –"

"And what, *primo*? Were you and he friends?"

To my horror, my cousin started crying. But before I could say anything else, my Aunt Laura came in. Elías hid his face, slapped a bandage on his side, and went to get his shirt.

"There you two are. Tamara, come. The magistrate is here, and we are going to have lunch. Elías, nice to see you." She swept out without seeing my cousin, assuming I would follow, which I did, after staring at my cousin. He refused to look back at me.

Soon I found myself sitting at a table on the terrace of Rodolfo's house. Laura and Rodolfo sat together, and Tomás Romero, who had on his politician's smile, was also there. His upturned lips, which showed neither genuine warmth nor indifference, were thick and surrounded by yesterday's beard.

He looked at me with his heavily lidded eyes, "My dear girl, what a welcome back to Manchay you are having – a murder, and your friend disappears. I am sorry this has happened. It is such a shame when these people go wrong…"

I did not know how to answer him. What people was he talking about? I looked at Laura, who leaned in toward Tomás.

"Tamara is good friends with K'antu, Tomás. She finds it hard to believe her friend is guilty of any crime."

"Ah," Tomás shook his head sadly, "It is a horrible thing, for sure, such a pretty little girl, but so many problems at home. Eduardo, you know, was abusive. She must have been driven to it by whatever latest foolishness her husband had her doing. One can hardly blame her for running away. So unfortunate she will be the one brought to justice when he was undoubtedly a big influence on her behavior."

He picked up a *tequeño*, dipped it into the green avocado sauce, different from guacamole from Mexico, and bit down. He looked like those goofy cartoon donkeys with exaggerated teeth.

"What do you mean 'foolishness her husband had her doing'? What was he doing that was wrong, I mean besides being abusive to K'antu?"

Tomás glanced at Laura, who nodded.

"My child, your aunt did not want you to find out, but because of the murder, I am afraid you must know. We believe K'antu has been and continues to be involved in the kind of activism that easily turns into fanaticism and violence – along with Eduardo and his brother Juan."

"What?" I nearly fell out of my chair.

"Sit down, Tamara. Let him explain," Laura said.

Tomás was nodding sagely to himself, "Yes, it is difficult to understand. The girl was beautiful..."

"What does beauty have to do with anything? Get to the point," I said.

"Tamara," Laura said, a note of warning in her voice.

"No matter, no matter, Laura. The girl is upset. Who can blame her?" Tomás focused his eyes on me, "Eduardo and Juan have been trying to wrest control of Manchay from me. Me, the

60

elected magistrate, if you can believe it. They've been at it for the past year – ever since the earthquake. They have incited their people, protested, thrown badly made smoke bombs into city hall, and broke into my office in a misplaced attempt to find evidence of corruption and misuse of monies – of which, I am happy to say, they found none."

I was shocked, not at the things he was saying, but at the fact that he would put all the blame on K'antu when, or if, she was found.

"Yes, indeed," he misunderstood my expression, "I can see you are surprised. Perhaps you do not want to believe it. But their activities are well documented. And, unfortunately, K'antu was involved in their exploits. No doubt Eduardo married her because of her expertise in weaponry –"

"That's a hobby," I protested, "she practiced it out of respect for her ancestors. She did not use it against anyone, ever. She wouldn't."

"Such loyalty is to be admired, my dear. But how well did you know K'antu after all? How well could you? You do not live here full time. You were here only for small amounts of time each year. No, I am sorry, my pet, but she was, indeed, involved in violent activism. And it has gotten worse since the earthquake," Tomás said.

"My pet?" I said, trying not to explode. Despite his condescension, he had a point. I was friends with K'antu, but I only saw her a few weeks out of every year. What did I know about her? On the other hand, she had saved my life. She had always been good to me. I felt in my bones she could never have murdered anyone. "I know her a lot better than you know me,

Tomás. And I do not believe you. Also, by the way, my name is Tamara."

"Tamara," My aunt said sharply. Then, as if none of the previous conversations had happened, she said, "Why don't we have dessert? Rodolfo, I hear your cook has made Tamara's favorite, *picarones.*"

"Regarding the earthquake," I went on before she succeeded in trivializing the conversation, "hasn't it made the poor of Manchay poorer? Isn't it acceptable for people to participate in activism to make sure the poor get the resources they need?"

Three pairs of eyes stared at me.

"Tamara, *cariño*, we do our best for the people of Manchay. You see how Elías has been cared for here... and my workers –" Laura began.

"Oh, I know you help, *Tía*. I don't doubt that. But does everybody?" I stared pointedly at Tomás.

His eyes showed a flash of some strong emotion for a second. But he smiled ruefully at me and said, "Such passion in the young. It is a good thing. Until it isn't."

He leaned toward me and said in a grim voice, "Resorting to violence cannot be allowed. To place bombs in government areas creates chaos and helps nothing. To trespass on my property is an invasion of my privacy and a waste of time. Now, getting back to K'antu, perhaps she got tired of being a pawn in Juan and Eduardo's violent game and killed one of them off. One could understand her motivation while at the same time abhorring her actions."

He went on without giving me a chance to respond, "Maybe she wanted to be more than a peon. She had, after all, as you say, been trained as a warrior before she married her husband. Maybe she wanted to be the one in power. Or maybe he struck her one too many times, and she hit him back, and it went wrong. Or she got angry. One way or another, she must be found and brought to justice before she disappears altogether, and Juan and the rest of them take it into their own hands to escalate the violence."

The other two adults nodded.

"So, it has to be K'antu? You wouldn't consider the possibility it is anyone else?"

"There is one other possibility –" Rodolfo said.

"Rodolfo, no," Laura tried to distract me from his comment, "Tamara, you need to try these *picarones*."

"No, I need to know what he means. Who is the other possibility?"

"Rodolfo, don't," Laura said.

But he ignored her. "Your cousin Elías had a contentious relationship with Eduardo."

"What?" I said. First, there had been the maids' rumors about Eduardo and Elías being mixed up in something terrible, and then I had witnessed my cousin's grief over Eduardo's death. Now this cryptic comment. Was there a connection between my cousin and the murdered man that I wasn't understanding? Not that I believed for a second Elías was a murderer, but maybe he knew something he had not told anyone.

Why was Rodolfo bringing it up? Did he, like me, not believe K'antu was guilty? Could I enlist him as an ally? It hadn't seemed so when he came to get me at Miguelito's house – but maybe he was genuinely concerned about me. I would have to talk to him later.

Laura laughed and said, "Rodolfo. You read too much into their relationship. Tamara, Elías was a close friend to Eduardo, but he had no reason to kill him. Not, unfortunately, like K'antu."

"Stop. Tía, I am surprised at you. Neither my cousin nor K'antu is a killer. And you know it. You will all have to look somewhere else,"

But they all stared at me sadly and dished out dessert from the plate a maid had put on the table. I couldn't believe they would go from accusing people of a major crime to stuffing sweets in their mouths. Well, I was not about to fall into the same dangerous assumptions they had. There was one thing to do. I had to find K'antu, and I had to do it before they did.

Chapter 7

"I am going to the bathroom," I stood. I could feel the magistrate's eyes on me as I walked toward the house. My aunt hardly paid attention to my leaving, which was a good thing. The longer they ignored me, the more time I had to get away. I went through the house and out through the side door. I fired up the dune buggy we had come in – silly of her to leave the keys – and drove to the offices of People Help. It did not take long to get there, and I was so focused on my mission I forgot to panic about being in the center of 'Rubbletown.' I pushed open the glass door. It swung open a lot faster than I expected, and I leaned back while at the same time reaching for it so it wouldn't bang shut. I went in, being more cautious with the loosely hinged door. The front room was dimly lit. Behind a small desk was a small but wiry elderly woman with a pair of reading glasses hanging off the edge of her nose. A metal-plated name tag that said 'Señora Helena Ramos' was pinned to the lapel of her jacket.

"I'm looking for Mario... Mario Alvarez Doñoso. Is he here?"

The woman looked up from the book she had been reading. She peered at me and said, "I believe he is. Let me go back and see."

She went away. The office was sparsely furnished, but the plastering of posters on the wall made the room look full. I went over and read one of the posters. It had information on People Help's mission. I was engrossed in reading until a sound from behind startled me.

"Tamara?"

It was Mario. I turned. We stood looking at each other. Out of the corner of my eye, I saw Señora Ramos go back to the desk.

"Mario, I have to find K'antu. And you need to help me find her. This time for real."

"No. You don't. And no, I don't. Forget about it. Please. Let the police do their job."

He turned to go back into the other room.

I rushed to get in front of him, blocking his way. "You don't understand. I have to get to her before they do. They think she is guilty. I was at lunch with Laura and your dad. The magistrate was there too. They all blindly assume it was K'antu."

The look Mario gave me could have withered a ripe plum into a prune. "I know. We have been over all this already. But what are you going to do with her if you get her? You don't even live here. How are you going to hide her?"

I hadn't thought that far ahead. Mario noticed.

"Look, Tamara, let them find her. Maybe you can convince your aunt to help K'antu once she is found and locked up."

Frowning, I said, "I don't understand why my aunt believes so implicitly in K'antu's guilt.

She knows her so well. Why would any of them believe it so easily when there could be any number of explanations? No, there is more to this, and the only way to find out is to find K'antu."

"Oh, there is more to the story, all right. But you getting any more involved will only get you – and K'antu – into more trouble." Mario said

"What is your problem? You were willing enough to help me find her yesterday –"

He put his hand up, palm facing me. "I was trying to divert your attention away from Patabamba. I didn't want you to get lost going there."

"That... that's not... but..." Tears welled up in my eyes, so I looked down at the herringbone-patterned parquet floor. It was a series of pretty blues marred only by a few streaks of dirt. Mario was a jerk. I had come here because I was still afraid of going to Patabamba by myself. But if I tried hard enough, I could find the courage. I swiveled to leave.

Mario's voice came from behind me, sounding soft and inviting, "Why don't you come inside instead of leaving? I will introduce you to the people who work here, and you can see the plans we have to help rebuild houses. Your Aunt Ada is going to be one of the recipients. You can look at the options she chose..."

It was a compelling invitation. It almost worked. Outside, I fired up the dune buggy and checked the cooler in the back. It was empty. I got in and zipped out of the parking lot, so the tires squealed. I stopped at the corner store where the owner insisted on making me two large *butifarra* sandwiches at no charge.

"No, Señor, I cannot allow you to give me these for free. Please, let me pay you."

"Señorita, my son works on your aunt's land. She has done so much for him. This is the least I can do to repay her. Please, take them and enjoy them."

He added fruit, bananas and figs, and a couple of *Sublimes* – my favorite Peruvian chocolate. He carried all the food to the dune buggy and packed it carefully in the cooler, adding ice packs to keep it all cool. I thanked him and drove off. The office of People Help was at the edge of town closest to Laura's property, so I did not have far to go before reaching it. The danger would be to drive to the back of the property before anyone saw me and tried to stop me. If Laura had noticed I was gone and that the dune buggy was missing, she might guess my plans and intercept me.

People were busy in the vineyard, so they did not notice me. As I got closer to the house, I slowed the buggy, hoping the crunch of gravel would not make enough noise to call people out of the house - especially Laura.

The buggy glided by the house, but no one came out. Next would be to get to the path. It led up the foothills to Patabamba and lay among a cluster of desert plants, including *huarango* trees and several types of cactus, all with prickly spines. The *huarangos* were everywhere in the Perúvian desert terrain. They were short trees without much of a trunk, and their branches spread in all directions like an umbrella. The dark green leaves gave off lots of shade. Not that they needed to, it never got all that hot.

I passed the cluster of trees and made a sharp left turn, continuing up the steep, hilly incline. I continued patting myself mentally on the back – until I saw something ahead of me. My heart almost stopped.

A dark figure stood at the entrance of the oasis. It blocked my way, leaning casually against one of the trees. Its wavy hair curled in the humidity, and the green eyes looked in my direction. Mario. I stopped the buggy only inches away from him.

"Get out of my way, Son of Rodolfo."

He grinned, "You've managed to make it sound even more offensive than it was before. But don't worry, I am not offended. I will still go with you."

He climbed in. I tried to push him, but he held on tight.

"So now you want to come with me? After your spiel back there about leaving things alone? And how in the hell did you get here so fast?" I asked.

"Get here so fast? Well, that wasn't hard. I came the back way. Didn't you? Ah, I know, you took a long time at the store. I hope you got enough for both of us." He reached toward the cooler.

I slapped his hand. He laughed but withdrew it. His face got serious.

"But seriously, I'm not letting you go there alone."

"Why not? I can take care of myself," I bristled.

"I can see that," he said, looking at me.

I tried to punch him in the arm, but he twisted out of the way, "If we are not going to eat, let's get going before someone catches up to us."

"Ugh, fine, you can come with me if you want. But don't try

to stop me from looking for K'antu. And I'm in charge of what we do and how we do things."

"Yes, ma'am." He sat back. "I assume you know the way to Patabamba?"

"Of course, you go up this path."

"Whatever you say, you're in charge."

I felt evil satisfaction in seeing his body jerk when I purposely accelerated quickly and then slowed down abruptly to navigate the entrance.

"Hey, take it easy, Miss Driver. You're about to go up a pretty dangerous path..."

It was my turn to find humor in the situation. "Scared? You can always jump out."

"No, I am not scared. Just don't drive me off of a cliff, okay? I'd like to live to become a doctor."

"Of course, you would," I said through my teeth.

The dunes of the foothills of the Andes are bleak. Besides the occasional *huarango* or cactus, they looked very much like gigantic piles of sand. There was never much wind, and it hardly rained at all, even though the air was humid.

Patabamba wasn't far from Manchay as the crow flies, but the road up took time because it was winding and narrow. We were both lost in thought. I kept driving. It seemed like an eternity. Not long after we had left the oasis, Mario said, "There's a cluster of trees ahead. Why don't we get out and eat? I'm starving."

I kept driving, passing the trees.

"Oh, come on, Tamara. You bought those sandwiches. I saw you from across the street. So, you must have had a plan to eat them. What do you say? We don't have to stop for long, and I can drive if you want, after lunch.

"All right," I sighed loudly, "we will stop. But I keep driving when we get back in."

"Suit yourself."

Backing the buggy up, I guided it toward the trees and parked. Mario hopped out and grabbed the cooler. I reached under the seat and found a blanket, which I spread on the sandy ground under the shade. We sat munching on sandwiches. I ignored him for a while, concentrating on what I would say to anyone we met in Patabamba until he spoke.

"It's nice here, isn't it?"

It wasn't. Not to me. I am not the kind who appreciates endless desert scenery. So instead of saying something vacuous, I said, "So really, why are you here? Back at the People Help office, you were totally against me trying to find K'antu."

"I couldn't talk freely there, Tamara. The walls have ears. Things get around. They should think I am discouraging you from finding her."

"Then... you think it's good I'm looking for her?" I was surprised.

He peeled a banana, concentrating on it. "I know something is off. And I don't like my father's easy acceptance of K'antu's guilt."

"Or Laura's," I said. "Neither do I," I got up.

Suddenly there was a rumbling noise, and the ground started shaking. I tripped and landed back on the blanket, grabbing it with both hands. Even though logically, I knew that would not help me hold on to the stable ground, it was a natural reflex. My body tensed, and I couldn't move. My mouth fell open, but I uttered no sound.

In a flash, it all started coming back. Everything that had happened last year. The darkness... The weird greenish glow in the air... The ground was rolling like it was doing now... all of the cries for help, including mine – and those of some who were doomed to die... I was stuck... my leg – I had known I was about to die.

"Tamara."

Someone slapped me. I opened my eyes. Mario was holding me and gazing intently at my face.

"You were screaming, and you blacked out. But you are okay. It was a tremor. But it is over now. Everything is all right."

My senses started to come back. I was shaking, and my heart was pounding. No, wait. It was Mario's heart. Why could I feel his heart? I focused my eyes. He had me in a bear hug.

Pushing him away, I looked around. The ground had stopped moving. I tried to relax, stood up, and moved to the edge of the hill. From that angle, I saw the valley below. I was looking for Laura's vineyard. Sun got into my eyes, and I squinted. I found what I was looking for and breathed deeply, not seeing any major changes in the landscape or any ant-like people scurrying around in panic.

"It must be all right. It doesn't look like anyone down there has been hurt..." I burst into tears.

Mario came and put his arm around my shoulder, "Come away from the edge there. Just in case -"

Whatever he was about to say, it wouldn't be something I

wanted to hear. I twisted away from him so he would stop talking.

"I am sorry, Tamara," he said, letting me go, "I didn't mean to say that. Everything is all right. It was just a small tremor."

"You were going to say, 'in case it happens again, and you fall off the cliff,' weren't you?" I was reacting out of a delayed fear. It wasn't fair to him, but it felt good.

"No! I… uh…"

I stomped back to the dune buggy and was about to get in when a voice coming from beyond the trees shouted, "Get down on the ground. Both of you. Now."

We did not do as the voice ordered. Instead, we stared at each other.

Something whizzed past us and landed with a thump. We both turned to it. Behind us, sticking out of the sand like the forlorn branch of a fallen tree, was the long handle of a macana, an Incan spear. My insides dropped into my feet.

"What the hell?" Mario shouted.

"I said get down. Next time I won't miss one of you," the voice shouted.

Mario put a hand on my arm, and we both got on the ground. I laid my head sideways, but Mario's face was three inches from mine, so I turned away, still unhappy with him. Sand fell off of my eyelashes but mercifully did not get into my eyes. But perhaps it would not have mattered since the tears of fear that started flowing would probably have flushed the sand out.

"Who are you?" Mario called in a muffled voice. He coughed, presumably having inhaled a mouthful of sand.

"Shut up," the voice called. It was getting closer.

"Oh God," I started crying harder. What was happening?

Mario whispered something to me, but I did not hear.

A shadow loomed, and the person was there. He, the voice was male, went to Mario first. I squeezed my eyes shut but could still hear. It sounded like he was tying Mario up. I wanted to know what was going on but did not dare look.

When our attacker came over to me and forced my arms behind my back, I thought of something I had read a few years ago about getting out of bindings. So, I tried it. I turned my wrists at a certain angle, fighting to keep them aligned, my thumb on one hand and my pinky finger on the other, even as the rope dug painfully into my skin. After they finished tying my wrists, they similarly disabled my feet and went back to Mario. He was taken away. I was sweating profusely with fear. This was worse than the tremor by far. Now I wish I hadn't reacted the way I did. Was I stupid? A dumb little movement of the earth... it was no scarier than a thunderstorm, right? Or a tornado? And I never fainted over those... Speaking of fainting, I felt like I would. But I couldn't. I had to stay conscious and get away so I could help Mario. A small surge of arrogance ran through me. He probably hadn't thought quickly of a way to escape his bindings.

While the guy was gone doing whatever he was doing with Mario, I was alone, so I shifted and tried to realign my hands. I sweated. It wasn't working. My heart pounded. But as I was about to give up, my wrists came together, and the rope loosened. I could hardly believe it. Who knew it would work? Then again, the person who was taking us hostage must not be very bright. He had not noticed I was doing strange acrobatics with my hands. That thought boosted my spirits considerably. I sat as quickly as I could and began pulling the rope off my wrists. It took a few seconds, but I finally got it. I began untying the rope on my feet.

Every half-second, I looked up. I needed to be quick. Whoever he was would be back for me in a moment. My heart lurched. Mario. What was the guy doing with him? I tried to work faster. If I could only get away, I could go get help. I would get an entire army of people to come get Mario back – people who knew these hills much better than I did.

Mario! I couldn't believe I was thinking of him right now. But it was my fault he had been dragged away. My fault... my mind went back to just a few minutes before when I had freaked out during the tremor. I had emerged from my stupor to the feel of his heartbeat.

No time for that. I shook those thoughts out of my head. I needed to finish untying myself and run. I had gotten the rest of the ropes loose when a damp cloth smelling of chemicals pressed against my face. Everything went dark.

Chapter 8

Somewhere between a dream and reality, I woke up. I was lying on soft, fragrant grass. I lay there, relaxed, with my eyes softly closed. There was a flute playing a soft melody somewhere in the background. A gentle breeze brushed my face. I hadn't felt this peaceful for over a year. Something came and blocked the sunlight from my face. I turned lazily onto my side. My eyes fluttered open. The first thing I saw was a pair of well-manicured male feet. My eyes traveled up and saw filmy white gypsy-like pants covering a pair of nicely shaped legs, visible through the opaque material.

His torso was bare – deeply tanned and well-muscled. I looked through my eyelashes.

"Mario."

"Shhh, be quiet. They'll come back..."

"Who will? Where are we?" I blinked.

"I don't know. I regained consciousness myself a minute ago. I was almost sorry to wake you – it looked like you had a good dream."

"What? You're crazy. I wasn't dreaming," I looked around. The room we were in had one window. It was a window like many in the adobe homes of the area - open to the elements with metal bars to keep people and animals out. There was a giant, hairy spider on its web in the corner of the window. I moved to lean on the wall and wiped the sweat from my forehead.

"We've been kidnapped," I said, realizing belatedly that my head hurt. I put my hand up and touched the back of my head. I have a lot of hair, and whatever hit me had not been hard enough to make me bleed, but I felt the beginnings of a bump. I looked at him. "Are you okay?"

Mario nodded. He went to a small table by the door. On the table was a pitcher with purplish liquid in it and a glass. He hesitated a moment, then picked up the pitcher and poured *Chicha Morada,* purple corn drink, into the glass, handing it to me.

"If you knew anything about me, you would know that I hate that drink . Take it away. And you go away too." I pushed the glass away. I was being rude to Mario, but my mind was fuzzy.

"I can't go away," he said matter-of-factly, "I am a prisoner too."

To illustrate his point, he rattled the doorknob. He banged his hand against the door in frustration. That made some of the liquid in the cup he was holding with his other hand splash out. He calmed down and wiped his hand on the side of his pants.

I turned away from him, knelt on the bed, and, trying to avoid the spider, peered out the window. Outside was a garden with fruit trees and a couple of dogs lying in a streak of sunlight between the shadows of the trees. A key rattled in the lock. I looked at Mario, who paled and stared at the door. A moment later, K'antu walked in, and a young man followed her.

"K'antu!" A rush of relief engulfed me. Everything was all right now. I tried to stand but got dizzy and had to sit back down.

"Tamara." My friend looked horrible. Her eyes were red with dark puffy circles underneath them. Her hair was stringy, and she looked thinner than she was two days ago. It was as if she had not eaten since she had found out about the death of Eduardo.

There was an awkward silence for a moment until K'antu's companion said, "Nice trick with the hands Tamara. You almost got away with it."

"So, you were the one who attacked us." If I hadn't been feeling a little ill, I would have punched him.

"Brilliant deduction, Tamara," he turned to Mario and said, "You. Come with me."

I panicked, "No. Wait. Where are you taking him? I want him to stay here with me."

The boy smirked, "It is not up to you. Let's go, Mario."

"Where are you taking him?"

"None of your business."

K'antu put a bony hand on the young man's arm, "Juan, be nice. There is no reason to traumatize Tamara. Tamara, this is Juan, my brother-in-law. Mario's room is the one next door. He will be fine. Please. Let them go. I need to talk to you for a while."

Mario was staring at me. We locked eyes. No one moved until Juan got tired of waiting and grabbed Mario's arm. "Let's go."

He shut the door. The lock turned from the outside.

"K'antu –" I protested, turning to her.

"Mario will be safe, and so will you. I promise you."

"But –"

"Please, Tamara. Hear me out. Isn't that what you were coming here for? To hear what I have to say?"

Yes, it was, although I had expected to find her on my terms. But I stopped protesting. I leaned against the wall and looked at the ceiling and the walls – anywhere except at K'antu. "So, am I in Patabamba?"

"Yes. And I am sorry you got here the way you did. You were followed yesterday when you went to People Help." K'antu began, sitting on the bed and speaking in a quiet voice, "They want to arrest me for Eduardo's death, but they know the people here would hide me well, so they let you go hoping you would do what they wouldn't be able to."

"Who is 'they?'" I said.

She looked at the floor. "The police."

"So, you had to kidnap me so they wouldn't find you."

K'antu had the grace to blush. "Well, yes, kind of…"

"Kind of? K'antu, I was tied up. I was hit on the head and was brought here by force. Now I am here behind a locked door – a prisoner. I would say that is more than 'kind of.'"

"You are safe here," K'antu said, staring vacantly out the window. "The people here are my people – and they hate the government and the police of Manchay. But they won't harm you.

Patabamba was a poor town, what they called an invasion. A generation ago, people from higher in the mountains had come down seeking a better life. With no roots on the coast and nowhere to go, they had taken over areas of the vast expanses of sandy hillside that were technically the state's property. They had eked out a living – and gradually built towns – like this one, Patabamba, above Manchay. Many of the workers on my aunt's vineyard came from here. It was because of this that I believed her.

"We are trying to figure out how to deal with the situation in Manchay."

"Who are 'we'?"

"The police won't look for Eduardo's killer, so we have to find who did it ourselves."

"We?" I repeated.

"A group of us," she said vaguely.

"K'antu," I said, my voice soft, "Please tell me there is a person who killed your husband and who isn't in this room right now."

K'antu flinched. Tears fell from her eyes, but she wiped them away and glanced at the door. "I thought you believed I did not kill Eduardo."

I was surprised. "How do you know?"

"A couple of people told me." Her eyes shifted sideways.

"Shit, gossip travels fast here. I thought you were in hiding. I don't think I have talked to anyone who knew where you were."

"If you must know, Mario told me."

I started. "Mario?"

"We've been in contact..." K'antu said lamely.

"What? How? I don't believe it."

"Well, not direct contact. Mario and Elías talked, and your cousin passed the word to us."

"Elías? How is he involved in all of this?"

K'antu ran her hand along an old scar on her wrist. "He and Eduardo were friends. Good friends... But never mind that. I also heard from Lorena you had been defending me to Tomás Romero."

That was just great. I threw my hands up. "Lorena – you mean the deputy magistrate? How have you not been caught yet? Everyone knows you are here."

"Lorena is – has been – our go-between. She is helping us figure out who is responsible for the theft of aid money. She would not turn me in."

"I am so confused," I said.

"Tamara, have a drink. You look pale. Sugar will do you good. I will explain everything."

"I hate –"

"Yes, yes, you don't like chicha. Fine. Here." K'antu pulled chocolate out of her pocket. I grabbed, unwrapped it, and stuck it in my mouth. She was right. I felt better.

"So, you know none of us received more than $500 after the earthquake. You also know the accounts don't add up. That means someone has been filtering money away from the people who need it and to themselves. We have been trying to discover who is responsible since before Eduardo was –"

Her voice trailed off.

"I am so sorry about Eduardo," I stammered, not knowing what else to say.

But K'antu hiccupped and stared at the ceiling. "Honestly, I don't know why I am crying. He – he was horrible to me – at least lately he was. He had become a completely different person. He and I – and now they think I killed him."

Leaning forward, I put my arm around her and murmured random platitudes.

"I did not kill him, *amiga*," K'antu said in a low whisper.

"I believe you," I said, "But –"

"But someone did." K'antu wiped her eyes with her sleeve. "And we need to find out why."

"Yes," I remembered what Rodolfo had insinuated. "What did Eduardo argue with Elías about, K'antu?"

K'antu shook her head, "No. Not Elías."

"But –"

"You would accuse your cousin, Tamara?"

"No… I… look, I heard they weren't exactly getting along. Maybe it went too far the other night… it would have been an accident, I know Elías would never do anything on purpose, but –"

"Forget it, Tamara. He did not kill my husband, and the reason they were having issues has nothing to do with why Eduardo was killed."

"How can you be so sure?"

K'antu got up and started pacing the room. "Believe me. He did not do it. It was someone trying to cover up the crime of stealing money from all of us."

"Who then? Who do you think did it?"

But K'antu did not answer. I changed the subject, "So where exactly am I anyway?"

K'antu's shoulders relaxed, "You are in the house of the unofficial mayor of Patabamba. He is an old man and senile. He keeps to himself at the other end of the house."

"This town is run by a crazy old man. And you have taken over his house to keep me, and Mario locked in it? What do you mean unofficial mayor?"

"I... I know it sounds incredible to you, Tamara. Patabamba is part of Manchay, but the people here do not recognize that government. The mayor has always been like family to everyone here. His was one of the first families to settle here, and he is well respected. Lorena is his daughter."

"His daughter?" So that was the connection.

"Yes. Lorena Guerra is his daughter. She helps with everything here."

"So does Lorena know Mario and I are here?" Tamara asked.

K'antu's face reddened. "Yes. We called her when Juan got here with the two of you."

"And she condones this? She is all right with you guys keeping us here?"

"Well, not exactly. But she won't do anything about it. She is on our side –"

"Whose side? What does that mean?"

"I mean, she knows about the government's corruption, and she believes I did not kill Eduardo."

"She knows the government is corrupt. Isn't she part of the government?" I raised an eyebrow.

K'antu sighed. "I mean, she suspects someone in the government like we do."

I stood and looked around. There was nowhere to go. I sat down again.

"Explain it all to me again, K'antu."

K'antu grabbed ahold of my hand and took a deep breath. "So, as you know, most people in this area are poor."

I nodded.

"You are probably also aware it is hard for anyone poor in Manchay to find an opportunity for a better life. It is not like in the United States, where you work hard and become rich."

"Well, that's not exactly the way it works –" I began. It had happened before to me. People made this assumption. The United States was the land of milk and honey. But K'antu was already moving on.

"Before the earthquake, things were bad, but afterward, it was much worse. Some people had friends and relatives from Lima help. They had money brought to them and food and people to fix the damage to their houses. The rest of us had to wait for public aid. Only the aid didn't come for weeks. And when it did, it wasn't enough."

"But that doesn't mean anyone was stealing it. Couldn't it have simply been not enough? Maybe there was too much damage and not enough money to distribute." I was playing devil's advocate. I knew the people in Manchay did not have enough money. My insides contracted at the memory of Miguelito. But what I didn't know was whether K'antu was entirely correct in blaming the government. Of course, I had been challenging Tomás Romero about it, but was he or someone in his administration a thief, or was it a lack of funds and shortness of time? Being kidnapped had made me more objective.

"What you might not know is Lorena is the liaison between Manchay's government and Lima. She saw discrepancies. She asked Tomás Romero about them, but he was able to explain them away in logical ways."

"So, what happened?" I asked.

"Nothing."

"Nothing?"

She shrugged, "These things take time."

A similar excuse to the one Rodolfo had given me.

"So, you are waiting?"

"Was. I – we – were waiting. Until Eduardo was murdered."

"K'antu?"

"Yes?"

"Why did you get married?"

She took her hand off of mine and turned away, "You wouldn't understand."

"You're right. I don't. You were way too young to get married. Laura told me you disappeared with him and didn't tell her about it. She also told me it looked like he was controlling you. Why, K'antu? Why were you letting him –?"

K'antu got up, went over to the little table, picked up the pitcher of *chicha,* and flung it at the wall. Purple liquid and shards of glass flew back toward the bed. I put my hands up to protect my head, but a large piece of glass hit me anyway. I screamed. It hurt, and my head wasn't in perfect shape, to begin with.

My friend turned to me. Her face was purple. "You are such a spoiled brat, Tamara. None of it is any of your business."

I cringed.

K'antu stood there for a moment, breathing hard, her fists

clenched, still in fighting mode. I picked up the corner of the blanket and blotted my forehead. There was blood on the cloth.

"I am sorry, *amiga*. So sorry. I should not have done that. Everything is so messed up right now." She started to cry.

I did not reply. My head hurt, and I could feel the blood dripping down my face. I stuck the blanket over the wound again, this time keeping it there.

Blubbering now, K'antu picked up another corner of the blanket and pressed it to her nose. "After my grandfather died last year, I lived off of Laura's charity. But that is not what I wanted. Eduardo's family is poor too, but they own land here in Patabamba. Together we were trying to support each other and improve our life. At least, that was the plan until something happened a few months ago."

"Why didn't you tell me?" I asked.

The look she gave me made me recoil. "Every time you have come to Perú, you have seen me at your aunt's house, and you assume everything is great. But you only see a part of it. I am Laura's employee. I have had to hide my pain and my poverty from you. It would have been unattractive to have whined to you about it."

"K'antu, I am your friend. You could have told me anything. I would have –"

"What? You would have what? Helped me? Thrown some money at me and left it at that? What were you going to do, Tamara? You can't solve my problems, so why should I tell you anything?" K'antu leaned against the wall and bent her knees, sliding down until she was lying in sticky liquid. She cried so hard I couldn't feel angry at what she had said.

"Okay, so you're right. Eduardo could help you. So, you married him."

"Maybe you think I am stupid, but yes, I thought that was the best thing I could do. I never thought he was –"

"He was what, a domestic abuser?"

"And –"

"And what?"

"Oh, lots of things. He and Juan spent a lot of time together. They were both angry about losing so much in the earthquake. When they realized what had been destroyed was not going to be replaced anytime soon, they became angrier. Eduardo started drinking. And when he was drunk, he would either disappear for days, or he would lash out at me. Then, two weeks ago, he came home, and he wasn't drunk. He was still angry, but he was sober. I was so happy. I wanted to talk to him, but he told me to go to bed. So, I did. Later, Juan came to the house. I got out of bed and went to the door to listen. They talked about the previous night. They had gone to someone's house and gotten something that made them happy. They were happy, but it was like an angry happy. I think they might have found something that proved we were right –someone was stealing money meant for the people."

"What was it? What did they find?" I asked.

K'antu's face had an anguished expression on it. "I don't know. I couldn't hear clearly, and Eduardo never confided in me."

"You don't know?"

"I don't, Tamara. I did not hear. I wish I had. I should have insisted he tell me. I should have told him to go to the authorities with whatever they had found. Maybe he would still be alive."

"Don't think like that. It is not your fault."

K'antu began to pick pieces of glass off of her clothes. When she had a handful, she put them down on the table. Then she wiped her hands on her sides and pulled the hem of her shirt out to check for more.

"Is there something else, K'antu?"

K'antu refused to look at me. "They did not talk about it after that. At least, not when I was around. But they had a lot of whispered conversations, and I heard the names Rodolfo and Tomás and…"

"And?"

"And Laura."

"Laura?"

K'antu hung her head. "I think they found something that implicated your aunt."

"My Aunt Laura?" I was dumbfounded.

"Yes."

I grabbed K'antu by the forearm and spun her, so she was facing me. "Did they – do you – believe Laura had something to do with embezzling money?"

K'antu looked back at her shirt.

"Do you?" I shook her arm.

"Tamara, stop. No. I don't. Not really."

"Not really?"

"Tamara, Laura has been nothing but kind to me. She has taught me many things. But she is good friends with Tomás and lots of other people with a lot of money and she –"

"She what?" My hand was still on her arm, and it was getting red. I loosened my grip.

"She doesn't fight for us." A stony look appeared on K'antu's face. She began picking at a string on her sleeve.

Letting go of her arm, I said, "What do you mean? She has never been anything but kind and generous to lots of people in Manchay."

K'antu continued the expressionless inspection of her shirt. "Yes, I know. But there is kindness, and then there is taking a stand against injustice. She does the first. She does not do the second."

She went on quickly before I could say something defensive, her expression softening, "I am not saying she is a bad person. But she won't defend us against the establishment. Maybe she knew about something and didn't take action."

"No. I don't believe it. She does help. She will help. She has nothing to do with it. I am sure of it. She will..."

K'antu sucked on her upper lip before saying, "Did you see her trying to stop them from coming after me?"

"Yes, I... I mean, of course, she did..." But the truth was I hadn't. My heart sank.

K'antu saw my distress and nodded.

"But K'antu, you did not kill your husband, and the police can't be stupid forever. Soon something must come to light that points away from you, and when they find the real killer, they will have found the embezzler also, and everything will be all right."

Her face was stained with tears as she said to me, "You are so innocent, *amiga*. They will not look for anyone else. They don't want anyone to know who killed Eduardo."

I ground my teeth. "So, we will have to find out whoever did it."

"Then... you will help us?" K'antu looked at me, her eyes wide.

"It is what I meant to do all along," I said, "I wish I could have done it my way."

K'antu laughed. I found nothing amusing about it.

"Don't look so serious, *amiga*. Now that you are going to help us, Juan will let you go around the compound freely. He will be back soon, and he will let us both out."

"Yeah, sure," I said, "just one more thing."

"Yes, *amiga*?" My friend had been moving toward the door as if someone were on the other side to open it immediately and free us.

"Why did the killer set it up to look like you did it?"

The weight of the world seemed to have left her shoulders. Had it been that important to her I stay and help?

She was jubilant, saying, "I think whoever did it, their aim was to weaken the bonds between the people who are fighting against them. By killing Eduardo with my knife, they could accuse me, and they would also force Juan to take action. With his brother dead and me in jail, Juan would get angrier. Everyone in Manchay and Patabamba knows him. He is volatile. They were setting him up to explode so they could arrest him too. With both him and me out of the way, there would be no one left to investigate the loss of the money."

"No one would step in and take his place – and yours?"

"I mean... there are others here, but they are not the kind of leader he is... I don't think they... I... honestly, I think they would probably go back to life the way it was – miserable and poor, but too tired and defeated to complain."

"So how did the killer get your *Tumi* knife?" I stood and stretched my legs, pacing, trailing my hand against the wall. It was cold and rough—Adobe, like my Aunt Ada's house. I glanced nervously out the window. I took my hand off the wall and sat back down, checking the walls for cracks.

"It is no secret I collect the ancient weapons of my ancestors," K'antu was saying, "As you are probably aware, the houses in Manchay are not the most secure. Any moron could break into our houses. It happens all the time. People are robbed daily around here. So, anyone could have found it and used it. It was in a box – and yes, the box was locked. But that doesn't mean much to someone determined to get it."

Before I could react, the door was opened, and Juan came back in.

"Juan, Tamara is going to help us," K'antu said to him happily.

The boy looked impassively at me.

"Isn't that great?" K'antu asked him.

He didn't answer.

"Sure." He fiddled in his pocket, looking for something.

"Let's go. I want to show you around *amiga*." K'antu grabbed me, and we went outside.

We stood under the shade of a covered walkway that ran around the courtyard between it and the building itself. Several teenagers were out in the courtyard. Each one of them had some form of ancient Inca weapon with them. They were practicing on different types of targets; canvas bullseyes, plastic models with human shapes, and pictures of real people pasted on the walls.

The sight of it took me back to the summers K'antu, and I would go out with her grandfather and train. We'd go to the hills behind Laura's, throwing macanas at targets in the cool desert air. They did not teach me any of the other weapons, but I loved to watch them as they wielded them. They laughed at me a lot the first year. I was gangly, and that made me clumsy. They laughed the second year also, and the third, until I finally began to improve. They taught me the art of weaponry, but I also learned not to take myself too seriously.

"Doesn't it remind you of when we were kids?" K'antu said, reading my mind.

Juan joined us, pushing Mario in front of him.

"Mario," I exclaimed.

"Tamara. Are you okay?" he asked.

"Yes, are you?"

"I am fine," he responded.

"Let's go talk to Lorena," K'antu said. She took me by the hand and led me towards a room on the far side of the complex. I turned and looked behind me, wanting to make sure Mario was following. He wasn't. He was standing with Juan watching the kids in the courtyard exercising with the weapons.

"Why aren't Juan and Mario coming with us, K'antu?" I asked.

"Oh, they'll come eventually. Here we are, let's go in."

This room had glass windows, and it was air-conditioned, and the walls were painted white. The furniture was new and well made, and there was an expensive-looking espresso machine on a long side table by one of the walls. Lorena stood up from behind a desk with a tablet on it. Even though she was short and square, the suit she wore, dark blue and well-cut, showed her figure off well. Her hair was slicked back and pinned in a bun. She had light skin and dark eyes behind dark-framed glasses.

"So, you have agreed to help," she said to me.

"She did. Have you discovered anything new?" K'antu replied before I could say anything.

Lorena's glasses flashed. She fiddled with the espresso machine. Once it was hissing, she put a mug under the nozzle and said, "Nothing good, I'm afraid, K'antu. They are building a fairly good case against you. Joaquin has not shown any willingness to look in other directions."

"What a surprise," Juan drawled, coming into the room. He was tall and muscular. His thick, black hair was shaved on both sides, and if someone looked closely enough, they would see an Inca warrior tattoo under the stubble on the left side of his head. He had a semi-permanent scowl on his face. Mario came in after him and stood awkwardly by the door.

"So, what is the plan? Are we going to run down the hill brandishing those weapons and scare them into finding the real killer?" I asked.

Juan's face darkened. He stood up and came toward me. His body was puffed out, and his hands were clenched. "Tell me," he looked me up and down, "is everyone in your country as ignorant and useless as you are?"

I raised my closed fist, ready to punch him if he got any

closer. But K'antu got between us. "Stop it, you two. This isn't helping."

"Get out of my way K'antu." He shoved K'antu aside and tried to grab me. I ducked and moved behind Lorena. He came after me and was about to grab me when something flew between us and tackled him. There was a short scuffle. Juan overpowered the figure, pinned him to the ground, and punched him hard.

"Mario!" I cried as blood spurted everywhere.

Chapter 9

The kids who had been training in the courtyard all gathered in the doorway. For one agonizing moment, no one did anything. I screamed at them to help Mario. I ran to them and tried to pull one of the boys inside so he would help. He backed away, so I turned to another, but before I could grab him, the kids were pushed aside by a man with Juan's same build and pepper gray hair.

"Juan," was all he needed to say; the attacker stopped and sat back on his heels.

"Take him away," Lorena told the man, who pushed Juan out the door.

"Somebody get a doctor." I knelt at Mario's side. I tore at the hem of my shirt, trying to get a piece of cloth to wipe the blood away.

Someone touched my shoulder. I looked up. Lorena tilted her head, gesturing for me to move away. She had a wet cloth in her hand. I stood up and supported myself on K'antu, who had put her arm around me. Lorena ministered to Mario, who had only opened his eyes briefly during the aftermath of the attack. Her hands felt his face and upper body.

"Is he..." I stammered.

Lorena smiled grimly, "He'll be fine. It's only a bloody nose."

"Only? That kid is crazy. He needs to be –" I started, but K'antu shushed me. The gray-haired man was back. Another man accompanied him.

"This is a doctor. Let him see the boy," the first man said. Then he disappeared.

As the doctor examined Mario, Lorena pulled me to the far end of the room, "Tamara, please, don't antagonize Juan."

Incredulous, I stared at her. "Me? He was the one being insulting."

"Please, keep quiet for now. As soon as Mario is okay, we will all talk. I will go see if Juan has calmed down."

She left the room.

I turned to K'antu, who looked away. She seemed upset, but at me, not at the situation. I shook my head in disbelief. Then I went to Mario and the doctor. "Is he okay?"

The doctor had cleaned Mario and bandaged his nose. Mario refused to look at me. "He will be. He should keep the ice pack on it for a while, and you can give him these if he complains of pain."

He pressed a small bottle of pills into my hand and left.

I turned to Mario. He was trying to sit. I helped him, and K'antu brought a chair.

"Mario, I... thank you for defending me... I -"

He put his hand up to stop me. "Don't worry about it. He is a bully. From what I hear, he's getting worse. I would have done the same for anyone."

"Oh. Well, when you are feeling better, we need to talk to Lorena," I said. We can't hang here and do nothing. We have to find a way to clear K'antu's name.

"I'm ready. Let's talk now." He stood up slowly.

K'antu looked nervous. "I think it would be good if Lorena came back in here. I will go get her."

She walked out the door before either of us could say anything. Mario leaned back on the chair. He still had the ice pack to his nose. He had not looked directly at me since he had been attacked. As we waited, I picked at my nails. We waited in silence.

When K'antu opened the door again, Lorena was behind her. I could hear shouting and cheering. K'antu came in, and the noises were muffled when Lorena shut the door. They brought chairs over to be close to Mario.

Lorena sat rigidly; her feet crossed at the ankle. She took off her glasses and let them drop to her chest, hanging off of their chain. She peered at me and put her glasses back on. "Are you willing to do whatever it takes to help us, Tamara?"

I glanced at K'antu. She nodded her head. "I... I guess."

"Then I am afraid we are going to ask you to do things you might not be comfortable with. But please hear me out before you say anything."

I looked at her and then at K'antu, who had a pleading expression on her face as if she were anticipating my reaction already. My eyes went to Mario, and I was surprised to see he was staring at me, his eyes dark and the rest of his face impassive.

"Go ahead," I said.

Lorena breathed. "All right, so far you are aware K'antu has been accused of murdering her husband. You also know you have been brought here, perhaps not under the best of circumstances –"."

I blew air through my lips and rolled my eyes.

Lorena saw the gesture, "You are right. It was horrible the way it happened. It must have scared you to death. But I am afraid we are desperate. Here is the situation. They are going to charge K'antu with Eduardo's murder – probably tomorrow morning. After that, we will all become accessories if we continue to hide her. So far, she is here under the protection of the people of Patabamba because they know how these things work. They believe she is being set up, that Tomás Romero had Eduardo killed because he was close to proving Tomás has stolen thousands of dollars - maybe hundreds of thousands – from the people of Manchay and Patabamba. K'antu is here, and the people will do anything to protect her from the injustice of the charges. For the most part, the kids who know where K'antu is hiding are intelligent kids who are desperately poor and fed up with being bullied by the government. Unfortunately, they have chosen as their leader an irrational and unpredictable man, Juan. In the past year, he has shown himself to be an aggressive but charismatic leader. I am afraid you have only seen his bad side, which has become worse since his brother's death."

I huffed again but said nothing.

"I am here unofficially," Lorena continued, eyeing me, "and I can move between here and my office of deputy magistrate because I was born here in Patabamba, and the people trust me. Tomás sent me here ostensibly to calm the mood of the people. He does not know I know where K'antu is. Joaquin, our chief detective in Manchay, has already been here and, naturally, did not find her."

"So? What have you done to help?" I said.

Lorena glared at me. "No one knows exactly what Eduardo found out. He was killed before he could reveal the information. But K'antu believes he had hard evidence of corruption."

I looked at K'antu and narrowed my eyes. K'antu was nodding at Lorena and avoiding my gaze. That had not exactly been what K'antu had told me earlier in the room. What was K'antu up to?

"If we could find that evidence, we could arrest somebody –" Lorena continued.

"Who?" I interrupted.

Lorena stood and went to fill her cup with more espresso. "We are not sure," she answered with her back to me, "That's what we need to find out. I have worked with Tomás for years, and if he has been stealing the aid money, I have not found proof. It could be someone else, not him."

"Who?" I repeated.

"I don't want to list a bunch of names without a little bit of evidence they could be guilty," Lorena said pompously, "Suffice it to say there are several people who might have found a way to siphon money away from People Help."

She stared at Mario with a pensive look, but he was lost in his thoughts.

"Anyway," K'antu's voice was loud, "if we can find out who has been stealing the money, we might also be closer to discovering who killed Eduardo and why. Then I could come out of hiding, and we could start the process of justice for the people who need the aid money without Juan getting any further involved."

"You make it sound so easy," I said, "but so far, neither of you has suggested anything specific."

Lorena turned and looked sharply at me. She was about to speak, but K'antu said, "No, Señora, let me."

She turned to me, "*Amiga*, you've been through a lot in the last couple of days. Of course, this won't be easy, but I believe we can do it. Especially with your help – and Mario's."

She blinked a couple of times and opened her eyes wide, pleading with me.

"You didn't tell me you knew Eduardo had evidence of corruption back when we were in the room," I said to her.

K'antu's eyes widened. "I did."

"No, you didn't. What you said was you didn't know exactly what they found."

K'antu shifted uncomfortably and looked toward Lorena but talked to me, "I meant to say I was pretty sure they had evidence. I'm still not completely sure. Please, Tamara…"

"All right, K'antu. It's okay. Go on," I said.

"We need to have Juan open up to us about what it is Eduardo found. He's not ready. But I'm working on it. I need you to be patient. Please." K'antu looked between Mario and me, including him in her appeal

"Yes, and if you kids find anything out, you must bring it to me - and only me - no matter what," Lorena said.

"What will you do with it if we do find something?" I asked.

Light flashed in Lorena's glasses, "I will use it to clear K'antu, of course."

Would she? Or would she take it to Tomás or Laura first? I looked again at Mario and was surprised to see him looking at me. He nodded slowly at me.

Sighing, I said, "All right, K'antu, I said I would help you, so I'll go along with this for now. But what about Laura? She must be wondering where I am..."

"I will have a quiet word with her. She cannot know exactly where you are, but I will tell her you are with Mario." Lorena picked up her purse and prepared to leave.

"And Juan? I can cooperate, but it doesn't seem like he wants me here. What if he locks me into the room again? What if he -"

"I will talk to his father. He has considerable influence on Juan."

"And I will talk to him too," K'antu said, "He will be reasonable..."

I rolled my eyes.

That night I sat outside next to K'antu on a cheap plastic lawn chair. There was a bonfire in a fire pit in the middle of the courtyard. The kids who had been playing with weapons earlier were all there. Bright lights ran under the awning that made the roof of the covered walkway on all four sides of the courtyard, and the fire provided warmth in the chilly mountain air.

K'antu and Lorena had talked to Juan. He told them if Mario and I were locked in at night, we could be let out during the day.

I had protested, but K'antu looked so tired and scared. Eventually, I gave in. Mario continued with his vow of silence. He didn't care what happened to him – or me.

Juan smirked across the flames at me before launching into a long-winded account of his prowess beating a boy, who was from a town higher in the mountains, at spear throwing.

"What a windbag," I muttered to myself. Mario, who was sitting next to me, overheard.

"He is the typical jackass everyone admires because they have to," Mario said through his teeth.

"Shut up, you two," K'antu hissed under her breath, "Let's get through tonight at least without another incident."

I turned to her and said, "Sorry, K'antu."

I might have kept whispering to Mario, but Juan had other ideas.

"It is time to go back to your cages for the night, little birdies. K'antu, come with me."

I was about to ask why K'antu had to be locked up too when Juan whistled, and two other boys came over, forced Mario and me to stand, and prodded us along toward the side of the compound toward the bedrooms. I turned, searching for K'antu. She and Juan were following us. Juan had his arm around K'antu. She was looking at his face, listening intently to what he was saying. I looked wildly at Mario, but he was lost in his thoughts.

They thrust me into my room. Someone shut the door. The key turned in the lock. Another door slammed—Mario's.

Light coming in through the window let me see the room. It was dim but enough to see there was a new, clean blanket on the bed. I sat down. The mattress, plastic covered, was thin, and the wool of the blanket was coarse. There was no pillow. My foot hit something under the bed. I got on my hands and knees and looked. It was a ceramic bowl – a bedpan. I figured no one would be coming to take me on a bathroom break in the middle of the night, so I was supposed to use the chamber pot. I stood and dusted my hands off. The floor was grainy like they couldn't keep the sand outside from spilling in. I turned. The table was still there, but the pitcher of *chicha* had not been replaced. With any luck, I could wait until morning and go to a real bathroom.

I sat on the bed and leaned against the wall, knowing I would never sleep. This room reminded me of my Aunt Ada's house, and since last year I could not think of that house without remembering the earthquake. There was nothing like Mother Nature's occasional temper tantrums to remind people they have no control whatsoever over their lives. I had been peacefully ignorant of that fact – until the longest and strongest earthquake in Manchay's history had ripped the blinders off of my eyes.

Breathing deeply, I practiced the meditation techniques a friend in Chicago had encouraged me to do after getting back. I had spent months jumping nervously at any trembling ground; a truck on a bridge, a loud blast of lightning, and floors shaking.

I shifted, trying to get a little more comfortable. K'antu was hiding something. Was she nervous because the police were looking for her? Or could there be something about her husband's death she had not told me? Was my blind faith in my friend foolish?

I didn't want to think about all this and started to regret staying. I should have told Lorena to tell Laura to come to get me.

But K'antu needed help. She was hiding something. I needed to know what. There was so much conflict going on inside me. Drop everything and go back to safety. Who cares if it was important to me? Or stay and live my fears over and over? It had been a long day, and my eyes were heavy. I fell asleep sitting up.

The next morning, I was in the courtyard seated next to Mario. There was a plate of warm bread, small, dense rolls, and a stick of butter in front of me. These buns were famous in the area. Usually, I scarfed down several at a time, but this morning I had little appetite. I picked at one and studiously ignored Mario. Two could play at that game.

We were on the side of the courtyard close – but not too close – to some kids who handled *ayllos* trying to control the erratic movement of the weapon. They brandished the devices like lassos at life-size plastic mannequins, every once in a while succeeding in entwining them in the 'victims' feet, causing the plastic figures to fall.

"Why are they training anyway?" I said, "Do these kids think they are going to go to Manchay, yell a war cry and entrap someone with those ridiculous things? Are they going to snare the magistrate and solve all of their problems?"

Mario's lips pressed together. "Probably not, but they are proud of their heritage. It is good exercise, and it's better than other alternatives – like building bombs."

"Whatever." I hadn't thought of it like that.

Juan sauntered over and sat down in between us. We were forced to move. "So, what do you think of my little army, Tamara?"

"Army?" I began, looking with fascination at the tattoo on

Juan's head. I would have said something else, but Mario made a kind of choking face at me, so I controlled myself, "Impressive, Juan. You are doing a great job of keeping these kids occupied while you plan your meetings with the government."

Juan turned to me, a supercilious look on his face. "Do you think this is a game?"

Immediately, I regretted saying anything. "No... I mean..."

"Get up," Juan ordered.

"What?" I was surprised and more than a little uneasy.

He stood and leaned over me, his shadow covering me.

"I said get up." He turned and called to one of the boys who had been throwing a *macana*. "Oliver, come here."

Oliver glided over. In his hand was the short wooden spear the Incas used to throw at, or club, their human prey. Many of the weapons I had seen thrown so far that morning had simple lead star-shaped ends on them. Some were made of copper or silver – all were star-shaped. Oliver's was made of gold with a burnished wooden shaft with a couple of Incan carvings near the end. It was by far the most beautiful one of the group. He looked inquisitively at Juan.

"Give Tamara your spear," Juan demanded.

"But..." Oliver was hesitant to give over such a prized object.

"Has everyone gone deaf this morning? I said give it to her." Juan snatched it out of Oliver's hands and shoved the other boy away. Oliver stumbled but stayed standing. His face went pale. When he recovered his balance, he stalked over to the shade and grabbed a plate, slopping food onto it so forcefully some of it fell on the ground. A dog wandered in and lay in the sun, ribs showing and scrawny belly expanding and contracting.

"Come with me," Juan said. I looked at Mario, panicking. But he was staring at his plate. Shoulders slumping, I turned and followed Juan, who had started, confident I would obey his order.

He led me to a spot in the courtyard. "Stand here. Take the spear and throw it toward the target. Try to hit at least the edge of it, all right?"

He laughed at his wit, and several of the other kids who had stopped what they were doing to gather around also found him funny. Someone made a joke about *gringos*, and the general merriment increased.

"Silence," Juan said. The single word was said in a low voice, but somehow the crowd immediately got quiet.

So, this is what he wanted – to embarrass me because I ridiculed him. No problem. He must not know about my sessions with K'antu and her grandfather. I held the spear. It was beautiful, cool to the touch, smooth, and not too heavy. It had an energy coursing through it like it was alive and ready to do my bidding. Or perhaps I imagined it. I looked around. The kids had all stopped and turned to face me, blending in a homogeneous mass of black hair and flat, sunburned brown faces. Only one person stood out: a pair of green eyes, wavy hair, expressionless face.

"Throw it," Juan all but screeched – but in a low whisper that brushed at my face.

I looked at him.

"Do it, Tamara." K'antu's voice was like a blast of fresh airbrushing the back of my neck. "Throw it."

Turning, I assessed the target Juan pointed to. It was nothing but a square of soft wood . There were a couple of star-like dents on it already, not on the edges, but nowhere near the middle. Oliver had been practicing on this block of wood before Juan called him over.

"What are you waiting for? Throw it," Juan yelled, losing his patience.

Muscles I hadn't used for a while fired up. I threw it and turned away, not caring what the result was. I walked toward K'antu. Behind me, there was a dull thud and a collective gasp. K'antu smirked and grinned at me. The kids stood silent, but Mario's voice rang out, cheering me. I turned, seeing Juan before anything else. His face had a crafty, thoughtful look on it. K'antu took my arm and turned me all the way around, pointing toward the target. It had a perfect star-shaped dent in the exact middle of the block of wood.

Chapter 10

The desert can be a tricky place - miles and miles of nothing but sand, burning the eyes, sucking the energy of one's spirit. And then, in the middle of nowhere, an oasis appears with trees and water. I was in one of these this morning, but it wasn't a relief to be there. From here, I could look down and see the town of Manchay. The houses appeared tiny, like miniature matchstick models, obscured by the greenery of vineyards.

Even though I could see the town, I did not want to, so I turned my head. Looking the other way, I saw the river which originated higher in the Andes and ended as a trickle of cold water barely gurgling over a rocky bank to drip into a small lake in the middle of the oasis.

To the left of the river was a prominent symbol made of rocks spread over a patch of sand. It was a collection of stones collected together to "write" something in the tradition of the Nazca people, who drew oversized animals and figures on the desert floor, presumably as a kind of communication device. No one really knew. The ones I was looking at were copied from that style in modern times.

I admired the ability of the artists to make a sign they could not see until they had stepped far away, even if the modern ones were politics and advertisements, not animals and geometric symbols.

"Quit daydreaming and get over here." Juan had woken me at daybreak. It was the day after I had hit the target. He had terrified me by coming into my room in the dark and shaking me awake. At first, I had no idea who he was. When I finally fully woke up, he stopped shaking me, throwing me a banana, and telling me to get up and come outside in two minutes.

Once outside, I was herded into a dune buggy. Oliver and K'antu were there as well, their faces grim. Mario was absent. Where was he? Juan had driven about forty minutes before we ended up at this oasis.

I did as Juan asked, approaching the rough wooden bench he was sitting on. He contemplated me.

"You showed promise yesterday. Maybe you are exactly what we need. But I must be sure. So, you are going to do some drills up here. If it turns out it wasn't a lucky break, you can join our group."

"Join your group? What does that mean exactly? What makes you think I want to join any group of yours? And what if it was just luck?" I asked.

Juan stood up. He took off his t-shirt, walked over, and grabbed K'antu. He took her over to the pond, forced her to her knees, and dunked her head underwater.

"Stop it. What are you doing?" I screamed. Was he insane?

He let go of K'antu and stepped away. I ran to her and helped her up. She sucked in the air. I wiped K'antu's hair out of her face and ran my hands up and down her arms to warm her in the chilly morning air.

I glared at Juan. He took no notice. He was back on his bench, chiseling at a piece of wood with a small knife. I looked at Oliver, who had the same non-expression on his face, there since I got in the dune buggy.

"What did you do that for?" I said.

For an answer, he came over and shoved me away from K'antu, grabbing her neck again. I fell on my butt, threw up my hands, and screamed, "No, don't."

His eyes, dark and calm, met mine. He said nothing, but there was a question there. He pushed at K'antu like he would dunk her again into the water, staring at me with a sneer on his face.

"All right, all right. What do you want me to do?" I said, my voice low and as steady as I could make it. K'antu gasped in air. I could tell she was trying not to cry. "I'll do whatever you want. Leave her alone. Please." I added the last word as a hasty afterthought.

He grunted.

"But I am not as good as K'antu. She can't be replaced. Please. Don't hurt her. She is valuable to you. I –"

Juan let K'antu go and came to stand right in front of me. "Get up."

I stood. He was at least four or five inches taller than me and a lot bulkier. He leaned toward me and said, "I will decide if she can be replaced or not. So shut up."

Straightening my spine, I stared into his eyes. "Fine."

He went back to the bench and motioned me to sit with him. He continued to whittle on the wood. I looked at the carving that was taking shape. It was good.

"We will wait until it gets lighter," he said, shaving off little pieces of wood.

There was silence for what seemed like an eternity. The block of wood changed into a llama. He started using the tip of the knife to form details, like fur.

"So, tell me what your group is all about." I tried to make conversation, while out of the corner of my eyes, checking to see if K'antu was okay. She was still kneeling by the pond. I couldn't tell if she needed help, but I did not want to call attention to her again.

"I'll tell you about it when I am ready to." He peered through the tree branches. "Looks like the sun is coming up, time to throw. If you can hit the ten targets like the one you did yesterday, I'll tell you all about my little army."

He stood and pointed toward a box of sticks.

"Pick one and throw. The targets are all set up. Let's see what you can do. Oliver," he called to his friend, who was standing straight and rigid like a statue, "Go to the viewing point. You can report to me from there. I will watch from here."

I glanced at K'antu, who nodded at me. I took a deep breath and walked to the box of spears. I glanced inside. There was no fancy gold one in this box. I reached in and picked up each one, in turn, laying them on the ground. There were two rough sticks with lead ends: a thin stick with a copper star and a metal stick with silverpoints.

"You'll throw them all," Juan directed me, "and we'll see how you do with each one."

Holding each stick separately, I assessed their weight and balance. The silver stick was the heaviest and the copper one the lightest. Both lead sticks had similar weights, but one was longer than the other. K'antu had also had several types, so it should not be too hard to use these.

"Hurry, girl, we don't have all day." Juan had lit something that looked like a cigarette. I grabbed the longer lead spear, took aim, imagined Juan's head, and threw the *macana* at the first target. It made a mark right in the middle of the soft wood.

Juan exhaled and jumped up, shouting for me to continue. He looked amazed but happier than I had seen him so far. I kept going. There were many targets, so it took me a little over forty minutes to finish the regimen Juan had assigned. By the end, I had hit the targets about eighty percent of the time, and my arm could barely move. I looked toward Juan, expecting praise, but his face had changed. He was pacing the ground me. He moved his arms restlessly like he was talking to himself. His eyes were wide, and he kept looking over his shoulder.

"They are coming for us," he whispered loudly, "You're done, no more throwing. We have to go. Now. Oliver, get the dune buggy."

My heart pounded. What was wrong? I looked at K'antu, who shook her head and put her finger to her lips. We all piled into the vehicle. Oliver drove, and Juan turned his head, owl-like, to survey the surroundings.

"Do you see them, K'antu? They are coming for us. Tamara, get ready with the macana."

I squirmed. We had left the spears back at the oasis. I had no weapon with me. K'antu touched my arm. We looked at each other. The only thing I could figure out from K'antu's expression was I should keep quiet.

By the time we reached the compound in Patabamba, Juan was in a disturbed semi-trance, muttering to himself about the enemy.

"Go to your room," Oliver told me. He struggled to get Juan out of the dune buggy and too busy to notice K'antu came with me. Before we went to the room that was designated for me, K'antu looked back. Oliver had disappeared with Juan, so she went and knocked on Mario's door. He answered, but it was locked, so he could not come out.

K'antu went away without saying anything. She came back with Oliver and a set of keys. I looked warily at Oliver.

"It's all right, Tamara. We are going to get Mario out, and then Oliver will explain more things to you."

Oliver came in, followed by Mario, and gestured for us to sit on the bed. A small girl brought in a tray with coca tea and sandwiches and set it on the small table. K'antu passed out cups of hot tea made from coca leaves, not the drug cocaine until processed, but with beneficial properties which alleviate altitude sickness and increase energy. We all picked up a sandwich.

Standing at the door like a prison guard, Oliver looked at both Mario and me. "I am not going to lie. Things are a mess here."

I exhaled. "You can say that again. Juan is a psycho. Is this whole town going to let him imagine he can lead an army of freaks down to Manchay with spears to attack the magistrate?"

K'antu's mouth dropped open. "Army of..."

Oops. Blood rushed to my face. "I... I don't mean you guys..."

Oliver sighed. "I can understand your anger, Tamara, and your frustration. Juan is not a bad guy -"

"Seriously?"

Mario turned to me and quietly said, "Tamara, hear him out. Please."

I was hungry despite the morning's upsetting activities, so I picked up another sandwich and bit into it.

"Go on, although I can't imagine why you are defending him, Mario," I muttered with my mouth full.

Oliver talked for a while. The town of Patabamba, as he explained, had originally been a *"pueblo joven"* or, as the government liked to think of it, an invasion. These were areas of land outside of cities, mainly Lima, and Manchay, where poor people from the mountainous regions set up camps to live and find opportunities on the coast. Their camps usually started rough, a cardboard box, buckets of water, no plumbing or sewage. Little by little, these camps became small villages. As more people came to live close by, people started building more permanent structures with adobe bricks. Eventually, the governments in the larger cities would go and install rough forms of water and sewage for the people.

Over time, several of these invasions turned into lower-middle-class towns with more advanced infrastructures. But some, like Patabamba, had remained poor. For decades, the government of Manchay had not helped Patabamba, and over the years, little or nothing was done to advance the town's services. Juan, Eduardo, Oliver, and K'antu all came from Patabamba, as had Lorena –

although she had left for Lima with family when she was ten. Education had been limited for lots of the children of the town. These four kids' parents had been lucky enough to find employment with my family. Laura had made sure her employees got enough food and sent their kids to the public school in Manchay. The school was not as good as the private ones, but much better than the one in Patabamba.

Still, life was difficult. Their homes were nothing but crude adobe huts, dark and dusty with basic plumbing and no heat for the cold desert nights. The kids who grew up in Patabamba and went to school there did not know anything else, but the ones "lucky" enough to go to school in Manchay were forced to face daily examples of the vast inequalities of life. In many ways, that made them more unfortunate than the kids who had not gone to Manchay.

Kids like Oliver and K'antu had enough to keep them happy: their families, while poor, were in no way stupid. They taught their children the old ways of life - traditions that dated back to the Incas and further. They led a simple life, but a happy one, so the kids were happy too. They had hope for the future and faith that they could change the government and improve the lives of their people when they were older.

But Juan and Eduardo did not have the same experience. Their parents worked for Rodolfo, Mario's father – I saw Oliver look at Mario as he talked about Rodolfo – who was, according to Oliver, not as socially aware as Laura. Juan and Eduardo's father was an alcoholic and died when the boys were young, forcing their mother to work harder to support them. They had had a younger sister, who had disappeared when she was twelve, two years after the death of their father. Their mother had nearly died from the grief of losing both her husband and her only daughter. Rodolfo treated her kindly, but the boys had quit school and begun working.

Eduardo started drinking around the time of his father's death, but after he and K'antu married, it got much worse – I looked at K'antu when Oliver talked about this. She reddened and looked down at her hands – Oliver kept talking. Eduardo drank, but he was intelligent, and when sober, he seemed like he could have made a difference for his family and the rest of the town. He had been instrumental in convincing Rodolfo to let Elías, Eduardo's best friend, use the empty workshop to start his glass-blowing business.

"Really?" I said, interrupting the lecture.

Even though the information was mainly for me, Mario and K'antu both waved at me to be quiet.

Oliver continued. Right before the earthquake, Eduardo seemed to be at his best. He had stopped drinking as heavily and was focused on working with People Help. But then the earthquake had hit, and he and K'antu had gotten married. He felt the strain of supporting her, so he worked harder but was not making the kind of money he wanted to. He began disappearing for long periods. Sometimes Juan went with him, or Elías – Oliver looked to K'antu for confirmation of this. She nodded – At other times, no one knew where Eduardo was. Right before he had been killed, he seemed jubilant and resolute about something. But he had not told anyone what it was.

"And then he was killed," Oliver broke down. K'antu started

crying too. I handed each of them another cup of tea, and Mario handed them napkins.

Oliver got ahold of himself and continued, "Juan was often with Eduardo at People Help. He has changed a lot since his brother's death. He was volatile before, now he is spinning out of control. He has started smoking *paco* and talking endlessly about forming his "army" to take control of the situation which, as you know, has deteriorated since the earthquake."

I nodded. It had. The destruction was impossible to miss – even without people like Mario dragging me to unfortunate people's houses.

"Is that why he was so weird this morning? Because of what he was smoking?" I asked.

Oliver nodded, and K'antu said, "Yes, that was *paco*."

"I don't understand why everyone is letting him control them. He's a loose cannon, a drug addict, and no one is acting against him."

"He can be intimidating, Tamara," K'antu said, "But he is kind, deep down – at least to people who he knows have been taken advantage of. Also, he is the only one making enough noise about the situation here to attract any attention. He is the only one who dares to go far to get what he wants. Maybe he is the one with the least amount to lose. I think the people hope he will do something to Tomás Romero, who they all hate."

I gave her a dirty look, but she paid no attention, so I said, "Those are great excuses for him, K'antu. But he nearly drowned you this morning. There's no excuse for that."

"He is our only hope," K'antu said stubbornly, "we have to put up with the bad to get to the good."

Oliver nodded. "The people here are tired. They have not seen anything change in decades. Things only get worse. So, when someone like Juan comes in and takes charge, even though he is unpredictable and increasingly violent, people accept him – warts and all."

I held up my hands. "Hold on. Things are bad, people are poor; all of that is true. But how is this crazy guy going to help get K'antu out of the mess she is in?"

"Don't underestimate the rest of us, Tamara," Oliver said, "none of us wants K'antu to go to jail for something we are sure she did not do. We are working with Lorena to get more informa-tion on Eduardo's death, even if Juan is focusing on other things. Hopefully, something will come to light, and K'antu will be free to go back to Manchay soon."

"But what can Mario and I possibly do to help you guys? Why are we here?"

Oliver avoided my eyes.

"I'm sorry, I am. But now that you are here, and Juan has focused his attention on you, I will try my best to protect you. Unfortunately, Juan is not a big fan of yours. You seem to be rubbing him the wrong way. Plus, a rich American coming into 'help' - that's been tried before, only to have the magistrate get richer and the rest of us get poorer."

"I'm not rich, and I am not trying to help solve the poverty problem here. I wanted to protect my friend. Besides, you, and everyone here, knows Laura and my grandparents have always tried." I had had enough. I stood and walked toward the door.

"Tamara, don't –" K'antu began.

"And you," I turned to my friend, "I saw the way you looked

at Juan yesterday. What's up with that? Are you in love with him? Helping him run his little terror organization? Do you realize how frightened I've been in the last two days? You were the one who taught me to throw those macanas, do you remember? And now that son of a bitch is throwing it into your face, saying maybe I'll "replace" you, and you're just taking it. Weren't you abused enough with Eduardo? Now you're going to repeat that mistake with Juan? I don't want to do this anymore."

Mario had a slight smirk on his face, which made me angrier. I got up, pushed past Oliver, and ran to the courtyard. Looking around wildly, I spied the front door and increased my pace. I grabbed the handle and pulled the door. It opened. I couldn't believe my luck. I did not care how far away I was. I would run, walk or crawl back to Manchay. But my hopes were dashed the minute I got the door completely open. Two boys sat at a small table playing cards.

"Hey, get back inside," one of them called to me as the other stood up. A quick appraisal of them, taller than I and muscular, had me rethinking my escape.

With slumped shoulders, I went back inside. K'antu, a sympathetic look on her face, waved me toward the kitchen. I might as well eat. The food here was simple but delicious.

Chapter 11

That night I lay awake thinking. Some of the other kids had caught sight of me storming out of the room, so after our meal, they had called to me to come over to them. They wanted to see me throw *macanas*, and one of the girls taught me a trick with the *bolas*. My friends left me alone for the rest of the day.

Aesthetically, of all the weapons, my favorite was the *Tumi*. *Tumis are* a symbol of good luck. All of the *artesanales*, craft shops, sold *Tumis* in varying forms; paintings, gold figures, silver jewelry, on T-shirts – all kinds of things. But the box of *Tumis* was unused at one end of the courtyard. Did the kids avoid using them because of what had happened to Eduardo? At one point, I asked why they trained with all of the weapons, but they shut down on me, so I did not insist.

The rest of the afternoon and evening was spent talking to them. They asked me many questions regarding the United States, and I learned about their lives here in Patabamba. These kids had grown up with very little. Most of the time, they had barely enough food. Their homes were rudimentary, and their opportunities for even basic jobs were scarce.

All afternoon there was genuine laughter in the exchanges between the kids. They joked with each other and had fun. They had all seen the destruction of natural disasters and felt loss every time a service or product was denied to them via government agencies. But they were happy and optimistic. Not like me. And I had every material thing I needed.

Having spent the day soaking in their joy, I found myself reluctantly evaluating my own life. My house was well built and not in an earthquake zone, the food I had, all of my clothes and my things, my excellent school. I had it all, but did I have happiness – the pure kind where if everything was taken from me, I would still have it? I wondered who

the "poor" people were, them, or me?

I was deep in thought when the noise started. At first, it was a quiet scratching. It got a little louder and stopped. Then it continued until it got louder and stopped again. This pattern kept going. It made me nervous. I got out of bed and went to the window, but all I saw outside was dark shadows. Maybe it was an animal... I went back and was about to lie down when I felt something on the bed. It was warm, and it had a pulse.

Scared out of my mind, I screamed. The form moved swiftly, and something covered my mouth almost before the scream ended. I couldn't breathe. I flailed my arms, trying to make contact so I could separate myself from the person who had grabbed me.

"Tamara, be quiet. They'll hear you, and they'll find me."

Widening my eyes in surprise, I stopped fighting. The figure let me go. I turned.

"Mario. How... how did you get in here?" Going to the door, I tried to open it. It was locked.

"There's a little opening between these rooms. It is like a dog door or something. It hadn't been opened in years, or at least it took me hours to get it open. I have been working on it all day while you were – doing whatever." He pointed to a hole in the wall close to the ground by the corner near the window.

"But the walls are so thick..." I said, but I felt guilty. I had not thought of him all afternoon. "They locked you back in your room?"

"Right after you stormed out."

"Hey, it is what it is. And it turns out it was to my advantage."

"What do you mean? You are going to take advantage now that you are in my room?"

"Not 'take advantage,' Tamara. Finding this doorway is our ticket to freedom."

Now I was confused. "What do you mean?"

"The walls are thick. You are right. But this one was built oddly. Maybe they kept a dog here before, or maybe it was a secret escape for whoever lived here. The little door in your wall leads to a space between your room and mine."

"It does?"

"But the best part," he went on happily, "is it is a tiny passage. There's another little door between ours leads outside. We can get out of here. I have been waiting for hours to tell, and now I have. So, let's go." He reached for my hand and started toward the little square in the wall – our escape route.

"Wait, no," I said.

He turned his head to face me. There were two deep vertical lines between his eyebrows. "What?"

"We can't go. What about K'antu?"

Mario pulled at me. "Don't you think we can help her better from Manchay?"

To stop him, I planted my feet firmly on the ground and tried to pull my arm away from his grip. "How? What are we going to tell the police? What will we tell your father and my aunt?"

"I…" He stopped trying to force me toward the door.

We stood in the dark for several minutes. Finally, I had an idea. "Mario?"

"Yes?"

"I have a crazy idea."

"It can't be crazier than what we've been through in the last few days. What is it?"

"Let's go look around. We'll get a feel for how far we can get and where we can go. We can do a couple of exploratory missions, and in a day or two, we can make it down to Manchay. Since no one will know we are gone, and no one in Manchay will be expecting us to be wandering around at night, maybe we will be able to find something that will prove K'antu is innocent. That would be better than just escaping and leaving K'antu here. Wouldn't it?"

Without waiting for a comment from Mario, I smoothed back my curly mop of hair and wound a band around to hold it in a ponytail. Then I stripped the bed and formed a body-like figure out of the sheets, fixing the blanket over it. I was assuming he would agree with my plan.

"If they come in again, they'll see me sleeping," I explained, looking over my shoulder. "What are you waiting for? Crawl back and do the same to your room. We probably shouldn't be gone for more than an hour this first time."

Silently, he went through the little door, presumably to do as I said. Moments later, we breathed in the sharp, cool air of freedom.

"Do you know where we are?" I asked Mario.

"More or less. This compound seems to be on the eastern edge of Patabamba, farthest away from the road, goes to Manchay. Further to the east, the hills get rocky."

"Lorena said Joaquin had come here looking for K'antu the other day…" I said.

"Yes, and it was probably easy enough to hide her amongst the rocks and trees," he replied.

"Yeah, but he will be back, I'm sure. And when he comes, he may surprise them." I was observing—the wrong thing to do out loud.

"Yes… all the more reason for us to leave – go back to our families." He still wasn't entirely on board with my idea, and I had reminded him of another reason not to like it.

"I can't leave K'antu, Mario."

"Yes, yes. I know. I will go along with your plan – if you promise that if it doesn't work in a few days, we will leave."

I nodded. "I promise. But we will have to be thorough. There simply has to be something we can find to exonerate K'antu. This might be the only way to find anything out."

I surveyed the outside wall we had emerged from, committing it to memory, and said, "I don't understand why Joaquin, or one of his men, isn't here all day every day lying in wait for her."

"They probably figure she can't hide forever, and it'll be less work for them when she comes out on her own. It is not like she'll go anywhere else but Patabamba. Or maybe they are biding their time to make a surprise raid and find something else to blame on her or Juan. Or..." He stopped.

"Or what?"

"Maybe he doesn't want to find her."

That was a weird thing to say. I looked at him. But he did not explain what he meant. Without speaking, we started to walk.

K'antu had explained the compound to us earlier. It had once been a group of individual homes. Someone at one time had walled them off, presumably to keep them safe from robbers. The homes within the compound were better built than anything else in Patabamba, owned by the area's wealthiest family. The term "rich" was relative, of course. The homes were still basic adobe structures. We had come out of the little secret passage directly to a grove of *huarango* trees and a rough path leading up toward the mountains. Going around the wall of the compound would put us on the main road of Patabamba.

"Which way should we go first?" Mario asked.

"I think for tonight we go up, don't you? From there, we can look down on what we are dealing with."

"Okay," he agreed.

The going wasn't easy. We walked through a small *Loma*, an area with a lot of vegetation that got its water only from the early morning fog. It did not rain here. After that, the ground became rocky. There were no flat surfaces. We had to step cautiously from stone to stone and weave amongst different prickly plants. Since we did not have a flashlight, we relied on the light of the stars. We climbed for about twenty minutes before I stumbled on a loose rock, lost my balance, and was almost going to crash into a six-foot cactus. Mario lunged for me and caught me right before I impaled my entire side on the cactus' spiny surface.

"Whoa, be careful, Tamara." He dragged me into an awkward embrace to steady me. When my feet were standing firmly on the rocks, he reached toward my face. My heart lurched. But he touched my cheek gently and took his hand away. We both looked at it. There was blood on it. I reached toward my cheek, which was burning – with embarrassment and because of the cut.

"Thank you, Mario. I'll be more careful." I said stiffly, avoiding his eyes. Why he was doing all of this with me instead of running off back to Rodolfo. I wasn't going to ask. "It looks like there is a little flat area over there. Should we sit?"

"Yeah. Sure." He sounded distant, so I stopped him before he could make his way to the small plateau.

"Mario."

"Yeah?"

"Look, I... uh... I appreciate what you are doing…"

"Hey, Tamara, no worries. All right? Let's go. We can't be out here much longer."

"Okay. Let's go over there and rest."

We made our way to the little area. It was grassy, and if it were daylight, it would be covered with the shade of the rim of trees surrounding it. We sat on the ground. I lifted my shirt and pressed it against my cheek, which was still bleeding. I hoped the cut wouldn't be too noticeable to K'antu – or Juan.

"Mario," I said after a minute.

"What?"

"Why are you still here?"

"What?"

"Well, I know why I'm here. I have to support K'antu. But why are you not on your way to Manchay right now?"

He did not answer.

"Mario?"

"What?"

"I asked you a question, Rodolfo's son. Why aren't you answering me?"

"You don't want to know the answer to your question."

I looked at him. He was lying five feet away from me. He had his eyes open, and he was staring at the stars.

"Do you know the constellations here, Tamara?" he asked, not turning his head.

Looking up, I said, "I only know the Southern Cross."

"Yeah... a lot of people from the north know that one. Some people don't know that the constellations are all different in the Southern Hemisphere."

"Do you know them?" I wasn't going to get an answer to my other question, so I might as well play along.

"My favorite is Apus, the bird of paradise. I've always liked that plant, and I guess it's why it is my favorite constellation."

"Oh yeah?"

He lifted himself on his forearm and turned to look at me.

"It's a burst of color in a dull green plant. Something about the flower says, "I fought, and I made it, so look at me". I like that."

He lay back again.

To keep him company, even though the ground didn't look all that comfortable, I went and lay next to him. He stayed still. After a minute, I put my head on his chest. His breath caught. His left hand hovered over my hair before touching it. I stayed where I was, and so did his hand. A falling star streaked across the sky, and I tried to see if the moving light was another dimmer one or an airplane.

"It is for you," he said.

"Huh? What is?" I had almost dozed off.

"The reason I stay. It is for you."

I turned to him.

He avoided eye contact. "At first, it was for Laura. She asked me to look after you on this trip to Perú. Everyone knows you went through a hard time in the earthquake, and she wanted someone to take care of you while you were here this time. To help you forget. So, you would like it here again. But then..."

I got up and brushed my butt off. "Forget? And you thought you could 'help' me do that? That's the problem with everyone here. Everything is so easy to forget. The rich people forget about the poor people, the poor forget they're poor, and the people in charge of distributing money forget to distribute it. But it's not so easy for me. How am I supposed to forget what happened last year – it was awful."

About to continue my rant, a piece of his little condescending explanation connected, and I stopped in mid-attack, "Wait, did you say, "but then"? Then what?"

"Then, I don't know... I guess now I am doing it for you. I am not going to leave you alone with that whack job Juan, and I can't convince you to leave, but I don't want you to get hurt, so I will stay and do what I can to make sure you aren't."

Turning, I walked away from him. Something scrambled behind me. I assumed he was getting up. But I did not look back.

"Look, Tamara, I get it. You are angry about how things work around here. It's not making me happy either. But we have to step back and let them be."

"What does that mean?" I stopped walking. I could feel him near me.

"I mean, you want to help K'antu – but maybe you can't. At least not in the way you want to help her. And you want Laura to do more – but it's possible she's done all she's capable of doing."

"So, I should let a psychopath help K'antu and Laura should continue to look the other way at people's problems?"

"I am just saying you cannot change everything, and people aren't all bad. Like Juan, for instance – he is crazy, that's for sure. But he is passionate about helping his people. And Laura treats people ten times better than my dad does and a hundred times better than other rich people in Manchay, even if she does have her moments of being a diva. Sometimes you have to look for the good and deal with the bad."

"I am not good at that," I said.

"So, you tend to see the bad side of people? That's not exactly a nice trait. Should I judge you for it?"

It hit me what he was doing. I didn't want to face my hypocritical behavior. I started to walk away again, but he pulled me to him. A pair of green eyes met my own. He caressed my cheek again, but instead of wiping the blood away, he cupped it and brought his lips to mine.

Lost in the moment, I let it happen but then pushed him away. "We can't do this, Mario. Not now. Not here."

"Fine. Let's go back."

He started walking, calling back over his shoulder, "Tomorrow, we need to make a better plan than coming out here and looking around."

"How about if we walk toward Manchay and figure out how long it'll take us," I followed after him, a little nervous. Was he upset I had pushed him away? Or was he going along with me as he had been doing before? I was confused about the kiss. Did I like him? I wasn't sure. "Then the next night, if we know we have time, we'll go and find something to prove K'antu didn't kill Eduardo. Or at least that someone else could have."

"Deal. Now let's get back before someone finds out we're gone. And Tamara?"

"Yes?"

"This will be over soon. You will see. And then, well... everything will be fine."

We smiled at each other. I was relieved we were going to sweep the kiss under the carpet. I guess I was more like the people here than I had previously acknowledged – avoiding subjects because they were uncomfortable. But I had no time to think now. We turned the way we thought we had come and taken a few steps before realizing we were going the wrong way. Turning back, we went in the other direction. I stumbled. Mario caught me again, but this time we both fell. Mario put out his hands, and as we landed, something squelched underneath him.

Peering more closely, I realized what it was we had fallen on. I jumped up and screamed. Mario threw his arms around me, carefully keeping his dirty hands from touching any part of my body. We had tripped on the semi-fresh remains of a llama. It was torn in two. Its blood was covering the ground. A crude, heavy lead *Tumi* lay to the side of the dead animal.

"What happened?" Nausea boiled in my throat.

"Juan."

I scraped my feet to rid myself of any llama parts that might have stuck to them and ran my hands along the parts of me which had made contact with the ground. Mario had gotten the raw end of the deal – literally. I did not want to look at him because of the gore on his clothes.

Mario gagged. He stood up and went past the line of trees to the riverbed above. I followed.

"Look, Mario." I sucked in my breath, swaying a little. It was still dark, but I saw several animal carcasses in varying stages of decay - all cut savagely in different ways.

"He's been practicing. But did he... could he have –"

"Don't say it. Don't. Let's get out of here."

We headed back as quickly as the incline would allow. Back at the compound, Mario whispered to me to shut my little door tightly and rub dust from the floor on the wall, so it didn't look like it had been recently opened. Neither of us had any idea whether Juan or any of the others knew about the openings.

My hands shook as I did as he said. I remade the bed, wiped my hands on the bottom of the blanket, and lay down. I couldn't sleep. My mind switched between images of the dead animals and what had happened with Mario.

Sleep eluded me. I closed my eyes and tried to think pleasant thoughts about the boy in the next room. Suddenly someone was coming toward me. Then I was being pushed from behind. Someone was screaming, but there was a roaring sound drowning out everything else. I tried to prevent it from coming, but it came anyway. Despite my efforts, my cousins fell one by one, crushed, blood everywhere. Then they were whole again, except they had turned into zombies. The zombies all split in half and rushed at me. Gore splattered all over the room. I fell, spinning into a dark hole.

Chapter 12

Utensils clinked against dishes. Kids talked with their mouths open. The smell of fresh bread and scrambled eggs filled the air. A dog barked. Someone laughed. Another person yelled in the kitchen water splashed in the sink.

I picked at my food – a roughly cooked omelet with limp onions on top. Mario had not shown up to breakfast yet. Juan was in the courtyard showing a little girl how to use the *bolas*. I shuddered, envisioning him cutting the little girl. But as I watched, he laughed affectionately at the girl's attempts and applauded loudly when she finally looked like she got the hang of it. She put down the weapon, and Juan bent to talk to her. He gave her money from his pocket, which she looked like she needed – she was emaciated. He hugged her and walked her over to a boy, her brother. The two boys did a knuckle touch: the younger boy looking grateful. I watched the entire transaction in disbelief. He was like a completely different person. It was weird.

"What's the matter, Tamara?" K'antu came up behind me.

I shoved my plate away. "Nothing."

"Are you sure?"

"I didn't sleep well."

K'antu grimaced. "I know how much you are sacrificing for me, Tamara. And I want you to know how much I appreciate your friendship and how sorry I am that you've been caught up in the middle of it all."

She put her hand on mine. I did not take it away, even though I felt like it.

"K'antu, you're my friend. I can't let you go to jail for something I know you didn't do." I paused, then I said, "I haven't asked you how you are... you must be grieving while being a fugitive. It isn't fair."

K'antu took her hand away and looked down, her hair falling in black waves over her face. I hugged her.

"Go ahead and cry, K'antu, it is okay."

K'antu raised her head. She was angry. "I don't grieve for him, Tamara. I'm glad he's gone."

"Glad? But surely..."

At that moment, Lorena came running up. "Girls, there's someone here from People Help. You must both hide. Where is Mario? He needs to go with you."

K'antu grabbed me, towing me by the hand and calling Lorena, "He must still be in his room. Send him to the tunnels."

"Tunnels?" I panted, looking back as she dragged me. K'antu was making us go at a quick pace.

Behind us, Lorena was mobilizing the other kids, and there was general chaos in the courtyard. The kids milled about and spoke a little louder than they might have. Many of them started clearing the breakfast dishes, and others brought out books and a whiteboard as if they were going to have class. A few of them gathered in a group directly in line with me and K'antu as if blocking anyone's view of our retreat and argued about a chemistry problem they had supposedly been working on.

We ran toward the back of the compound - but on the other side, away from the bedrooms. Lorena had sent one of the boys to get Mario, and they caught up with us by a door in the wall. The door looked like every other door, but when K'antu threw it open all I saw was darkness. The boy whispered loudly, telling K'antu he'd shut it behind us and reminding her there were flashlights on a shelf after the first flight of stairs."

"Stairs?" I said.

"Shh, don't talk until we're away from here," K'antu warned.

We shuffled carefully down the stairs. Mario and I coughed. It smelled musty. The walls were adobe brick without the thin layer of plaster rooms in the rest of the buildings had and a little damp. At the bottom, K'antu grabbed a flashlight, which was more like a lantern, from the shelf and turned it on. She shined it around, and we took in our surroundings. We were in a small anteroom. The shelf that the lantern had come from was in a small alcove. On the wall of the alcove was a miniature painting. I recognized it as Santa Rosa de Lima. The shelf had two other flashlights, not as big as K'antu's, but Mario and I each grabbed one. With all the light, we saw another staircase on the far side of the room.

"Let's go, you two. We can get outside from here and to the hills," K'antu said.

"What is this, K'antu? Why is it here?" My voice echoed in the chamber.

"Back in the '90's Perú was having problems with terrorists, who built these so they could go back and forth unnoticed."

"Seriously?" Mario sounded impressed. "I haven't ever heard about that…"

"That's the point," K'antu said.

"Yeah, but you would think that I would have heard rumors about it at least…" he sounded pensive.

"Let's get out of here." I was trying not to take any deep breaths.

It was chilly in the tunnel, and the other staircase was farther than it looked. When we got to it, we went up the stairs and faced an opening crudely shut with a wood plank.

"That should have been opened recently, but it doesn't look like it's been touched for a long time…" K'antu sounded worried.

Mario moved her aside and pushed on the wood. It popped easily out of its holdings, and light shone in from above, making the three of us blink.

"Looks are deceiving. It must have been opened recently, K'antu," I said. I climbed the final stairs and found myself standing in a grove of trees breathing in fresh air.

"I hadn't been through the tunnel before," K'antu said.

"Is that how no one from Manchay has found you yet? You've been escaping through tunnels?" I asked.

She looked up and did not answer, so I followed her gaze.

"We seem to be in one of the hills, but I don't think it's the same one that – "I began. Mario interrupted me.

"Yes, and look over there," Mario said. "K'antu, you would

know the area best. Maybe you should go find a place for us to hide in case someone finds the tunnel."

K'antu gave us both a suspicious look, but she went.

"You almost gave it away," Mario hissed.

"What do you mean?" I said, blustering. "Surely we don't have to keep it secret from K'antu that we're sneaking out at night? We are doing it for her after all..."

"Yes, that's true. But remember, she spends a lot of time with Juan. If she finds out, she might tell him, by accident – or on purpose. Let's keep it quiet for now," he said.

"All right, all right, you are right," I remembered the way I saw K'antu look at Juan the night before.

K'antu came back. She was about to say something, but a sound scared us. We ducked behind a tree and huddled together as close as we could. Someone called to us. It was the same boy that had closed the tunnel door behind us.

"They are gone. But you'd better come back. They must have told Lorena and Juan bad news. Juan is furious, and Lorena is making plans to leave."

We didn't move. The boy came around the tree. We must not have been hidden well.

"Come on," The boy insisted.

Instead of going back in the tunnel, we followed him down a narrow path. He was one of the kids who lived and went to school in Patabamba, so he knew the area well. The path led to the wall of the compound. He opened the door. We walked past an orchard of mango and *pacay*. Beyond the trees was a small chicken coop and several piles of discarded scrap metal. A savory smell emanated from the kitchen, which was where we were headed. It smelled like *aji de gallina.* My stomach growled.

As we entered the kitchen, the two cooks, a pair of older kids, yelled at us to hurry. Lorena was looking for us. We walked through the cramped and smoky room, out through the hallway, and into the courtyard.

Juan was in the middle of a tantrum, bashing a chair to pieces with another chair. No one tried to stop him. Several people stood at a respectful distance, boys slightly in front of girls to protect them. Lorena was nowhere to be seen. When the chair was reduced to a pile of sticks, Juan stood staring at it, his chest heaving. His face was wet. It might have been sweat, but I thought it was more tears.

"What—?" K'antu was about to say when a boy standing next to her flung out his arm, hitting her on the shoulder.

During the few moments we had been there for Juan's outburst, I had watched him staring in awe at Juan, his eyes wide with fear.

"Don't call attention to us. It might make him more pissed off than he already is," the boy whispered.

But Juan must have heard him because he looked up, his eyes flashing in our direction. He dropped the leg he had been grasping – the only part left of the chair – and strode over to where we stood. I held my breath.

"Juan, what happened?" K'antu asked, her voice shaking.

Juan ignored her and grabbed my arm. "Let's go, *gringa.* You come with me."

"I'm not going anywhere with you." I tried to shake him off, but Juan twisted around and lifted his other arm as if he were about to backhand me. I shrank back but still managed to glare at him.

"Tough girl, huh?" he sneered. "You're lucky I have other things on my mind, or you'd be unconscious. Let's go."

I looked at K'antu, silently willing her to help me, but the look on her face was an odd mix of jealousy and fear. I wouldn't be getting any help from her, I figured.

Juan dragged me toward the front of the compound. Where was Mario? Why wasn't he coming after me? I turned my head and saw why I hadn't heard him protesting. Three boys held him back. One of them had put a cloth over his mouth. He was trying to resist, twisting his body, but they were too strong for him. Juan kept dragging me, and before I could fight more, he forced me out the front entrance and into a car.

Juan drove carefully. For someone with such erratic and violent moods, that surprised me. The car slid down the hill at a reasonable pace. Nevertheless, my heart was beating twice as fast as usual. I stared out the window, refusing to give him the satisfaction of asking where we were going. We drove down the winding road toward Manchay. Right before we reached the edge of town, I heard a strange sound. I turned and looked at Juan. He was laughing.

"What is so funny?" I asked.

"You know, Tamara, for being a filthy *gringa*, I kinda like you."

"Gee, thanks." It was foolish to be flippant. The guy scared the crap out of me. But I couldn't help it. My mind had lost control of my mouth.

"You got yourself into quite a mess, didn't you?"

"I'm here for K'antu. And that's what you should be concen-

143

trating on too, instead of trying to drown her, throwing tantrums like a toddler, and dragging unwilling victims around."

He stopped laughing, but I went on.

"Did you smoke anything today?" I said.

He rolled his eyes. "No. I didn't get a chance. And I don't have time now."

"I wasn't suggesting you do. You shouldn't smoke that stuff."

"Yeah? And who are you, the drug police? What do you know?"

"I know it only makes things worse."

"What could be worse than this?" He took both hands off the wheel and gestured to the small, disheveled huts that lay on the outskirts of Manchay. The car swerved. He grabbed the wheel again and laughed. "To be high, it makes this look better. It helps me do what I need to do."

"What you need to do is be there for your family and find out who killed your brother so K'antu can lead a normal life."

The car ground to a stop, startling the two dogs lying asleep on the side of the street. They barked briefly at the car and vanished around a corner.

"Figure out who killed my brother? That's what you think I should be doing?" He glared at me.

Sitting up straight, I said, "Yes."

"And how the hell should I be doing that?"

I was unable to come up with an answer.

"Exactly. You see, Tamara," he drawled, "the police here do whatever they want. If they are convinced K'antu killed Eduardo, then she did. It doesn't matter what any of us say. She'll go to jail eventually. It's either that or disappear back up to the mountains."

"Do you believe she killed him?" I was curious.

His nostrils twitched. "No, dumb ass. I do not think she killed him. Haven't you been listening to me?"

He paused and looked out the window. "But, actually, now that you mention it, she probably could have killed him."

"What? That's crazy. I should never have asked you."

"No, it's true, he was a violent son-of-a-bitch. Maybe she did get rid of him –"

It was my turn to laugh.

"What are you laughing at?" Juan's creepy eyes locked with mine. I looked away.

"You said he was violent."

"Yeah? What's so funny?"

"It's just that if I were you, I wouldn't criticize other people for being violent." I knew I had gone too far as the words were coming out. We were still stopped. Maybe I could get out of the car now. I grabbed at the handle, but the door wouldn't open.

Juan smirked, "Don't bother. Child locks."

Well, at least he did not hit me for what I had said. I held my arms against my chest.

"I may be violent, but I've never hit a woman," he said in a quiet voice. "Eduardo used to beat the crap out of K'antu."

"You never hit a woman? Didn't you dunk K'antu's head into a pond yesterday? Didn't you grab me against my will and take me away?"

He looked at me. "You needed to be taught a lesson. So did she."

145

"How dare you –"

"Shut up. We are at war here. You can't get all squeamish at what happens to K'antu right now."

"I am not at war with anyone. And neither are you."

"That shows you know nothing about what you've gotten yourself into. Anyway, getting back to Eduardo, he abused her – really abused her – stuff much worse than getting her face a little wet."

"It was her whole head, Juan. You nearly drowned her."

He went on, ignoring me. "He was a real bastard. But really, you could hardly blame him. He led a shitty life. All the cards had been stacked against him. It wasn't exactly his fault…"

"Nothing is ever the guy's fault, is it?" I said bitterly.

"Now you're catching on," he grinned.

"She didn't want to tell me about Eduardo. Why didn't she get help from somewhere?"

"And again, I say, didn't you notice? It's the fact that people don't pay attention that makes it hard for victims to speak up. If your friends and relatives can't see bruises and cuts, maybe they aren't there."

I let out a breath and put up my hands, "I did. I did notice. Oh my God, I did. But I didn't say anything. I thought… I thought she would tell me. I didn't think –"

"Exactly. You didn't think. You don't have to. You were born with that silver spoon stuck down your throat. Well, but Eduardo's treatment of K'antu is ancient history now, isn't it? He's dead." He made a kind of braying sound.

"I know… I… I'm sorry… But… wait, why didn't you do anything to stop your brother?" He had been leading me down a path of guilt – manipulating me – but I didn't see K'antu often. "You noticed it and did nothing. Why?"

He looked at me and back at the road. "Don't you want to know where I'm taking you?"

I looked back at the rear window. Maybe someone had followed us down and would come to get me. We had been stopped here long enough... But there was no car coming. The street was deserted.

Juan started the car again. "Let me explain something to you, *gringa*. This morning we received a visit from those wonderful people from People Help. They told us ever-so-nicely that the high school, which was supposed to have been rebuilt starting last year, will be underfunded for another year at least. When Lorena asked why they gave their typical bullshit answers about lack of money and how they need to do more fundraising."

"Uh-huh," I said, squinting my eyes and waiting for the cavalry to come. I was still facing backward.

"Uh-huh?" His voice cracked, his anger returning. "Is that all you can say?"

"Well, it sounds like they are having a hard time raising funds. It's tough luck."

"Tough luck? You sound like all of them 'We'll try harder. Money will come.'" He said in a high squeaky voice, "It's all lies. It will never come. None of us will graduate from high school, and we'll be stuck here for the rest of our lives."

He slammed his hands against the steering wheel.

"Yeah, it sucks, but aren't they trying to get the money? Isn't Lorena –" I began.

His eyes glowed with a strange light, "Oh yes, indeed it does suck, *gringa*. And it's about to suck worse."

"What does that mean?"

"Shut up."

We had arrived in Manchay Juan slowly pulled up to a four-way corner. He got out of the car and slammed the door. The next thing I knew, he'd opened the door on my side and pulled me out by the arm.

"By the time we are done here, *gringa*, you'll know what tough luck is."

Chapter 13

The school was deserted. Still dragging me by the arm, Juan led me to the door and kicked it open.

"Oh, that's great. Why don't you add to the damage?" The acid in my stomach bubbled to my throat, but I couldn't keep my mouth shut. Also, I talked because I didn't want to imagine what his intentions were in bringing me here.

"The door was a piece of crap even before it all happened," He said, "But wait, it only gets better. Look."

He grabbed hold of the back of my head, so I was forced to face inward. There wasn't much light filtering in, but I could see the cracked walls of a dim hallway and faint outlines of piles of rubble scattered on the floor. The air smelled like dust, and the complete absence of sound filled me with a desperate desire to escape.

"Let's go." Juan shoved me forward. We started down the

passage. I tripped a few times on various jumbles of adobe bricks. My feet, clad in thin black sneakers, started throbbing.

"Ouch," I protested after about the third toe-stubbing, "okay, Juan, I see now. I understand what you were talking about. They haven't gotten around to rebuilding your school yet. You don't have to show me more. I believe you."

"Shut up." He moved behind me, his hands gripping my shoulders as we emerged into a large open area surrounded by the rest of his shabby-looking school. "See that?" he said, his voice breaking. He pointed to a rough structure in the middle of the courtyard. It looked like it had been woven out of reeds, and it was the size of a large gazebo.

I could feel the sweat on his hands. His grip on me was weakening. I angled my body and thrust my elbow backward, but I didn't have enough room to make an impact. He grunted and pushed back, knocking me down. I fell face-first on the dry, sandy ground, swallowing a mouthful of it. Tears burned my eyes. My ears rang. But it wasn't loud enough to drown out Juan's growling.

"I said, 'see that?'" He said through his teeth, pulling me upright. I cried out in pain. My knee was bleeding. Mercifully, though, he stepped away from me, leaving me to at least stand on my own.

I sidled away from him a few inches and turned away, croaking, "I see."

"What do you see?"

"A courtyard –"

"Describe it to me." A match struck. I turned back. He puffed into my face.

Coughing, I looked again at the structure, but my mind wasn't on what it looked like because it wasn't a cigarette, he had lit. Remembering his behavior the last time he smoked this *paco*, I felt an electric current of fear sizzling in my gut. I had to get out of here.

"What are you waiting for? Describe it," Juan said.

I took another tiny step to the side and swallowed hard. "It appears to be a wooden frame, about thirty feet by a little more than twelve –"

The sound of a quick inhale followed by a puff came before he interrupted me, "Feet? Feet... I don't know feet. Tell me in meters."

My mind went through a series of steps to figure it out. I wasn't good at converting to the metric system, so it took me a while. Finally, after stepping a little farther away from him – tiny bits at a time so he wouldn't notice, I said in a shaky voice, "Nine meters. I would say the structure is about nine meters by four meters."

"Walls?" he barked, inhaling.

"N... no. There aren't any walls."

"No walls? Why not?"

"I... I don't know."

"Think, dumb ass." He stepped toward me.

My skin turned to ice. But he was not focusing on me. "N... No money for walls?" I ventured a guess.

"You're catching on." He dropped something on the ground and stomped on it. "Do you have any idea how cold it gets here in July?"

He stepped closer to me. The space I had put between us disappeared.

"Well?" His voice was raspy, and his eyes blazed.

"It can get down to about fifty degrees," I continued quickly, stepping back to avoid physical contact.

He stalked over to the wall of the original building and punched it. A large piece of plaster fell off, nearly striking him. He ducked, gagged, and shook white powder off of his head before taking a breath. "Fifty? That would burn us all up."

Closing my eyes, I moved my lips, thinking. Now that he had walked away from me, if I could keep him focused on my ignorance of the metric system, maybe I could make my way to the hallway. "Fifty... yeah, um in Celsius that would be pretty hot I guess... let's see, fifty, subtract thirty-two, times five would be, wait, no –"

"Son of a bitch, it is simple math." The speed at which he had slithered back to me took me by surprise, and I gasped as he took hold of me again. "It can get down to ten degrees here in our lovely town of Manchay in the middle of this beautiful, windy desert. Ten degrees. No heat. No walls."

His face, purple with rage, was inches – or maybe better put – centimeters from mine. I gulped and choked on my saliva. Juan let go of my arms, so roughly, I stumbled backward.

"I'm sorry –" I said, "I am. I know it's a bad situation."

"Spare me your false pity. You were so smart, you said we don't study in the building. You were right. We study out here. Or we are supposed to, anyway. Do you have any idea what it is like to sit here day after day in the cold, trying to learn from teachers who are so badly paid it is amazing they show up and so cold themselves they can hardly teach? We have no walls, no food, and only a few school supplies that some aid agency gave us because they are sorry for us. We can't have computers, because where are we going to plug them in? And now they come and say funding has been delayed? It's been over a year. We have lost a year of school. Some of the students will never come back."

He went over to the flimsy structure and started kicking one of the wood supports. I stood there, frozen to the ground. It had been several days since I began suspecting he was the one who had killed Eduardo, but right now, as the grief and pain of all the loss he had endured during the earthquake and subsequent events poured out of him, I could almost understand him - this boy: my tormentor. Then I shook cobwebs out of my head, trying to rid myself of the empathy I felt. I still needed to get away from him.

I began moving snail-like toward the hallway opening. I was almost there when he emitted a strangled scream. He had stopped raging long enough to look toward the area I had been standing. I saw him swivel his head around and catch sight of me.

I turned and ran, but he was too quick for me. He caught me and pulled me over to the only chair in the entire courtyard, a plastic lawn chair that might at one time have been white. He forced me to sit down, then fumbled in his pocket with the hand that wasn't flat on my chest.

"What are you doing?" My voice trembled.

He ignored me. I lost all the resolve I had been holding myself up with. "Please, I won't run. I'll stay. You don't have to –"

He slapped me hard across the face.

Tears blurred my vision. Through the hand I had put up to cover my burning cheek, I said, "I thought you said you don't hit women."

"You made me do it." He said, leaning in toward me. I sensed something pricking me in the arm. I put my hand down, blinked several times to clear my vision, and looked.

"Oh my God... what did you do? What is that?" I panicked. Juan had a syringe in his hand and was injecting the needle into my arm.

I struggled, but he was able to push down on the plunger, and liquid flowed into my blood. I went weak. I slumped down further into the chair.

"What did you put into me?" I mumbled.

"A little something to make you feel chill," He cackled, "something to keep you from running.

Cackling sounds. There was a witch here. Where? Where was I? I blinked again. Not a witch, a llama. No, that wasn't right—human, not animal. Or maybe animal... but the face was green. The hair was black. A sick witch. No, not that kind of green. With a wart. The witch. And sharp teeth. It needed to brush... No, not a witch, a wizard. Definitely a man. A man with a green face. Brown face. Oh yeah, I remembered. But wait, what was his name? Jose. No. Not Jose. It started with a 'P.' I was sure of it. So, it couldn't be, oh who the hell cared? What I needed to do, I nodded sagely to myself, was push the fluffy white sheep off of the wall.

The traffic light was saying something to me. Suddenly my cheek stung. How can a fish slap me in the face? Oh. My vision cleared. Not a fish. Not a traffic light. My mind focused again. Juan. That's right. It was Juan. I put my hand to my cheek —déjà vu.

He was saying something to me. His face was distorted – clown-like – weren't clowns supposed to be nice? Something came out of his mouth. I was woozy. Suddenly I was moving. He said something about crosses. Were we in a church? No, not crosses, across... across what? A street. Usually, you cross a street. Then what? A school? What? I tried to take a deep breath. But that made it worse. Light flashed. I blacked out momentarily but was dragged. I tried to walk, I did, but I think I tripped most of the way.

"No," I shook my head, "Not... going... with you." But that didn't help. I was moving. Through the fog that was in my mind, I figured out that we were going down the hallway in the original part of the destroyed school heading for the front door. I saw rubble and a cracked wall. Just then, everything started shaking. I screamed.

"Oh God... s...stop... Stop! What tha? Whas movin?" I began clawing at the witch – no, at Juan and felt something clamp my arm tightly. It was him holding me to calm me. Suddenly a pipe from the ceiling rattled. I looked up. There was rumbling and a crack and the pipe came loose from its bearings and swung toward us. It missed both of our heads by a narrow margin. It all seemed like slow motion, and I ducked after it had already come loose. My knees felt a sharp pain. I had fallen on them and was kneeling on the ground. Something was next to me. It was a monster. Its eyes were also frightened – or were they frightening? I whimpered. No... it was Juan...

"Helicopter?" I whispered.

"You've never jacked up before, have you?" Juan muttered. "That was a tremor. And we nearly got beaned by that pipe. Do you see why kids can't study here?"

"Wha?" I asked the scarecrow.

"I said you've never been high before, right?" he yelled.

I gripped his arm, "Lion! I heard a lion roar. Lez run."

I was about to run – or try to in the state I was in when I looked and saw he was doubled over laughing. But then he looked back at the pipe, which was swinging from one last flimsy bearing holding it onto the ceiling, and then he said, "Let's get out of here."

"No." I grabbed his arm. "Can't leave, be killed."

"Don't be a moron. It is more dangerous here. Jeez, you are a pain in the ass. If I had known you'd react like this... But anyway, I need to show you the other school. Come on. You'll need to try to act normal as we cross the street."

"Normal. Got it," I nodded to the wizard.

He held my hand. His touch was gentle. Was this the same wizard who had drugged me? Oh yeah, it was. He started pulling me. We went across the street.

"Kansas," I murmured, wide-eyed.

"What?" he turned toward me.

"F'get it." I blinked. A tear of self-pity meandered down my cheek. No one ever got my Wizard of Oz references here in Perú. I was homesick – and physically sick. But there was no stopping. We reached the other side of the street, but no one would be kicking down any doors this time. This school had a thick concrete wall with barbed wire winding in a long swirl on top of it. The entrance was a black iron gate with a huge padlock. There was no one in the little guard booth between the gate and the street.

"Cl'sed. Tha' sucks." What was I saying? I struggled to regain control of myself. "Come back tomorrow. Hey, I have an idea. Let's go to my house –"

"Shut up. We're not going in this way."

He led me around the side of the building. The school fronted one of the main streets of Manchay, and on the side was a food market, also closed. Juan and I walked along the wall past the market and to the back of the school. There, like in the front, was an iron gate. This one, however, was the size of a door, not wide enough to let cars through like the one in front. And, this one was unlocked, the padlock nowhere to be seen.

"Wow, great security," I said, finally feeling normal enough to get a complete sentence out without dropping a few syllables in the process.

"Be quiet." Juan slipped into the school's yard, dragging me with him.

We went in a large, ornate wood door and through the back of the school to the foyer in front. For a moment, we both stood looking around.

"Iz beautiful," I slurred, the drug-taking control again. I was in a kaleidoscope. I spun around and then bent over. The floor was marble. I felt sick, so I stood up. The walls moved. They were covered in stucco and were moving like tiny ripples in water. My eyelids fluttered, and the ripples stopped. I shut my eyes for a moment, trying to remember what it felt like to be normal, but that made me lose my balance. I fell and ended up lying on the floor. Opening my eyes, I saw that the ceiling had been painted with a scene from the mountains so beautiful it had to have been done by a professional artist.

"'Mazing," I said.

"Get up. Let's go see the classrooms." He pulled me up and guided me around the school to the regular classrooms, each with a tablet on every desk, through the science lab that had various apparatus for experiments. Some I didn't recognize. But maybe it was the drug. We went on through to the cafeteria, which had three huge refrigerators and several pantries.

I opened one of the refrigerators. In it were fruits of all kinds and milk and cheeses. I reached in. Something moved.

"Juan," I said in a low voice.

"Yeah?" He was busy stuffing a ham sandwich into his mouth.

"The cheese moved."

He sputtered, spraying crumbs in front of him. He coughed, gulped Inca Kola, and looked thoughtful. "The cheese?"

"Yes."

"You say it moved?"

"Yeah. What should we do?"

A smile played on his lips, and he glanced sideways at me. "Kill it."

"Kill it?"

"Yes. It moved. It must be alive. So, kill it. Here." He handed me a heavy iron pan.

I took it and tested its weight in my hands. "I shud kill t'cheese?"

"Oh yeah," He said, "and when you are done with that, there are other things that might be alive in here."

His hands moved vaguely around, indicating the whole room.

Who was that person pointing at the moving objects? He looked familiar. I knew I was afraid of him. But I couldn't remember why. But he was right. I had to kill the cheese. And the other things. Before another tremor came. Before I died in the earthquake. Like last year. Wait. I didn't die, did I? I was right here. But this wasn't my house…

Juan came closer to me. A light shone from his eyes. It wasn't a pleasant one. I panicked and swung the pan. Juan's body dissolved like Pepto-Bismol in water. But his laughter hung in the air and grew. Things started breaking—lots of things. I swung and hit the inside of the refrigerator. The glass shelves crackled and broke, falling to the bottom of the refrigerator. Some of them dropped on the tile floor of the kitchen.

I moved on, determined to kill the cheese. Juan leaned against the wall furthest from me and watched, smiling, as I went around the kitchen, destroying everything in my path. At one point, I dropped the pan, picked up a piece of broken ceramic, and flung it at him. He stopped smiling. He ran out of the kitchen, but I picked up a coffee pot on the ground and followed him. I was about to throw the pot out of one of the front windows when he came behind me and lifted me, pinning my arms to my side so I couldn't move.

"All right, you've killed it all. You can stop now," he said.

But I pulled away from him. There was one more thing I had not yet killed – him. I threw the pot out the window. I plucked a broken piece of glass from the frame and came toward him with it. If I had been in my normal state of mind, I might have been happy to see the fear in his eyes. But now, all I saw was a living thing. "Yr wrong. Got to kill it."

"No, I... Tamara, put that down."

"Got to –" I sliced the air. He fell to the floor and grabbed me by the ankles. I hit the ground.

"It's dead! It's all dead. Let go of the glass Tamara," he yelled.

I gasped for the air that had rushed out of my lungs upon impact. "S'dead? All dead?"

"Yeah. You did it. Good job. I couldn't have done it any better."

He let go of me. I tried to get up, and in the process, I knocked my head against a side table. Momentarily stunned, I lay down and closed my eyes. The room spun above me. I lay there for a while. When things calmed down a little, I got up. Dizzy. I put my head between my legs and began to feel better. I looked up slowly. Juan was not there anymore.

Putting my hands down carefully on the glass-filled floor, I pushed myself to standing. It hurt. I looked at them. My hands were bloody and full of cuts. I didn't make it to the bathroom in time, so the foyer would have to be mopped and disinfected by someone on Monday morning. Not that they wouldn't have had to do major cleanup anyway...

Now that I had lost what was in my stomach, my mind started clearing. What had I done? I wasn't sure I wanted to know. I limped to the kitchen and stood, shocked, at sight. There wasn't one visible area immune to my rampage. Broken glass and pottery, mixed in with various foodstuffs, were smashed and strewn all over the floor. It looked like I had ripped the door off of one of the refrigerators. Angry gashes and dents decorated the walls, and a blade of the ceiling fan hung down, split in two.

Juan stood by the large center island, calmly munching on another ham sandwich.

"Well," he said, "That ought to teach them."

He laughed in between bites.

Chapter 14

The next day I found myself back in the tunnel. The police were raiding the compound looking for evidence. Juan had driven me back to the compound after finishing his sandwich. He had taken me directly back to 'my room and locked me in. I had fallen into a deep sleep until K'antu had raced in the next morning.

"Get up, Tamara. The police are on their way," she had said.

"Huh?" My mind was still a little fuzzy.

But K'antu had pulled me up and arranged my clothes. "We have to hide again. Quick, let's go."

"Okay," I had agreed, yawning.

K'antu had looked strangely at me. "What is the matter with you? What did you guys do yesterday?"

But hearing sounds in the courtyard, she had not waited. She had dragged me toward the tunnels, and we had gone in.

K'antu and I huddled together with Mario sitting not far away. Juan was standing. He was closest to the exit - the portal to the hills above. I had been in this same tunnel the day before. At least it looked the same. I wished it were my aunt and not the police who were out there looking for us. I wanted to go back to Manchay. Actually, I wanted to go back home to Chicago. But Manchay would be acceptable – better than this. Where was she anyway? Did she think I was having a party up here?

Juan leaned against the rough wall, whittling a piece of wood with his knife. From time to time, he would look at me and laugh softly to himself. Mario and K'antu stared at Juan, but I avoided looking at him. Although memories of the previous day were blurry, I had done bad things. I knew what he was laughing at. I was sure, though, whatever K'antu and Mario thought it wasn't that.

After what seemed like hours, Juan spoke.

"So, Tamara, I am impressed by what you did yesterday."

I cringed. I didn't want anyone else to know.

"What exactly did she do yesterday?" Mario asked, angry.

"Ask her." Juan waved his hand toward me.

Mario and K'antu both turned to me.

"I don't want to talk about it," I muttered.

Mario's face went pale, and K'antu frowned.

"She took some drugs and tripped," Juan said, "but don't worry, the only thing that got hurt was the school."

He laughed and laughed.

"The only thing that got hurt?" Mario said indignantly.

In one fluid movement, he shot up and over to Juan. His fist made contact with Juan's nose, and blood gushed. I started to scream, but K'antu slapped her hand over my mouth to warn me about staying quiet.

I blinked. K'antu let go of me and moved over to the boys, who scuffled on the ground. Speaking through her teeth, she said, "Stop it."

But they did not listen. Juan punched Mario. They continued rolling around, trying to gain an advantage until I went and hit them each on the head with my lantern. They separated. Mario recovered quickly enough to grab me in a bear hug, trying to turn me away from Juan's revenge punch and putting himself in harm's way. But he wasn't fast enough. Juan hit me in the ribs before stepping away, panting.

I would have fallen if Mario had not been holding me. The force of the punch knocked the wind out of me for a moment. Mario lowered me to the ground. Everything hurt—my hands and head from yesterday, and now my ribs. Maybe I was in a war.

K'antu went to stand by Juan.

There was nothing but our clothing to clean the boys' bloody faces. K'antu ripped the bottom of her t-shirt and started wiping Juan's face. Mario did not stop the blood from dripping out of his nose and other scratches on his face. I did nothing for him either. Yeah, he had tried to save me, but I was still angry at him. It was unreasonable, but he and K'antu could have kept Juan from taking me yesterday.

I breathed shallowly and tentatively felt my side, trying to assess the damage. Soon my breathing went back to normal, and I decided he must not have broken any of my ribs. I sat down and brushed grit off of the knees of my jeans. Not that it mattered. There would be an equal amount of junk on my butt now.

Looking at Mario, who was nursing his wounds, something stirred in my gut, and I relented. He had, after all, defended me now. And I guess he had done it before. It wasn't his fault he couldn't yesterday. He looked like he had received several good punches, but not enough for emergency medical care - not that they would be able to get any here. So, he'd be all right. My gaze went to the other two. K'antu was wiping Juan's face. He was grousing at her about the pain. His nose did not look as straight as it had moments ago, and there was a lot more blood on him than on his attacker.

The school was vandalized, and the police were here to get the criminals – but the criminal was me. I was uneasy. So far, I had not done one thing to help K'antu, and now I was in the same situation. Did they know who had been at the school yesterday? Had there been surveillance cameras? That was a stupid question. Of course, there were, which meant they were looking specifically for me. I thought uneasily I did not remember for sure the exact damage I had inflicted – and about how hard it would be to prove it had been Juan's fault.

I looked at K'antu, who was looking at Juan. Juan, on the other hand, had his eyes closed. The look on K'antu's face angered me. How could she be treating him so nicely?

"K'antu."

My friend looked at me, startled.

"What?"

"What are you doing?"

K'antu looked a little guilty as her eyes went back to the sleeping boy. "I... I was..."

"You were taking care of your boyfriend," Mario said in a low voice.

K'antu was flustered, "I... I."

"You are, aren't you?" I whispered.

"No, I..."

"Don't deny it, K'antu," Mario also whispered, "we've all seen you guys together."

K'antu's eyes blazed fire. She tried to slap Mario, but I grabbed her wrist, feeling pain in my ribs with the movement.

Juan mumbled something. We all looked at him, but he kept his eyes closed, ignoring us.

"Mario, are you okay?" I said, reaching for him but turning to K'antu, who I still had hold of, "K'antu, hasn't there been enough violence here already?"

"It is none of your business what relationship I have with Juan."

I faced her. "K'antu, what is going on with you? Your husband has been murdered, and you are the prime suspect. And you're having an affair with his brother? A man who has no problem drugging me and making me vandalize a school? Worse, a man who almost killed you the other day?"

All of K'antu's bravado flowed out of her body. She slumped against the wall. She put her face in her hands, so it was hard to hear what she said. Mario and I both leaned forward.

"Every time Eduardo was with – was... too drunk to be a husband to me – which was pretty much every day, Juan was there. He helped me with the house and with... with... everything. I... we couldn't help falling in love..." she looked toward the sleeping boy.

"You couldn't help –" I couldn't keep the disgust out of my voice. I wasn't trying too hard.

K'antu's eyes pleaded with me in the light of the lantern, "Please, Tamara, don't judge me. You don't know the whole story. Juan was so sweet to me... he did everything for me. Eduardo was, well he was..."

"He was your husband," Mario interjected his opinion.

K'antu nodded. "Yes. He was. And he was fighting for my people - our people. But he was an alcoholic and also –"

"Also, what?" I asked.

"Never mind. It's too painful."

"K'antu."

K'antu took a minute before she said, "He used to hit me. I turned to a friend."

"You mean Juan, your brother-in-law," I said.

"Yes, Juan. So what?"

"So maybe he wasn't an appropriate person to turn to, that's what," I said.

"You don't understand," K'antu said, moving away from us.

I took a deep breath. I coughed, took another breath, not so deep, and said, "K'antu. You're in denial. He is a bad person. Your boyfriend injected me forcibly with whatever concoction he had in his syringe. He took me to the private school where he proceeded to break in and encouraged me to destroy stuff when I was having hallucinations."

Seeing K'antu's face, I continued, but in a gentler voice, "I understand you've been abused, both by Eduardo and now by Juan, so maybe you can't recognize how awful he is. When this is all over, we'll get you help."

K'antu started to cry. Moments later, there was a noise outside the tunnel. My heart lurched. We all bumped into each other in our hurry to get outside. I was in front, Mario was behind me, Juan and K'antu after him. People were shouting and banging on doors or walls. I got to the trapdoor and started pushing it. Mario helped. There was a loud thump from somewhere in the tunnel. A woman screamed.

"K'antu." I turned and tried to go back. Mario caught me.

"Let me go, Mario. I have to go help K'antu."

I pulled out of his grasp, pushed him aside, and went back. I couldn't see for a moment in the darkness. Then, as my eyes adjusted, I was able to see K'antu being pulled from where she had fallen by two men in uniform. I drew a breath to object, but someone covered my mouth. I tried to kick back to get loose, but the person lifted me, and my feet lost their traction.

"Stop fighting me, Tamara," Juan hissed in my ear, "There's no reason you should also be found."

Resigning myself, I went limp in his arms and watched as my friend and the two policemen disappeared down the tunnel.

"Promise me you won't make any noise," Juan said before releasing me.

I nodded.

"Good girl," Juan said, still standing too close for comfort.

I elbowed him savagely in the side and moved away. "You let them take her."

"What could I do? She fell, and they got her. What was your phrase for stuff like that? Oh yeah, 'tough luck.'"

"You could have helped her." I refused to listen to reason from

Juan. "Now they've got her, and they'll arrest her, and we'll never see her again."

I started crying. "She trusted you and you—"

Mario put his hand on my arm. "Never mind, Tamara, I hate to say it, but Juan is right. What's done is done. We'll wait a while and go back. The good news is we can go back to Manchay now and find another way to help K'antu."

"Go back to Manchay? No. You two are staying here in Patabamba," Juan said.

"Staying? No. I want to leave. We are leaving. I have to go help K'antu. I was done doing what Juan wanted. "Let's go, Mario. We can walk from here."

Walking away seemed easy, but soon there was a muffled cry behind me. I turned. Juan was standing with a knife to Mario's neck – a *Tumi*.

"You're staying," Juan snarled. He pushed Mario down into the tunnel. Then he came after me. I ran but did not get far before feeling something whiz past my head. I stopped. The *Tumi* was jutting out of the ground in front of me.

"I won't miss next time, Tamara. Come here."

"Why are you doing this, Juan?" Tears of frustration ran down my face.

"Get down there." He approached and was about to shove me like he had Mario, but I pushed back at him.

"Don't touch me. I will come with you. You could have killed Mario by pushing him down there."

Doing what I said I would before he could 'help' me, I went into the tunnel. Mario was sitting by one of the walls rubbing his leg.

"Mario, are you all right?" I went to him.

He raised his hand to keep me from touching him. "Yeah, I will be. Give me a minute."

"Okay, your minute is over. Let's go back to the compound." Juan stepped down the last stair.

To avoid more physical conflict, I pulled Mario up with me. I didn't look at Juan. He could have killed me with the *Tumi,* and I doubted he cared one way or the other. But the other thing was, Eduardo had been killed with one. Maybe Juan killed his brother. That would make a lot of sense to me. Juan wanted K'antu, and he probably saw how badly Eduardo treated her, so he killed him. Or there could be another rivalry going on between them, something I did not know about. One of them could have been stealing the money from People Help, and the other found out. If it was Eduardo stealing, that could be a motive for Juan to kill him – he certainly had the temper for it. Or, if Juan were stealing and Eduardo caught him, killing him would be a way to cover up his crime.

When – or if – I ever got back to Manchay, those were the first things I would tell Laura. Unless I yelled at her first for not coming to get me. Didn't she guess I was up here? Where were my rescuers? I squeezed Mario's arm and helped him walk, limp-ing, through the tunnel.

Once we were out, blinking in the sunlight, Juan uttered a terse command, "Follow me."

He took us to the front room – the one we had previously spoken to Lorena in.

"Sit down," he said, opening a drawer in the desk. He pulled out an iPad and began searching for something on it.

"Are you calling someone to go help K'antu?" I asked.

Silence.

"Well, are you?"

"In a way," Juan said, "now be quiet."

"What does 'in a way' mean?" I would not be quiet while he sat there arrogantly ignoring me.

He glanced up from the screen. "I am calling a friend who is going to help us get to Tomás Romero. The only way to help K'antu now is to point the finger at someone else. But we need help for that."

I sat. Mario, to all intents and purposes forgotten by Juan, stood close to me.

A minute later, Juan started a conversation with the person he had called, "Taki, hi. I am glad you are home. I need you to talk to a couple of idiots for me."

I exchanged a glance with Mario, who shrugged. On the other end, the female greeted Juan and agreed, asking who she would be talking to.

He spoke to the screen, "You remember, the niece of the rich winemaker lady, Tamara. Tamara, meet Taki."

He turned the screen. I saw a girl sitting on a bed.

"Hi," I said weakly.

"Hi, Tamara. I am Taki." The girl sounded polite but kind of cold.

"And this is Mario," Juan said, "Taki, give Tamara and Mario a little tour of your house."

The girl complied, turning her device around the room, and explaining a little of what we were seeing. The home was one room. In one corner was a rough kitchen. The bed was directly opposite. A large screen T.V. with a diagonal crack across the screen covered the wall directly on the other side of the front door. The kitchen area covered the wall in between. There was another door by the kitchen, which presumably led outside. There was a pot boiling on the stove. Rice, Taki told them. The floor was dirt. Taki and her brother had never had the money to build a floor. I knew from previous trips here that the poorest inhabitants of Manchay somehow found ways to have cell phones or iPads – the basic communication necessities – so the dichotomy did not surprise me. It would have been strange to my friends in Chicago, though.

"Now tell these guys why you live in such a small, shitty house," Juan said, focusing my attention again on the girl.

"Juan." I should not have been surprised he would talk to anyone that way, but jeez.

He looked at me. "You want me to lie?"

"You could at least stop being so direct."

He laughed. "That's a good one, coming from you, Tamara. Taki, please continue."

He threw me a sarcastic "Acceptable?" look.

In return, I gave him an icy stare. He jabbed his finger toward the screen. I focused on it again.

Taki said, "I come from Patabamba like K'antu and Juan. But I live here in Manchay with my brother. We moved here a couple of years ago after our parents died. We thought here in Manchay, things would be safer for us. I started working for one of Tomás' assistants as a maid. The pay was horrible, and the conditions weren't any different."

"The man used to leer at me, and I was waiting for the day

when he tried something. But his wife was bigger and stronger than he was, and she was not a stupid woman. She was there the day he touched me. She beat the crap out of him. But she also hit me. I ended up in the hospital. She had broken two of my ribs, fractured the proximal phalanx of my left hand, and given me a concussion."

"That's criminal," I frowned.

Taki shrugged, "Anyway, while I was in recovery, Tomás Romero made one of his annual 'visits to the less fortunate. He saw me, and he was back the next day offering me a job. Now I work for him."

"Doing what?" I suspected that I did not want to know. Taki had the dark, shiny black hair of the region. She looked petite and on-screen; her bone structure was perfect. She was beautiful.

"I do lots of things," Taki said vaguely.

"Lots of things?" I asked. Juan spat on the floor. I made a disgusted exclamation at him. This room had a tile floor. The glob of spit sat there and glistened. Juan gestured for me to keep looking at the screen.

"I know what you are thinking. But it is not so bad. And my life is better now –"

"Better than what?" I said. I looked at Mario. He shook his head sadly at me.

"I have security now. Tomás will never let anything bad happen to me, or my brother, ever again. I get enough to eat, and the work is not that demanding..."

"Your brother, where is he?" I asked.

"He is up there with you. His name is Oliver," Taki smiled.

174

"Wait," I couldn't help myself, "you said you have security? But surely what you have to do to get it – it is too much."

"What would you have me do?" The screen on Taki's end moved – the ceiling appeared and the floor, and then it came back to Taki's face, which was dark with anger.

"I... I don't know," I said helplessly, "but... but is he going to take care of you when you get old and unable to work? Would he take care of you if you got pregnant?"

No answer. Taki had disconnected. I couldn't believe the story. How could Taki let this happen to herself? Although I guess that was blaming the victim. But there must be a way out... I stood up. I hadn't liked Romero before, and now I hated him. "The guy is a predator. He is taking advantage of her. It's illegal. He should be punished. He should be–"

"Oh, don't worry, we'll get him. Between Taki and me, we will arrange it, and now that you are with us, you are going to help us," Juan said.

I turned slowly and narrowed my eyes at him. What did Taki have to do with helping K'antu? I said, "So you believe Tomás Romero had something to do with Eduardo's death?"

Juan threw the device on the desk. "I don't believe, I know. It remains to prove it. Since Taki works with him, and he keeps her close, she is our best way of getting to him."

Amazed, and at the same time thrown off guard by how many sides of Juan I had seen, good, bad, and everything in between, I pursed my lips and nodded.

"Tamara..." there was a note of warning in Mario's voice.

"No, Mario. He might be right. Let's see what his plan is," I said. And to Juan, as an aside, I asked, "Why did you call Laura the 'rich winemaker lady'?"

"Isn't that who she is?"

"She is good to people. They don't hate her. Why should you?"

"People aren't as happy with your aunt as you want to think they are."

"What is that supposed to mean?" I said.

"Wouldn't you be resentful of her comfortable life if you lived the way Taki does? Wouldn't you hate someone who doesn't even lift a finger to change things in a town where these things go on, just because they feel they are treating their employees more fairly than anyone else?"

My shoulders slumped. "When you put it like that, yeah, maybe."

"Yeah, maybe," He imitated me. His face flushed a dark purple color, and he started to shake. He stared at me and pulled a knife, thin and sharp, out of his pocket.

Mario moved a little closer to me.

Chapter 15

Juan's demeanor traveled the spectrum from furious to calm. But I could tell it was a considerable effort. He opened a drawer, took out a block of wood, and started to whittle at it. "It's a nice knife, isn't it?"

"Do you feel like a man when you threaten us, Juan?" I breathed. There was a drop of sweat running down the middle of my back. Mario squeezed my shoulder tightly, but I shifted away from his grasp.

"What?" Out of the wood began to emerge the shape of a cute little alpaca.

"You could have killed me with that *Tumi*."

"Boy, you are paranoid. I wasn't even going to throw this," He waved the knife, "And learn your facts, this isn't a *Tumi*."

"Don't play stupid. I mean, back outside the tunnel. And just now, pulling the knife out, how did you expect us to react?"

He stopped his work and grinned, showing all of his teeth. "I could have killed you, couldn't I? But I didn't. And this – an uncle of mine taught me. He said it would calm me down. And he was right."

"You have a lot of skill with knives," Mario said. Juan and I both looked at him. He had been quiet throughout our whole ordeal in the tunnel and out.

"You could turn that into a career," Mario continued.

"Except..." I said, my voice trailing off.

Juan made eye contact with me. Slowly he put the wood and the knife down on the desk.

"Except what?"

"Where were you when Eduardo was killed?" I asked.

"Tamara!" Mario's voice was panicked. With wild eyes, he looked at Juan.

But Juan laughed. He scratched at the tattoo on his head with the knife. He looked nice when he smiled, I thought. I blinked and shook my head to get that thought out of it. I looked at Mario. He was pale, and his eyes had darkened. His face was a mix of fear and disgust – the latter emotion seemed to be directed at me. Had he read my mind and observed my random and hopefully short-lived admiration for Juan?

"Eduardo and I had our disagreements, to be sure. I could have killed him many times in the last year."

"Over K'antu?" I asked.

"That – and..." Juan's smile disappeared. He picked up his work again and focused on carving details on the alpaca.

"And what?" Mario asked before I could.

"Eduardo found something at Tomás' house. But instead of

telling me, he told Elías – your cousin, Tamara. He should have told me. If he had, he would not have been killed."

He slashed at the little wooden animal, making a large gash where there would not ordinarily be one. I made a little sound of protest. He slammed the wood and the knife onto the desk.

"I would have protected him. I did not kill my brother, Tamara. I know you think I'm crazy, but he is the one person who cared about me. I could not have done it. What happened to him was horrible. He should have told me what he had found, but instead, he had to go tell him –" He stopped. His eyes welled up.

"His what?" I asked. How much of his erratic behavior had to do with grief? Why hadn't I thought of that before? I had been quick to judge, although honestly, who wouldn't have judged him so harshly?

Nevertheless, It made me feel bad. I thought about my cousin. Why did he have the injury under his ribs? Had he fought with Eduardo? Had something terrible happened?

"His friend." Juan put a strong emphasis on the word 'friend'. He looked expectantly at me.

I stuck out my bottom lip. What game was he playing now? Was he trying to tell me something? Why didn't he come right out and say it? I wasn't ready to hear anything against my cousin, and I wanted to bury my sudden suspicious thoughts so deep they would never surface again. So, I said, "So he chose to confide in Elías – in his friend, so what? Maybe he didn't trust you. Maybe whatever he found had nothing to do with your crusade –"

In one fluid movement, Juan stood up and came behind me, grabbing my hair and pulling my head back, so I was forced to look at the ceiling. He had brought the knife along. He pressed it into my throat.

"Hey," Mario protested.

"You never stop, do you? I have been letting you ask so many questions. None of it is your business, but now that's over. Mario, your girlfriend here needs to learn respect."

I gagged.

"Let her go. Please," Mario begged.

Juan took the knife away and pushed my head as he had done with K'antu. Luckily there was no body of water here in the office. I fell forward onto the desk and bumped my forehead. I stayed where I was and shut my eyes. Everything hurt; my hands, my knees, my forehead…

"Go get her a bandage," Juan told Mario.

"I am not leaving…"

"She'll be fine without you. I won't touch her. Go."

Mario went.

"He is not my boyfriend," I said, choking out the words, my cheek resting on the smooth coolness of the desk.

"I don't care," Juan replied, "get up."

Painfully, I went to a chair and sank into it.

The little wooden animal was getting a few needed tweaks. Juan made short, perpendicular strokes, giving the alpaca 'fur'. It hid the larger gash he had made. Streaks of red soaked into the wood – my blood on the knife from the thin cut he had made on my throat. Strangely, it made the little sculpture look more artistic.

We sat in silence until Mario got back. He covered the cut on my neck with the bandage and gave me a bag of ice. My head was pounding, so I pressed the bag to it, grateful to him for thinking to bring it.

"Let's go." Juan started toward the door as soon as he saw me put the ice on my head.

A little while ago, I would have told him no or asked him where we were going. Now I got up and shuffled out of the room behind him, Mario behind me. Juan led us through the front door to the street. The office was close to the front of the compound, and we did not meet anyone on our way. Juan got into his car and barked at us to get in too.

Not this again, I thought wearily. But I got in. This time, at least Mario was with me. We set off on the gravel road to Manchay.

"You did not ask me where I'm taking you this time, Tamara." Mario and I had both opted to get in the back seat. Juan peered through the rearview mirror at me. The car swerved. I gripped the handle of the door with one hand and grabbed air with the other. My ice pack fell to the floor. Juan focused on the road again, spinning the steering wheel to straighten the car, and the ice slid under the passenger seat.

"Well?" He insisted while I debated whether or not to get the ice.

"Where are you taking us?" I said flatly.

"That's more like it. The two of you are going to go into Romero's house and search for anything to prove Romero killed my brother and why he did."

"How are we going to get into his house?' Mario asked.

"What a great question." Juan's body tilted to the left. With one hand, he fumbled in his pocket. I saw the dim light of a cell phone. Juan's head was down, and he only had one hand on the wheel. So much for being a safe driver.

Mario's voice was so polite that it wasn't. "Do you want me to call someone for you while you drive?"

"Shut up." Juan continued texting on his phone.

The car swerved again. Lights appeared on the other side of the road.

"Juan," I screamed, "pay attention. There is a car coming."

"I see it, I see it. Chill." He straightened the car before the other one passed. His phone beeped. This time he raised it to the top of the steering wheel.

I felt hot and cold at the same time. Nausea boiled in my stomach. I had to keep insisting. He would either kill me because I said something or because he was texting while driving. Either way, I had nothing to lose. "Please, Juan, put the phone down."

"Oh, don't be such a baby. I'm done with it anyway." He threw it down and raised his hands in a defiant gesture. The car stayed mercifully straight this time. Then, concentrating more on the road, he continued, "Taki has the keys to Romero's house. That's what I was going to talk to her about until you insulted her. Luckily, she just texted me back. She is going to meet us there."

"What do you mean? I was trying to point out how wrong her situation is."

"Yes, that's exactly what Taki needs to solve her problems – your indignation."

"I –" I was about to say something biting. But I couldn't think of a single thing that made more sense than what he had said. So, I kept my mouth shut and sulked.

A few minutes later, Mario and I sat on a bench in the park.

We were only blocks away from Tomás Romero's house. Large trees were scattered around well-manicured green triangles that sat between the X, making up the two pedestrian paths through the park. All the greenery looked grayish because it was now late evening. I looked uneasily around. Juan was sitting in a car not far away, watching and waiting also.

"I'm so tired," I said to fill the empty conversational space.

"I know –" Mario answered.

He turned his body toward me, but I refused to look at him.

"I'm sorry, Tamara."

"For what? This isn't your fault."

"I am sorry I haven't been able to protect you."

"Mario…"

"Yes?"

"Why are you doing this?"

He stiffened.

"You asked me already, and I told you – it's for you –"

"No, it's not. At least, that is not all of it. It can't be. You just met me. This is too much for anyone to go through for someone they hardly know."

He made a frustrated movement with his hand. "All right, you are right, damn it. There might be other reasons why I stay."

It didn't make me feel good to realize my guess was correct. When would I learn to keep quiet? Not anytime soon. I felt compelled to ask, "What other reasons?"

"Remember I told you my mother came from Patabamba too?"

I turned to him. "Yes, I remember…"

Mario breathed a little too long through his nose. "She was my father's maid."

"But... that's not so bad, right? Things are okay for her now, right?"

His face was expressionless.

"That is why you and your mother went to Spain, isn't it? And it's why you feel like you need to help get justice for K'antu – you know what is happening to her is unjust," I finished. He didn't need to be here. I could figure it all out on my own. Why I hadn't done it earlier was not important... I could not face yet another example of my ignorance tonight.

"Look, let's get this over with. Juan wants us to go in and look around, so let's do it," he said. "Where is Taki?"

"I'm so sorry, Mario, for everything," I whispered. He moved away from me and stood up, pacing in front of the bench. I looked back. Juan's car was still there. What if we were to make a run for it? Go back to Laura's house? What could he do to stop us? We both had an idealistic urge to help, but in the end, it wasn't our fight. What if Tomás Romero wasn't guilty – of murder, that is? Then this little excursion would be illegal breaking and entering for nothing. And Juan was keeping well out of it – a way to blame us in case we got caught? He seemed to have a way of sitting back and letting other people get in trouble for the results he wanted.

Why couldn't Taki do it? But then again, I didn't know her. Could I trust her? This could be my chance once and for all to find something that would point to someone – anyone else who could have killed Eduardo. Even if the magistrate were innocent, he could have information that would lead us to someone else. I wasn't crossing Juan off the list yet, even though he had been pretty convincing. He could have been lying. I knew already Tomás Romero did not like him. He might have had information on him.

Just as I had persuaded myself to stay, Taki finally showed up. She spent little time greeting us, saying merely, "Let's be quick."

Mario and I stood, and the three of us went the two blocks over to Tomás Romero's house. This part of Manchay was pretty; the trees and flowers, the pothole-free asphalt of the paved roads, the non-damaged houses. We walked along the sidewalk, passing wrought iron gates – a security tool used to keep intruders out while still showcasing the loveliness of the proper-ties inside.

The magistrate's house was a one-story, dark brown house. The roof, covered with curved tiles, jutted out slightly with the cream-colored corbels supporting the overhang contrasted nicely with the darkness of the rest of the facade. Bright lights shone from under the narrowly protruding roof, illuminating the house with a warm glow. Besides the garage attached at an angle to one wing, there were no ungainly corners to the home; it was all graceful curves.

Taki led us around the fence to a gate leading to the back of the house. She used her key, and we went in. A tiny baby llama cantered up to us as we crossed the lawn. A soft grunt floated in the air behind the baby animal, and I saw the outline of a larger llama.

"This is Baby," Taki said, "She is ten weeks old. Maria, her mom, is the other llama, and somewhere around here is JuJu, the dad."

"My aunt has llamas also. They do a great job manicuring the grass," I said, trying to be friendly.

"Tomás won't pay gardeners to cut it," Taki said bitterly.

None of us said anything. The comment was weird. Why have people cut the grass if the llamas did it for them? Baby followed me, so right before we reached the house, I spent a moment petting her. My hands disappeared in her soft fur. Maria, the mother, clomped up.

"Come on, Tamara," Mario said, "stop playing with the llamas. We need to do this as fast as possible and get out."

Taki led the way toward the house, and we entered through a small door on the side. The door opened onto a small room off the kitchen that was the size of a closet. It had a cot and a small table with drawers.

"This is my room when I stay here," Taki said.

"He goes all out for you," I said sarcastically, poking at the inch-thick plastic mattress.

Taki gave me a nasty look.

"Come on," Mario sounded testy, "we don't have much time. Taki, where is his office? It is probably the best place to start."

He started walking in the direction of what turned out to be the kitchen.

"Not that way," Taki whispered loudly, "follow me."

We went to the office, walking down a hallway filled with pictures of Tomás at different events. My heart jumped when I found a picture of him with Laura. They were smiling broadly and shaking hands in front of the private school. My head ached.

I felt like I hadn't seen my aunt in weeks. I did not like the smug look on her face, and I liked even less the sight of that school. It was the same one I had destroyed. But there was no time to think about all of that. I hurried along behind the other two.

When we got to the office, Taki waved her arm, telling me to open the door and go in first. I twisted the doorknob slowly and opened the door millimeters at a time, feeling like someone was going to jump out at me from the other side. Mario hissed at me to hurry, and when I finally got the door completely open and stepped in, Mario followed close on my heels. The desk was directly facing the door. On the desk was a small lamp, which was lit. Sitting on the chair behind the desk was the dark outline of a person. My heart skipped a beat. My instinct had not been wrong. I moved backward, knocking into Mario. I tried to turn and push him through the door, but before I could get us both out, he had reached around me and turned the overhead lights on.

I turned back to the desk. It was Lorena sitting there.

"Lorena, what are you doing here?" Mario demanded.

"I could ask you the same question," She responded, shuffling papers. She straightened her back and paused a moment, then said, "but I don't need to. I know why you are here."

"You came," she continued, propping herself on the side closest to us, "to find something incriminating against Tomás."

Staring at her, my heart beating, I tried to find something to say. I looked to find Taki, but the girl had disappeared. I racked my brains, but Mario was a lot quicker than me.

"No, no, of course not. But we don't believe it was K'antu who killed Eduardo, and we thought he might have files on... on Juan and the kids in Patabamba. Maybe if we looked at them, we could see something the magistrate hadn't – a detail that would lead to the real killer. Or a piece of information on how the money has been moving through People Help. If we could figure out where the corruption is, that could open up the suspect list, and the police would stop focusing on K'antu. I mean, not that we are smarter or anything, but information might mean different things to us –"

"Mario, don't worry so much. What you say makes a lot of sense. Perhaps we should have included the two of you in the investigation from the start. I understand how you might think K'antu did not kill her husband."

"You do?" I said, looking at her suspiciously.

Lorena leaned back in the chair, "Of course. I, myself, still believe she did it, but you may be right that it is in everyone's best interest to cast a wider net."

"Hmm..." I said.

"But regarding the movement of money, we have told you the truth, Mario. I know it has seemed wrong, but I have been over and over it. There simply was not enough for everyone. It is sad but true. However, next week I am going to Lima. I have meetings with several people there, and I am sure I can bring back more money. Don't worry, better times are coming for the people of Manchay. I promise."

Mario smiled. I felt comforted. At first, I was scared to find her here, but now I was glad we had run into her. She would make a good ally, even if she did not believe us as we did. At least she wasn't shutting me down entirely – like my aunt and the magistrate.

"As it happens, you came on a good day. Tomás is out of town," Lorena smiled. "He may not have been as amenable as I am to let you be involved. I see no harm in it, even though I wish you would have talked to me first."

"We, I –"

"But no matter," Lorena kept talking. She smoothed her already smooth hair with her thin hand, "Let's see, you were hoping to go through his computer? To see the files on People Help? Or the police report on Eduardo? I don't believe we have anything else."

She clicked on the keyboard of the computer.

"We... um... yes, whatever you have..." Mario stammered.

Lorena tilted her head, birdlike. "Don't be nervous, Mario. I am on your side. Why do you think I am here? I have been digging through his things this evening. Not that Tomás would be surprised to see me, as he would you."

"So... Did you find anything?" I asked.

"Find anything?" Lorena frowned.

"You said you had been digging..."

"Ah. Nothing," Lorena said a little too quickly, "nothing that would implicate anyone but K'antu, I am afraid. But please, have a look for yourself."

I let Mario go to the computer. He was more familiar with People Help than I was, and he could probably read through the paperwork from the police more quickly than I could. He grew up in Spain, so his Spanish was a lot better than mine – I spoke like a native, but reading official documents was not my forte.

"Thank you, Lorena," I said gratefully.

"Think nothing of it. So how did you get in here anyway?"

"Uh," I stuttered, not wanting to get Taki in trouble.

Lorena waited.

"Well, Juan... uh... he said..." I hesitated, not knowing whether it'd be good to mention Taki's name.

Mario had no such reservations. "Juan asked us to come. Taki came with us. She has the keys."

Lorena spoke as if to herself, "Ah, yes. Taki. Lovely girl. Smart, too."

"Can... can we do what we came here to do and get out?" I asked, "Juan is waiting outside. If we take too long, he might... he might..."

"He might what, Tamara? Is there something you need to tell me?" Lorena asked.

The office was a huge room, a little more than twenty by twenty feet square. The desk, accompanied by a soft leather chair, was large and made of mahogany – the room's centerpiece. In the middle of the room was a round table with four chairs. Behind it was a floor-to-ceiling wall-to-wall window facing the backyard where the llamas grazed, and a couple of fruit trees overhung a small pond. I moved to get to the other side of the desk, where Lorena was and peered out the window. There was a movement outside.

"Oh my God, Mario, something is moving out there. Maybe it's Juan. We need to find something quickly, or he will –." panicked. I doubled back and grabbed onto Mario's arm.

"Calm down, Tamara. It is probably the llamas," Lorena said, "besides, if you are afraid of Juan, don't be. He cannot do anything to you if you do not let him. You came with him, but you can leave without him."

"I don't see how." Hope bubbled inside me, but on top of it was a feeling of despair.

"You can simply leave here and go back home to Laura's house, can't you?" Lorena said.

"No, no, don't say that. He'd follow us, and I don't know what he would do," I said, my eyes widening.

Lorena and Mario both looked at me, Mario with surprise and Lorena with pity.

"Why are you staring at me? Don't you understand? He is crazy, and you both know it. I have tried to fight him, and it has gotten me in trouble – or injured."

Lorena grunted and gave up. "Well, if you say so. Then I guess you'll have to find something for him. Let's look through here then, shall we?"

She opened Tomás' desk and brought out a stack of papers. Lorena handed them to me. Mario leaned over my shoulder.

"These are the police reports of Eduardo's death," I said, reading through them anyway. Maybe there was something in this report that we didn't already know from the gossip and news we had seen and heard. I began reading. Eduardo had been found at home. K'antu and Eduardo had a small, unremarkable house near the center of Manchay. He had been found in the kitchen, lying on the floor in a pool of his blood. His throat had been slit. The murder weapon had been wrested out of the drying muck of blood; no fingerprints on it, no one but K'antu and Eduardo's in the kitchen.

"Didn't those two ever have guests?" I asked. "No one else left fingerprints in their kitchen?"

Lorena shrugged, "Maybe guests stayed in the living room."

I looked at her, then kept reading. The weapon had come from K'antu's collection. It was a *Tumi* made of a mix of gold and silver. *Tumi* knives were rounded at each end. The smaller end was the blade, a semicircle of sharpness. The other end was always the head of *Tumi*, the facial features of a warrior molded into the metal. The shaft of most *Tumis* were short, with just enough space for a person to grasp. This one had the design of a flower on its shaft - a long, tubular flower, flaring at the end with its pistil and stigma exposed at the end: a *K'antu*, or *Cantua Buxifolia*, the Perúvian national flower. It wasn't the easiest weapon to hurt someone with – I knew since I had been trained to use it. Maybe that is why Joaquín thought K'antu did it; she was an expert in its use.

There were interviews with neighbors indicating loud arguments between K'antu and Eduardo in the weeks leading up to his death. Eduardo had also argued with a male voice. But no neighbor had seen who it was. Or at least, no neighbor was willing to say who had visited Eduardo recently.

Eduardo had been killed the day of Laura's birthday party. K'antu had an alibi for various moments, but nothing that could be proven entirely. She had been seen running around town doing errands for Laura, but in the police timeline, she had an opportunity to have slipped back home to murder her husband.

"All the evidence is circumstantial," I said, absorbed in the reading. "There is nothing here that connects K'antu directly to the crime."

"True..." Lorena replied.

"Then why did they arrest her?" I said. My phone made a noise. I pulled it out of my back pocket. When I saw who had texted me, my hand began to shake, and I almost dropped the phone. "It's Juan. He says to hurry up."

Lorena gathered the papers. "Well, I am sorry we did not find anything –"

"But wait," Mario said, "what about the other drawers? Shouldn't we look more?"

"I have already looked," Lorena said. "In my opinion, the two of you should disappear out the back way before Juan decides to come in after you. Go home, Tamara. Go back to Laura. I will talk to Tomás about K'antu. I promise."

"Disappear?" Taki had appeared again.

"Taki, there you are. Where did you go?" I asked her.

"I had to get something from my room." Taki faced me. "Are you thinking of not going back with Juan?"

"Do you blame me? He did this to me." I touched my neck. Blood had seeped through the bandage.

"Lorena is right, Tamara, let's go to Laura's house. It won't take more than fifteen minutes to walk there from here," Mario said.

"But what if Juan sees us? Or what if he realizes we aren't in here anymore? He'll come after us. He's got the car…"

"We can go the back way. He'll never see us." Mario looked determined.

"I can go distract him," Taki said. "I can tell him you are only halfway done looking through Señor Romero's things. That will give you time to get away."

I looked at her, surprised. Mario nodded, agreeing with the suggestion.

"And I will clean up here and be on my way," Lorena said.

It was a good plan. Laura would help... I knew she would. "Okay, Taki. Thank you. And thank you, Lorena. You are right. Once I get back to Laura's I will be safe. He wouldn't dare try to get me out of there... and there is nothing here to help K'antu anyway. We will have to find another way."

"Exactly. So let's go," Mario said, pushing me toward the door.

We left Lorena there and headed toward the back of the house. Halfway there, there was a loud knocking on the front door. It was Juan yelling for someone to let him in. All the blood in my body drained to my feet.

"Quick, let's run," Mario said.

I did as he said. We ran to the back, out the door, and through the yard. A moment later, we heard the sound of Juan's fury. Taki yelled at him to calm down. Mario took my hand, and we ran faster.

Chapter 16

We ran, passing the docile llamas, and went through the gate. We made our way down the street. Soon, though, the sounds of a car coming up behind us made us jump.

"Quick, Tamara, this way," Mario croaked.

He led me into a small alleyway. The car's brakes screeched; gravel crunched under tires. The car moved on.

"He knows where we are going. He'll beat us there and get me before we make it," I panted.

His running slowed down. "You are right. So let's not go there."

"What?" I also slowed to a stop.

"Let's go to my father's house. Juan may figure out we went there when we don't show up at Laura's, but by then, it'll be too late."

I started laughing. I was so happy he had thought of it that I impulsively put my arms around his neck and kissed his cheek.

He reacted by pulling me closer to him. I tilted my head back, and our eyes met. He kissed me full on the lips. For one moment, I let myself escape into his embrace.

Gravel crunched again.

"We have to go."

"Come on, it's this way," Mario said, still holding my hand. We headed down the alley.

At the opening of the alleyway, we stopped to make sure Juan was not on the street. He wasn't. So we continued running, and before long, we found ourselves amongst rows of vines.

"This is the edge of Rodolfo's vineyard. We will be home soon. Quick," Mario whispered.

We sprinted under the vines, through the narrow arches of wire and leaves, ducking under the hanging grapes. Sand flew up, disturbed by our feet, and I tripped on a thick fallen plant near the end of one row, but Mario caught me. Rodolfo's house was fifty meters away from the end of the last vine.

Soon we opened the back door of Rodolfo's house, panting with exertion. We walked through. Mario beckoned me to follow him. He went through the house and knocked on a closed door. The sounds of shuffling got closer, and the door opened. It was Rodolfo's bedroom, and the man himself stood there.

"Mario, Tamara," He exclaimed. He had on a dark brown robe. Underneath was a pair of blue silk pajamas. "What are you doing here? I thought you were in Patabamba."

"We were," Mario said. We had planned out exactly what to tell him.

"But we needed to come back. K'antu had been arrested." I blurted out.

"Yes, I know," Rodolfo said. "So you came here in the middle of the night to tell me that?"

He did not look pleased.

"Please, Señor Alvarez," I sputtered, "I need to get back to Laura's house. Can you drive me... please? We will explain everything in the morning."

"Indeed you will. Give me a minute. Mario, go to bed. I will get Tamara home safe."

We had woken him up in the middle of the night, but he still seemed more angry than necessary. I gave Mario a questioning look. His face was sober, but he winked at me.

"Don't worry," He whispered.

"Easier said than done," I said back.

"Go get in my car Tamara," Rodolfo said, "I'll grab the keys and be right out."

I went to his car and got in on the passenger's side. I sat on a lump, so I reached under me and pulled out a small package. It was a plastic bag labeled "Eduardo". My heart lurched. I put it up to my nose. It was *paco*. What was it doing in Rodolfo's car?

Just then, he opened the driver's side door, so I stuffed the bag back under me. I felt him staring at me, but I leaned my head back and closed my eyes. "Thank you, Señor Alvarez, for driving me home. I've had such a bad time."

Displaying a great sense of timing, a tear rolled down my cheek. I sensed him turning forward. He started the car.

"Of course, Tamara. Relax. You'll be with Laura soon."

The following day Laura was spooning brown sugar into her coffee when I came down to breakfast. Rodolfo must have called my aunt before we left his house. Laura had opened the door to us and sent me directly to bed. As I walked to my bedroom, I had heard the two of them speaking quietly together.

"Good morning, *cariño*," Laura said as I kissed her cheek.

"Good morning *Tía*."

"So you've come back."

As if I had disappeared because I wanted to? Why hadn't she been more concerned? I was hurt but not willing to ask why she wasn't more relieved. I picked at the eggs I had served myself out of the platter in the middle of the table.

"I assume it is because you want to see K'antu," Laura continued.

"Yes, that is why we came back. *Tía*, we have to help her." I perked up at the mention of my friend. I had begun to be afraid Laura would dwell on how I had gotten home last night – or worse, bring up the issue of the vandalized school.

"Well, you will be pleasantly surprised to know I went yesterday and got her out of jail. She is here in her bedroom – probably still sleeping."

I almost dropped my coffee cup. "You did? She is?"

Laura smiled. "Did you think I would let her rot in jail?"

I blushed.

Laura stared. "You did, didn't you? You thought I would not take care of one of my own? Tamara."

"It… it's not that, *Tía*. It's… well… things are weird. So how did they let her out of jail so easily?"

Laura looked at the ceiling. "I simply pointed out that they did not have enough evidence. But she is only out on bail. They will be presenting their case to my lawyer in a few days. Until then, K'antu needs to stay here and not leave."

She looked pointedly at me.

"I want to talk to her."

Laura put out her hand, palm up. "*Cariño*, it would be better if you let her sleep. She will be down soon, I am sure. In the meantime, why don't you tell me what happened in Patabamba?"

"What do you mean what happened?" I had not gotten off so easily after all. I fiddled with my coffee cup.

"When I realized where you were, I knew that Mario was with you, so I didn't worry too much. But when rumors about the school started going around –"

"School?" I interrupted her.

"School," she continued, raising her voice, "people were saying that a girl with curly hair was with Juan when the school was vandalized."

I said nothing.

"And while they did not release the video from the surveillance cameras to the public, I saw it. You were on it. At least, a girl looking like you was there. I had never seen you like that before. I had a discussion with Joaquín, and now, somehow, the footage has been 'misplaced', so you should not have any issues, but Tamara. What were you thinking?"

"Misplaced?" I said.

"Misplaced." My aunt said firmly. "Do not ask me more about it. Just be glad it was."

"So if you knew it was me, why didn't you come to get me?"

Laura stood and went to the window. The sun was shining. "Excuse me?"

"I said why didn't you come to get me from Patabamba? Didn't you realize there was something wrong?"

"Darling," she did not turn away from the window, "I was busy here trying to convince the police it could not have been you. How was I also supposed to be up there?"

"So you used your influence to get rid of the evidence, but you left me to deal with Juan? *Tía*, he is out of his mind. He drugged me. That is why I did what I did. I was under the influence of whatever he gave me. Do you think I would have done what I did otherwise? He is crazy, and you –"

But I couldn't finish. My voice was thick with tears. I swiped at my eyes with a rough paper napkin.

Laura simply said in a faraway voice, "It is true, something needs to be done about Juan. He is an awful boy..."

I tell my aunt a boy kidnapped and drugged me, and that is all she can say? Does she feel so good about using her influence to save me from the police she completely misses the real problem? Because of her indifference, unwelcome emotions coursed through my brain, and the next words out of my mouth came as a surprise to me – except when I thought about it later, they were not entirely wrong.

"' That awful Juan' you say? You mean the boy whose life has been so shitty lately he cracked when he realized that instead of his school being rebuilt, the rich people of this town were just going to throw fundraisers where they can get dressed up in designer clothes and eat gourmet food and spend so much money there would be nothing left for the school children?" I couldn't believe the words coming out of my mouth. How could I be defending him? My aunt's cool dismissal of him and my situation annoyed me.

Laura looked equally surprised to hear me say those things.

She swiveled around and said, "Tamara, are you serious? There is no excuse for what Juan does. No excuse for what happened at the school. Sure, the public high school doesn't look so good now, but your description of how we do things around here is uncalled for."

"Have you been to the school, *Tía*? I have. It is unsafe. Nothing has been rebuilt, and it has no equipment or even a place for the kids to sit."

"*Cariño*, you are exaggerating."

"So you have not been there.'

"Well, no... but –"

"Then how do you know?"

"I know everyone on the school board. They all assure me–"

"The school board? Have they ever been there? How many of them send their kids to that school?"

Laura began to look mad. "Listen, Tamara, you have no idea what you are talking about. We are all trying our best to make Manchay a better place. These things take time. Keep in mind, we had a horrific natural disaster here last year. Buildings don't just pop back up after something like that."

"But if they had been built better before, like the private school – like your house –"

"Indeed – that is a great point. If life were a bowl of cherries, we would rebuild all of the houses of Manchay to be strong and earthquake resistant. But throwing money at the people who live here hardly solves the problem."

"What do you mean? No one is throwing money at them."

My aunt gave me a pitying look. "Have you seen any of the destroyed homes recently?"

"I have. I have seen at least two. Why?"

"Have you by any chance noticed anything like a satellite dish hanging off a roof?"

I looked confused.

"Because several of them have one. Those same roofs look like they are about to collapse again, and yet the owners decided to buy a satellite dish with the money they were allotted from People Help. Did no one mention it to you?" Laura demanded.

"No. But –"

"So you give someone money, and they have a choice: rebuild their house, or get satellite T.V. Guess what choice a lot of people made? Guess what kind of choice Juan made?"

"Does he have a satellite dish on his house?" I asked. I wanted to know.

Laura gave me a withering look. "No, in fact, he does not. But I am certain he spends his money on something else altogether. And it isn't the basic necessities."

I flushed. More than likely, a little of 'something else' had been flowing through my veins the other day.

"Exactly." Laura saw my discomfort and looked smug. She must have seen the flash of understanding in my eyes. "There is only so much anyone can do to help people. After that, they have to make their own choices – and not everyone makes good ones."

"So you don't think their claims of corruption in the government are true?"

"No, frankly, I do not," Laura said, standing up. "I thought K'antu might have killed Eduardo, but now I believe Juan killed him. He is on a vendetta against certain people in this town, and he works under the guise of fighting against government corruption. He has no proof, but he is charismatic. People believe him. That makes him dangerous. So we will be focusing on him now, not on K'antu. All we need is proof, and we'll lock him up and throw away the key."

I felt like there were two little people inside of me playing tug of war. The thought of Juan being hunted by my aunt and other influential people in town was extremely satisfying to the little person who had been tortured by him, but equally as strong was another little voice saying it was unfair. Why was I feeling sorry for him? He was a horrible person.

K'antu came in, so I metaphorically cut the rope so my insides could no longer argue and went to hug her.

"K'antu, Come, sit. Eat," Laura said to her. She then said something about needing to check the vineyards and swept out, much to my relief. I turned to my friend.

"I heard what she said about Juan, Tamara. But she is wrong. He is not dangerous, and he did not kill Eduardo."

"K'antu, I know you are in love with Juan or whatever, but my aunt has a point. Juan doesn't help himself with his behavior. And we have no proof there has been any corruption at all."

"But we do, Tamara. Or at least, we did. Eduardo had something. But it has disappeared."

"Mario and I were at Tomás' house looking for it last night..." I said.

K'antu raised an eyebrow. "And you expected to find it there? That is the last place it would be – if it still exists. No, no, I can't think that way. It must exist. It has to. We have to find it."

I faced her. "K'antu, how can you be so sure Juan did not kill Eduardo?"

"Why would he, Tamara? He has been fighting so hard for the people who suffered through the earthquake, and Eduardo was right there by him the whole time. I know you think Juan is a freak – a drug addict – violent –, but that is part of who he is. You don't know him. I do." K'antu got up. "I need to get out of here. I have to find the papers Eduardo hid."

"K'antu, you can't leave. Isn't that what Laura said?"

She sat back down. "Yeah. She did."

We stayed there in tense silence. Ten minutes went by before Daniela came in.

"Tamara, Mario, and Elías are here to see you. They are in the living room."

K'antu and I looked at each other.

"What is Elías doing here?" K'antu said ungraciously.

I frowned at K'antu. "Don't be mean. He is my cousin. And wasn't he friends with your husband? Maybe Eduardo confided in him. Maybe he knows where the papers are. Maybe that's why he's here now."

"Why now? If he knows something, why didn't he come forward the day Eduardo died?" K'antu said.

"I don't know. That is a good point. Maybe he hasn't had a chance yet. Maybe he is about to. But we won't learn anything by speculating, let's go talk to him."

We went to the living room. I went over and kissed Elías on the cheek in greeting. Then kissed Mario too – on the cheek. K'antu merely said hello. I glanced at her. This girl was so different from the affectionate one who had greeted me the other day. Who could blame her though, she had been chewed up and spat out several times recently.

Daniela brought in a tray of cookies and tea. I sat next to Mario on a loveseat. K'antu and Elías exchanged a weird glance. It looked like animosity. But I did not say anything. Let them work it out.

"Tamara," Mario said, "Elías came to me this morning with information."

"Information?" I looked at Elías.

"I know for a fact K'antu did not kill Eduardo," Elías started.

K'antu leaned forward. "Of course I didn't, you stupid ass. I would never have done anything to him. I still loved him, even if you and he were –"

"Before he died, he showed me some information," he interrupted her in a loud voice, his face reddening.

"He showed you information? Showed you? Information?" Spittle came out of K'antu's mouth.

"K'antu – let him finish," I said, glancing curiously at her. She slumped back in her chair, breathing erratically.

Elías looked nervously at K'antu. "Thank you, Tamara. Anyway, he showed me papers."

K'antu focused and leaned forward. Maybe she had been right. My head turned between the two of them like I was watching a tennis match.

"And what was in the papers?" I prompted him when he hesitated.

"I... I don't know," Elías said.

K'antu threw up her arms. "Well, that's that. Go away, Elías. I will have to find those papers myself."

"K'antu!" I admonished her. I turned back to my cousin. "What do you mean you don't know, Elías?"

"He showed them to me, but he didn't let me read them. But he did say they would prove once and for all money that was supposed to be going to people like my mom, and Eduardo was going to someone in the government."

"But Elías," I said gently, "if you don't know what was in those papers, we aren't any closer to proving anything."

He became indignant. He tried taking a deep breath but cut it short and put his hand over his ribs. "What about what Eduardo told me? Someone will have to believe me."

"Why would they?" Mario asked in a flat voice.

"I thought you were on my side, Mario," Elías turned to him.

"Dude, when you came to me with this, you did not tell me you had never actually read the proof. Otherwise..." Mario raised his hands in an I-don't-know gesture.

"Tamara?" Elías appealed to me. I looked up. I had been staring at his hand.

I shook my head, disagreeing, "Elías, this whole business has been so ridiculous on both sides. You all keep insisting the government is corrupt, but there's no proof. The police keep insisting K'antu is guilty, and there's no proof of that either. I am sorry. But until you come up with something concrete, no one is going to believe it."

"Tamara and her aunt don't think the allegations of corruption have any basis in fact," K'antu said resentfully to no one in particular.

"I know something weird is going on, but there are more sides to that story." I thought about what Laura had said. "And even if there is corruption, why would they kill Eduardo? He was not powerful enough to harm anyone."

"He had proof." Elías's voice was shrill, "But since you don't believe me, I will leave."

"Oh, come on, Elías, don't be like that. We will still look for what you say exists."

I thought his head would blow right off his neck. I suppose I should not have worded it that way exactly.

"I have to go to work." He stormed out.

"You say there is no proof I am guilty, but what you mean is there is no proof that I am innocent, right, Tamara?" K'antu said, her arms folded across her chest.

"No... K'antu, come on. Don't be unreasonable. That is not what I said." I was losing control of the situation – the situation I hadn't created.

But K'antu turned and also stormed out of the room. Mario put his hands on my shoulders. I turned.

"Has the entire world gone crazy?" I said.

"I know I have. I have gone crazy for you, Tamara."

I pulled away from him. "I can't do this right now."

"Can't do what?" he said.

An idea had been brewing in the back of my mind. It was a crazy idea. Under normal circumstances, I would never have said it out loud – probably I would never have thought it. But I wasn't entirely myself. It spilled out of my mouth before I could stop it. "You've been following me like a shadow ever since Eduardo was killed. Maybe you killed him, and you're sticking with me to make sure I don't find anything to prove K'antu didn't do it."

"What?" His mouth dropped open. "Why on earth would I kill Eduardo?"

"You say you've been working with People Help for the last year. Maybe you are the one siphoning off money." I looked at him in horror as the last phrase came out of my mouth. What was I thinking? Did I believe that?

He stared at me. "Wow, Tamara, you can find the bad side of people, aren't you?"

"Mario, I..."

But it was too late. He turned and stormed out.

"Mario... I didn't mean..." I said to the empty room. But did I? After all, he had been everywhere I was – and he had not saved me from Juan... had the kiss just been a way to make me think he cared?

I threw myself down on one of the sofas and cried. At that moment, all I wanted to do was go back home to Chicago. A few minutes later, while I was still crying, Daniela came in.

"Tamara, what is the matter?"

"It's nothing. I'm tired." I sat up, wiping my face.

But Daniela nodded. "Manchay, it has a way of making people cry... I know it well, Tamara. But that is why the people from here are so resilient. We are strong. We survive."

"I'm not from here, Daniela," I hiccupped.

"No, but you have the blood of your people running through those veins of yours. You'll get over it – whatever it is. And I will make you a nice *ceviche* dinner to help you."

She talked to herself as she left the room, mentally going over any ingredients she would need to send out and carrying the tray, which none of us had touched.

"Maybe she's right," I thought to myself, "maybe I need to calm down. Aunt Laura and K'antu will probably have gotten over being mad at me by dinner, and then I'll make Laura drive me to Rodolfo's house, and I can apologize to Mario."

Feeling better, I got up and headed toward my room. On the way down the hall, a door opened, a hand grabbed me, and I was pulled into K'antu's bedroom. Once inside, I was pushed toward the bed. K'antu was already on it and had to move quickly to the side, so I didn't careen right into her.

When I had recovered from the forcible manhandling, I looked for who had dragged me in here. What I ended up staring at was the muzzle of a gun. It was no great surprise to me that Juan's hand was at the other end. His eyes were wild, and his hand shook a little. I looked over at K'antu, who shook her head.

"So, you ran, huh? Well, you won't run from this. Now, let's get back to Patabamba."

"This is a nightmare," I thought as the car sped up the hill.

Chapter 17

I stumbled into the second room I had been forced into in a short matter of an hour. I had not even stood up yet when someone grabbed the back of my neck. I was yanked back and thrown again. I smashed against the wall.

"What the hell were you doing? You think you can go back?" A strong waft of moon-shined alcohol, probably Pisco, accompanied the question. The voice was low and had a deadly angry quality to it.

"I wanted –." I choked.

"I don't care what you wanted," Juan snarled.

I coughed and pressed my mouth directly against the wall to stop myself from saying anything else – or crying.

My lack of response seemed to make him angrier. He grabbed me again and shoved me toward the bed. I went flying and landed, hitting my head on the wall.

"Now talk," he said.

Momentarily stunned from the blow to my head, I tried not to let him see the tears that had welled up in my eyes. He stood there watching me, his shoulders tense and his fists clenched. When I could, I said, "About what?"

His body relaxed as if he had been waiting for me to talk back to him. "What did you find at Tomás' house?"

I rubbed my head and wiped my eyes. A goose egg was forming above my left temple. Pretty soon, my body would be a museum of injuries. "We didn't find anything."

He stepped forward lifted his arm to smack me, but I got up and ducked, moving behind him. I tried to open the door, but he had locked it. So I screamed. I yelled for help and then just plain screamed, and soon people started making noises on the other side of the door.

"Open up, Juan." It was Oliver's voice.

Juan fumed but opened the door. Several people came into the room, including K'antu. I was pushed back to the bed, this time from the impetus of the crowd. I sat and rubbed my head more, not wanting even to think that K'antu had been free to come in this whole time.

"Juan, what are you doing?" K'antu asked.

"What is all the screaming about?" Oliver wanted to know. Juan turned to him and said something in a low voice. Oliver left.

K'antu said, "Tamara, what happened to you? Let me go get ice."

"Leave her alone. She is fine," Juan told her.

At the same time, I grabbed at her and said, "Do not leave."

Oliver came back in and nodded at Juan.

"Let's go," Juan said to us, waving his arm toward the door.

I got up, swaying a little. K'antu put her arms around my shoulders for support.

We all went to the side of the courtyard closest to the kitchen and sat on a wooden picnic table. Juan called to the girls in the kitchen, and they brought out coffee, and bread, ham, butter, and avocado.

"Eat," Juan ordered.

I sat and picked at a roll. K'antu put avocado on bread, salted it, and ate.

"Eat Tamara. You'll need energy for what you are going to do later," Juan said.

K'antu stopped eating. "What is she going to do later?"

"You'll find out. eat."

"Oh God, will this never end?" I said softly.

No one answered me.

Later on, Juan took us to the office and ordered us to stay there. But that was unnecessary because when he left, he locked the door. We could hear him calling the other kids. Sounds of metal clanging, wood being sawed, and hammering started.

Time passed. We sat. After a while, K'antu said, "I am sorry about yesterday, Tamara."

"What do you have to be sorry about?" I said. "I should be the one sorry. You think that I think you are guilty. At first, I was sure you weren't, and I started having doubts. But I should have faith in you. I should have never doubted. It's that... it's... Juan..."

K'antu drew in her breath but changed her mind about saying something. She turned away from me. We sat in silence until Juan came back in.

"Let's go, Tamara."

Blood pounded in my head. I wanted so badly to tell him to go to hell, but my injuries told me not to. I followed him out. We left the compound.

"Get in the car," he said.

I got in.

Juan drove in the direction of Manchay again. It was early evening as we rolled into town, so there were people all over. I was surprised to find that we were entering the magistrate's neighborhood. I shouldn't have been surprised at anything this boy did. Juan spat out the window as he passed the large homes. All of them blocked from view behind tall wood fences with no spaces between the slats or equally tall ironwork fences with vegetation planted so thickly next to them it was impossible to see beyond.

We pulled up in front of Tomás Romero's house. Juan got out and rang the bell. His voice was calm and almost sweet as he announced his presence to the microphone. The gate clicked, unlocking. Juan pulled it open and came back to the car.

"I made an appointment," he grinned, noting the look of surprise on my face as he got back in the car.

I said nothing.

"Tamara, get out and make sure that the gate doesn't swing shut again for any reason. We may need to make a quick exit."

"What?"

"Get out. Hold the gate open. How hard is it to understand?" he said through stiff lips.

Getting out, I went and held on to the gate.

The house's lights had not come fully on yet. The way the house was angled, I saw the garage face-on from the street and most of the rest of the front of the house. The only part that was obscured by the garage was the front door.

I stood there, holding the gate, and sweating despite the chill in the air. What was this meeting about? Why had he brought me with him? Why would he need to make a quick exit? About twenty minutes later, the car came gliding out of the gate. Juan was driving. When he had cleared the entrance, he opened his window and called for me to get back in the car.

I opened the passenger side door and got in, fastening my seat belt. He lit a cigarette. I sniffed the air like a nervous rabbit, but it was only a cigarette.

He started driving.

"Well?" I said.

He puffed smoke through his nose, "Well, what?"

"Did you have a conversation with him?" I asked.

"Oh yeah," he laughed.

"What was it about?"

"It was about freedom."

"Freedom?"

"Yep." He flicked the cigarette, half-smoked, out the window, hitting an old woman in heavy woolen clothing. She waved a fist in the air and cursed, but Juan took no notice.

"K'antu's freedom?" I asked.

Juan laughed more.

"Come on, Juan. You drag me into these situations, the least you can do is explain what you are doing." I lost my temper, not thinking about what he would do.

Tires screeched as Juan applied the brakes. He turned to me

and said, "You want me to explain? You think you are entitled to an explanation?"

I put my head back on the headrest and looked out the window. A woman in a white maid uniform was walking down the street. A dog was sleeping on a strip of grass outside the fence of someone's yard. The whistle of a fruit cart vendor pierced the air several times and stopped. "Never mind. You are right. I should not ask. What do I care anyway?"

"Oh, you'll care, all right. Oh yeah, you will care. Everyone will care. This time that arrogant bastard will feel the pain of what he has done."

I sat up straight. "What do you mean? Who?"

"Who? You want to know? You need to know? Fine," he got out of the car, walked around to the passenger side, yanked me out, and dragged me behind the car.

He popped the hood, put his hand to the back of my head, and moved it, so I was looking inside. I gave a start, which forced my skull back into Juan's hand, and my heart skipped a beat. I blinked several times. I pushed away from him, stumbled over to the side of the road, and vomited. Juan's rolling laughter followed me. He slammed the hood of the trunk hard and yelled at me to get back in and hurry, but to make sure I wouldn't be sick again first. I closed my eyes, but that did not get rid of the image of what had been inside the trunk. Lying curled in a lifeless heap in Juan's car was the lifeless body of Tomás Romero.

Chapter 18

How we got back was a blur to me. I got out of the car and somehow made it back to what I had come to know as mine, closing the door. Nighttime fell, and I lay on the bed feeling nothing until somehow, I fell asleep.

In the morning, there was a strange silence on the other side of the door. I looked up, seeing not for the first time but noticing now the network of cracks that ran along the ceiling's white paint. They could split wide open anytime.

But there were more important things to worry about now – like protecting Juan from what he had done. I lay there, horrified at that thought, and fought against the girl I was becoming. I didn't hate him, a person who was unstable and undoubtedly a killer. Rather, I understood so much clearer the shades of gray we all are and increasingly justified his behavior. What was wrong with me? But there it was. There he was. Juan: evil, but gentle with his people, and with a vision for them – a violent vision, but one that could be seen as working toward a goal for the betterment of people who might not otherwise get it. In contrast, my aunt Laura, who was so good to people, but was so blind to situations, had been someone I looked up to before. Juan was hardened by life. My aunt was blessed by it. I had been blessed but was becoming hardened – and unfeeling towards people who loved me, like K'antu, Elías – and most painfully – Mario. I hardly recognized myself. And I didn't care. I thought about Tomás Romero. But the thoughts weren't of grief or sadness. They were of what we should do now. We?

A gentle knock failed to rouse me from the stupor I was in. But the knock had only been a courtesy. K'antu had a key. She pushed it open and came in, a tray in her hand. She set the tray on the table and turned to me.

"We only have a little while before they come for him. We will have to be ready."

I did not reply. K'antu poured strong, black coffee into a mug and came to the bed. She gestured for me to sit.

"You will have to get up, Tamara. Juan wants you in the courtyard." K'antu looked confused and a little resentful.

In answer, I stood, took the cup from her, drank a little of the hot liquid, and put it on the table. I went back to the bed and lay down, turning away from K'antu, who fidgeted.

"Tamara, you need to come with me. Juan will be angry if you don't hurry."

I pulled the itchy blanket over my head.

K'antu sighed loudly and left the room.

I wanted to stay there but how could I? He would come to do worse than she had done to get me to do as he wanted. I got up and kneeled by the little door that would lead me to the passageway and out. But the door was stuck. I tried to pry it open, but it would not budge. I stood and looked around and then went over and grabbed the butter knife from the breakfast tray.

Voices were coming closer to the room from the courtyard. My breath came quickly as I shoved the knife into the crack between the little door and the wall. I was pushing it, trying to find the catch of the lock, when Juan and Oliver came in.

"What are you doing?" Juan snapped, "I need you here to talk to Tomás."

"Tomás? But... isn't he dead?" Was that who K'antu meant? I thought she meant Juan.

Juan laughed. "You thought I had killed him? I am not that stupid. Besides, we need him."

"So he's..."

"Alive as you and me. Although you aren't looking too alive this morning." He eyed me.

"He... when I saw him in the trunk... he looked... I thought..."

"Yeah, I'm sure you did. But no, I did not kill him. He is much more useful to us alive. I merely knocked him out. It was the only way I could convince him to come with me. But hey, I'm sure glad I didn't tell you he was still alive. Your reaction was awesome."

He laughed again.

"You are cruel, Juan." I started to shake. I had believed that the man was dead. Now, to find out he was not, well, it was a relief, but now what? He was alive, and he was in the same situation I was in – a prisoner of this lunatic.

Juan rolled his eyes, "Yeah, cruel. Life sucks. Blah, blah, blah. Let's go. We have to talk to Romero and make a plan."

"Make a plan? Don't you have one already?" I squeaked.

Juan sighed. "Yeah, sure. That's what I meant. For him to get out of here alive, he needs to agree to let K'antu go and give all of us back all of our money. You are going to help me convince him to agree to this."

"What?"

"Get out here."

He stalked off. Oliver stood with his arms crossed. I gave him a dirty look and went into the courtyard. At first, I saw nothing but a bunch of kids sitting around, not talking. They were all facing my way, and when I squinted through the sunlight, I saw what they were all avoiding looking at.

I started running. I ran after Juan, who was walking along a little path through the kids. I ran fast and passed him. When I stopped, I was directly in front of a cage. The cage had not been there before. All the clanging and hammering that I had heard yesterday made sense now. Tomás Romero was inside the cage. He sat in a chair and stared out at nothing. He looked dusty and tired but otherwise okay. I gripped two of the bars of the cage and stared, speechless, at the man inside. His eyes slowly focused and came to rest on me. We made eye contact.

"Sir, are you all right?" I asked.

"Well," he said slowly, "If you don't count the fact I am your prisoner, yes. Yes, I am mostly all right."

I recoiled. "Not *my* prisoner. I have nothing to do with this."

220

"That is not what this young man seems to think," The magistrate nodded, indicating something behind me.

Juan was there, basking in his cleverness.

"Tell him I had nothing to do with this. Tell him I didn't know —"

"He wouldn't recognize the truth if a llama spits it into his face. Anyway, Tamara, what Tomás Romero knows is you, and I want K'antu exonerated. And he is the man to do it. Isn't that right, Romero? You can tell everyone what a mistake it was to accuse K'antu of murdering her husband, can't you? And while you are at it, you can give us all back the money we should have gotten after the earthquake. You do that, and we'll open the cage, and you can go home, right Tamara?" Juan took a pack of cigarettes, put one in his mouth, and lit it.

"Juan, please. Taking this man prisoner is not going to solve your problems. Let him go. Lorena has been working on K'antu's problems, and so will Laura now. They will figure it all out. Meanwhile, there is nothing to indicate Señor Romero stole any aid money."

Juan looked furious. "That's the problem with people like you, Tamara. A rich man with a nice suit looks a little pitiful, and you believe he's worth your while. Well, don't we all look pitiful? Look behind you. See the kids here? Shouldn't you be defending them?"

"Juan..."

"I said look at them."

I knew that tone of voice. I looked. There were a lot more of them today than there had been previously. Today there were younger kids too, a rag-tag group. They had the dark, sunburned

221

skin of mountain people, but their faces were covered with the dust of the coast. They all wore several layers of clothing, none of it individually sufficient for cold temperatures, and as a whole, also painfully inadequate. Their presence made the compound look shabbier; the tan-colored, dusty adobe had crumbled bits in various areas.

During my crazy moments here in the compound, the kids had been generous with their food – but they had little to share in the first place. What they had was basic: rice, potatoes, corn, onions, fresh cheese and occasionally eggs, bread and butter for breakfast, a rare piece of chicken. Many of the kids were painfully thin. Several of them had a haunted look that said they had not smiled a real smile in a long time.

"Don't you feel sorrier for them than you do for this man here?" Juan asked. "You should."

Sometimes he made way too much sense. He was crazy but not altogether illogical. I turned back to Tomás Romero.

"Señor Romero, why have you been leading a witch hunt against K'antu?"

The man in the cage replied, "There was a lot of evidence against her."

"But it was all circumstantial. Why were you only focused on her? Why couldn't you question other people also?"

"She's guilty, young lady. Accept it. And now you are too. You have helped a fugitive, vandalized a school, and now you have assisted in kidnapping a government official. When I get out of here, you will be held accountable. I don't care what your aunt says."

"You don't understand. I am also a victim here. I was forced -"

Romero got up and came toward me, our faces blocked from touching only by the crude bars of the temporary jail. "There is nothing you can say to make me care about your sad little story. I will make sure you are punished for your part in all of this."

He took a deep breath and continued, "But I would be open to lessening the charges if you open the gate for me right now and let me go."

I looked at Juan. He was looking regal, his nose in the air and his arms crossed across his broad chest, a knowing smile lighting his handsome features. Based on the thoughts of the morning, I should have been prepared for the surge of affinity I felt for him at that moment, and yet they still took me by surprise. But the man in the cage was showing himself to be a little too arrogant for someone in his situation.

Looking back at the cage, I tried one more time. "What about the money, Señor Romero? Where is it?"

Romero's face went purple. "I have no idea."

"All of these people here are poor. They were supposed to get money after the earthquake to help them rebuild their homes and pay for food and medical expenses. Where did that money go?"

He snorted. He wagged his finger at me and said, "Not that I am required to explain anything to you, Tamara, but each one of these people was given their money two weeks after the earthquake."

"Only five hundred dollars. What about the rest?"

"They were given much larger sums than that. Whoever told you five hundred lied to you. And as far as what they did with it, it is not my responsibility to govern how they spent it."

"I don't believe you," I said.

He sputtered. "Well, that is your problem. The issue is whether the government of Lima and the aid agencies believe me, and they do."

He went and sat back down on the chair.

"I went to see a family the other day. The boy in the family – his name is Miguelito. Does the name sound familiar to you?" I said.

Romero's face was stony, but his eyes shifted a little. Or it was the shadows of the overhanging roof.

"He has two younger sisters. His parents died – his grandparents died. It is only him, and his great-grandmother left to take care of the two young girls. That family can't afford the drugs the children need for their asthma. They either eat, or they buy medicine."

Romero shook his head sadly. I could practically feel the insincerity from the other side of the cage.

"Their house has never been rebuilt."

He stayed quiet.

My voice got louder. I was still gripping the bars of Romero's prison.

"The public school might as well fall all the rest of the way down. That is how bad it is."

He folded his hands and tapped his fingers.

"They have no supplies. They have nothing. The school kitty-corner from that dump has everything they could want."

Still nothing from the man in the cage.

"Do you think these things would still be true if people had received a fair amount of money?" I yelled at him.

Finally, he spoke. "Life is not fair, Tamara. Deal with it. The public school got their funds. I do not know what they did with them. And they are due to get more in a year or so, although I might want to oversee the distribution. As you say, it sounds like someone misappropriated it..."

"You might want to oversee...? You should have been doing that all along. Aren't you the magistrate? Aren't you there for, and because of, the people of Manchay?"

He came back to me. "When you visited the poor, did you bother to get any real information on how much money they got? Any proof?"

I frowned. "Miguelito said he spent the money on medicine. That must mean there was little since now they can't buy more medicine, and their house is still a wreck."

"Anyone else? What about him?" Tomás pointed at Juan.

I looked at Juan. He shrugged sheepishly.

"Juan?" I asked.

"Don't let him make this about me. You saw the school yourself, Tamara," Juan said.

"He squandered his money on drugs," Tomás spat, "the police have been watching him. We know how he spent the aid money he got. They all squandered it – drugs, T.V.'s, and who knows what else. This boy is making you his patsy. And his punching bag looks like. Think about it, Tamara."

That rang painfully true – literally and figuratively. I let go of the bars.

"You are right, Señor Romero. So right. What the hell am I doing here?"

I turned and started walking toward the front door.

"Do not leave me in this cage, young lady," Romero called

behind me, "I'm warning you, you had better help me. Come back."

"You should never have patronized and threatened me, Señor. Not diplomatic of you," I called over my shoulder, "I am better off with you here until I get on an airplane back to the U.S. Good luck with Juan."

I felt weirdly jubilant. Screw them all. I was leaving, and this time I would not let anyone stop me. I kept walking and talking, "Juan, you can shoot me if you want, but I am walking out the door."

But I didn't get far before K'antu stepped in front of me.

"Tamara, please don't go."

"Don't try to stop me, K'antu. I have tried to help you, I have. But this situation is a quagmire. It keeps getting worse, and soon no one will be able to fix it, especially not me. I am going back to Laura's house, where I will demand she take me back to Lima and the airport."

I pushed past K'antu, whose begging I steeled myself against, and opened the front door. I stopped short. There was a small army of men standing around the building. Several of them were holding guns. One of them turned to look at me. I slammed the door shut again and faced K'antu.

"K'antu, what is that about?"

"The guards? Juan kidnapped the magistrate. We needed protection -"

"' We' need protection? Actually, yes 'we do. Your precious boyfriend has gotten me into deep shit. And now I can't get out of it." My voice had gone higher and louder as I spoke. One of the men outside opened the door and demanded to know what was going on.

K'antu reassured him and turned back to me as he closed the door again. She held her hands in a supplicating gesture. "You are right, Tamara. I realize I have gotten you into the most horrible situation, *amiga,* and I will never stop apologizing for that. But if you leave now, things will get worse."

Juan came up to us. "Hey, I've ordered everyone to go on with what they were doing as if that animal weren't caged here. So I am going to start training some of these newbies in fifteen minutes, okay girls?"

Was he acting so normal? That rubbed me the wrong way. "Train for what, Juan? Are you seriously going to go "Inca" on someone? Who? You are insane. Are you planning on siccing a bunch of scrawny kids on Romero while he's in a wood cage? "

I laughed. It was funny. To me.

Juan glowered. "We train to give them confidence. Make fun all you want. And I said it before, Romero is staying here until someone comes with a guarantee K'antu will go free, and everyone here will get their money back. And before you say anything, Tamara, I know you feel sorry for the fat-rich guy, and you believe him because he lives in a nice house and doesn't seem to break the rules, so let me explain something to you. It is true, many people went out with their first installment and bought luxury items. But they live a miserable life. They work hard and get paid shit. They have not been educated like they deserve to have been. So what if they buy something that makes them happy? Do you think the paltry amount they got from the first check was enough to rebuild

227

as much as a new room for their house, much less a whole home? So since they couldn't rebuild, they made other decisions – maybe not great ones, but ones that brought at least a little happiness to them. And I should stop calling it the 'first installment. It was the only one, and from what Romero was saying just now, it was the only one."

He stalked away, calling back to K'antu to be ready in ten minutes.

Speechless, K'antu and I stared at each other.

"Oh my God, what he says makes a lot of sense. Why is it that everyone's logic sounds like the correct version?" I said, pulling at a curl of my hair.

"Things are never exactly as they seem, *amiga*. And everyone interprets situations in their way," K'antu said quietly.

"Even Eduardo's murderer?" I retorted.

K'antu walked away.

"Oh shit," I muttered to myself. I ran after my friend.

"K'antu, I am sorry. But I need to understand what is going on. Why are you in a relationship with Juan? What happened between you and Eduardo? I mean, whether people believe you or not, there is a certain amount of evidence that says you did it. Why would someone else kill him?"

K'antu merely said, "We need to get back."

"Please, K'antu." I stopped.

K'antu came back and stood in front of me.

"Okay, I will tell you. But we have to be quick."

I smiled. "Good. I am ready."

K'antu did not smile back. She glanced around, saw no one was around, and whispered, "My husband was having an affair long before I got involved with Juan –"

"An affair?"

"Keep your voice down. Yes, an affair. But it wasn't only that."

"What do you mean?"

"He was sleeping with your cousin Elías," She deadpanned. Then she started walking again.

My jaw dropped.

Chapter 19

I sat with my back against the bars of Tomás Romero's prison. They were wood slats about two inches wide and spaced four inches apart. I sat there as the man in the cage talked to me. He seemed to be talking for talking's sake. I listened, but not whole-heartedly. I picked up the gist of his talk and instantly forgot the details while he waxed eloquent for at least twenty minutes about his job as magistrate of the town he loved. I had my face to the sun, soaking in its heat. I thought about what K'antu had told me. Why hadn't I known that about my cousin? I guess I had not paid enough attention in the couple weeks a year I was here. He had never told me anything… I sighed.

"Tamara, are you listening to me?"

Resentful he had interrupted my thoughts, I turned. He was in the shade. It took a moment for my eyes to adjust. I blinked a few times, and the colored blotches faded. I wasn't about to tell him I had spaced out. I was tired of listening. I had heard him say stuff regarding his job - going out to visit the people in their various stages of grief after the earthquake, trying to keep up relationships with them while juggling the often slow and combative city council and the government in Lima. He talked about the people at People Help and how he had gotten to know them. He mentioned Juan and Eduardo in better times. He even mentioned the little old lady receptionist at People Help, Señora Ramos. He babbled on about how he had appointed Lorena the intermediary between the government and the aid organization and all of the work she had done – her dedication, her constant involvement in everything. His voice got more and more distressed the longer he talked, especially by the end, but by then, I had checked out almost completely.

"I am sorry. What was that last part?" I asked.

"I said, 'Don't you agree that is strange?' Weren't you listening?" he sounded like a petulant child.

"I apologize. I was thinking... well, it is not important. Please, repeat what you said. I am listening now; don't I agree that what is strange?"

"Never mind, it is probably not important. Out of all I have done, Tamara, maybe most of it hasn't been perfect, but I have tried my best. Just because I live in a big house doesn't automatically make me a bad person."

I could not think of anything I wanted to say to that, so I merely muttered, "Uh-huh..."

He sat down heavily on the only chair in the enclosure. "What are you doing here, Tamara?"

"Excuse me?" I was startled enough to shift my position and stare at him.

"Why have you been sitting here? You aren't keeping me company because you haven't been listening. Are you hoping when the police finally get here, you will be let free because you sat here with me?"

Sighing, I said, "I'm just sitting here. No reason. Yes, I want to be let go, yes I want K'antu to be exonerated, and I want to go home, but right now I am just sitting."

In truth, I was concerned this man was being held against his will, and for some reason, I did not like the thought of him sitting here by himself. I guess I did feel sorry for him. But I was not about to tell him that. And I certainly wouldn't tell Juan. Was Juan right? Did I have a bias for Tomás Romero because he was rich? Were the poor kids that filled the courtyard less worthy of my pity somehow? I was afraid to answer my questions.

Romero got up and came over to me, squatting down and looking me in the eyes through the slats. He lowered his voice and said, "Listen, Tamara, we can make a deal, you and I. You get me out of here, and I will drop any charges against you. You can be on a plane back to Chicago in less than forty-eight hours, with the freedom to come back and visit your family whenever you wish."

I stared. This was corruption in action. Should I bite? "What about K'antu?"

He thought for a moment. "She is more difficult..."

"No deal then." I had been tempted. That is how corruption works. I fought through it.

"Don't be stupid, Tamara. Make the deal. It makes sense for us both," he said. "I will be honest with you, the boy scares me. If you get me away from him, I will be in your debt."

He shuddered.

"I am not surprised," I said. "He scares a lot of people."

"It would look good for you if you were to help me escape. And K'antu will be treated fairly, I can promise you that. The judge will consider the fact that Eduardo abused her."

"No." I did not have to think. Why, after all, had I gotten myself into this mess? For K'antu. Without a promise to help her, I could not help him. I did not trust him.

"No?"

"I will not make any deals with you unless the police start looking for Eduardo's real killer. And they would have to begin doing it before I let you out. I would have to see them making an effort."

He grasped at the wood bars and let them go as quickly. With his right hand, he picked at a splinter on his left forefinger. As he tried to extract it, he talked.

"Tamara, honestly, there are so many things that point to K'antu being guilty. Who would the police –?"

Shaking my head, I said, "You see? You were never going to help her at all, were you? None of the evidence so far has been enough to prove her guilt. And there must be someone else. Eduardo was trying to find out what happened to the aid money – it must have made someone angry. It could have made you angry. How did your house get to be so beautiful? That takes money…"

"So you accuse me of killing Eduardo? I can see you did not

hear a word I was saying, Tamara. I was explaining my situation. Look, the house was my father's, and it was his father's before that. They made their money by working hard. They made it honestly, as do I. The city council has to approve my salary every year. It is public information. I have not ever siphoned money off of the aid organizations. How can I? I do not have direct access to it. If you and your cronies would only take the time to do the research, you could find all of it out yourselves."

I rolled my eyes. "Oh, please. I know records can be made to look spotless. The fact that you didn't pay for your house doesn't mean the money is going where it should. If you are not stealing it, why haven't people gotten the money they need to get simple medical attention, food, and basic rebuilding of their homes? Juan is right; five hundred dollars is not enough to fix even one room of a destroyed home."

Romero sucked on the finger that had a splinter in it and looked over his glasses at me. A slight frown appeared between his bushy eyebrows. "Believe it or not, those are questions I have been asking myself lately, too."

"What? Oh, sure, you say that because you are locked in here. If you are completely innocent, why didn't you try to help the people more before? Why now? Because Juan took you prisoner?"

He took his finger away from his mouth and said, "Tamara, at this moment, there is nothing I berate myself for more –"

Before he could continue, one of the men who had been guarding the compound raced past the makeshift jail cell. I looked at the retreating figure uneasily. He ran across the compound and knocked on the door where Juan and the others were gathered. Juan opened the door. The man spoke to him. I saw Juan nodding calmly. It must not be an emergency. He caught my eye and waved at me to join him. I glanced at Tomás Romero, who stared blankly back, and started walking toward Juan.

"Think about what I said, Tamara," he called after me, "all of it."

I did not look back. But he was making me uneasy. Was he trying to tell me something? Had I missed something important?

When I got to Juan, he said, "I told you not to go over there, Tamara."

"I was–"

"Never mind. This," he pointed at the man I had seen running, "is Antonio. He says Lorena has brought Mario and your Aunt Laura here. They are insisting they be allowed to talk to you."

My heart skipped a beat. I searched Juan's face looking for his reaction to that news. He was paler than I had ever seen him. His face was heart-shaped, and he normally sported a closely trimmed goatee, but today he looked like someone had vacuumed the air off his cheeks. The hair of his chin was several different lengths, with a little gray patch on the left side. Surprising. He was only twenty years old, but today he looked twice that.

"I–" I began.

Juan raised a shaky hand. "But I am not sure if I should allow it."

I crossed my arms in front of me, stood in the sunlight, and said, "Then why did you call me over here?"

He went on as if I had not spoken, "They are not the people I was waiting for. Not the people we need to get us out of this situation. We need to talk to people from Lima. People who can get us the money we want. And the assurances K'antu will be all right."

"But it is good they came. Maybe they have news. You can't ignore them."

"Nah, you are wrong. I will send them away. Antonio, see to it." Juan turned to go back inside.

I grabbed his arm. "Juan, no."

Antonio looked at me in surprise. He looked at Juan to see what his reaction would be. Juan's face darkened, and his body tensed.

"Juan, look, we can't stay this way forever. You need to fix this situation – to start negotiating. Let me talk to my aunt. She can help us. Please." I said all of this quickly before he could lash out at me.

"Wait here, Antonio." Juan turned and disappeared.

The two of us stood awkwardly at the closed door. I looked at Antonio's shoes. They had been brown but were now a dull, grayish color, worn almost to the point of being useless. He wasn't wearing socks, and his pants were several inches too short. His skin underneath the greyness was blackened from the sun.

Juan opened the door. The two of us were still standing there. His eyes narrowed. He put his hand in his pocket and pulled out a pack of cigarettes. I looked at them, as I did every time he was going to inhale something besides air, but they appeared to be normal tobacco-stuffed rolls.

"K'antu points out," he said, a cigarette bobbing between his lips, "that Laura might be the connection to Lima we need."

He cupped his hands to light the cigarette, an unnecessary gesture, I thought to myself, since there was no wind. There was never any. He leaned over and blew the first puff of smoke in my face. "So fine. We will let her in. Antonio."

The man snapped to attention. Whether cowed by the younger man, or a great admirer willing to accept a much younger leader, he seemed way too ready to do Juan's bidding.

"Go get Señora Villanueva and bring her to me. And you should bring Mario also," he leered at me.

My hand itched to smack Juan's smug face. K'antu, coming up behind Juan, read my thoughts. She touched my shoulder, "Tamara, why don't we get the coffee ready for everyone?"

"Fine," I said.

We went to the kitchen, and K'antu began making coffee. I inspected the pantry. I grabbed a package of *Doña Pepas* and another of *Margaritas* and started putting them on a tray. K'antu and I had not talked since her revelation about her husband, and I did not know exactly what to say. Elías had been with me during last year's earthquake, but I had left him here to go back to my life in Chicago. The burden of guilt I felt was heavy.

I didn't know what to say to K'antu. So I said nothing. It was easy to say nothing. I had recently accused my aunt of doing nothing... but it was different when I did it, right? I had a good reason... I kicked myself mentally.

The bell tinkled on the coffee maker, and K'antu poured the thick, dark liquid into a large thermos. She put it on a tray and looked at me.

"I can see you are uncomfortable with me, *amiga*. I want you to know I understand. None of this is easy for you. I am so sorry. Again. You have suffered so much on my account." She wiped away tears.

I did not reply. K'antu nodded, misunderstanding. Silently, she took the plate of cookies from me and began walking out the door.

"K'antu," I said. The other girl stopped.

"Can we... can I talk to you?"

"They'll be looking for us..."

"Please," I pleaded.

"Okay," K'antu said. She put down the tray.

I saw the same gauntness in my friend I had noticed on Juan. Everyone was under stress. K'antu, perhaps, had the most to lose, but for the first time, I wondered if Juan did care, in his own messed up way, about her.

"K'antu, what you told me earlier -"

"Don't, Tamara," K'antu held up her hands. "It is okay. I know I should not hold anything against Elías. We were all to blame for how things ended up. I... I mean..."

I nodded, "I know. You are not talking about Eduardo's death."

K'antu smiled a tight-lipped smile, "I don't know why Eduardo married me."

I was about to murmur platitudes when K'antu continued, "No. That is not true. I do know. I was his, how do you say? His cover."

"Cover? Oh, you mean his beard..."

K'antu frowned in confusion and played with the cover of the coffee pot, turning it around and around until it squeaked. "No one wanted to say that Eduardo was gay. Not Eduardo, not his family – no one. We don't talk about things like that much here in this small town. The world has grown, but our towns stay behind. In several ways."

I laughed ruefully, "Yeah, I know. Did... did you love him when you married him?"

"Yes. I did. We might have married early, and I got married for security, but I would never have married someone if I hadn't loved him. It was after we got married, I found out. I guess I was a fool."

"It's not like you could have guessed, K'antu. I know Elías, and I didn't know about him. He did not make it obvious. Eduardo must have been the same."

We smiled at each other.

"You are right..."

"Juan?"

Why didn't you tell me about your problems?" I took K'antu by the hand, stopping her from pouring the creamer from its jar to a mug and back again.

"I didn't tell you because we don't talk about those things –"

"Yes, you don't talk about those things here in Manchay. But K'antu, we are friends. You could not confide in me and let me help you – or at least listen and support you?"

"Juan did not want me talking about it –"

I let go of K'antu. "And we are back to Juan."

K'antu continued fiddling with the creamer. I stepped away.

"K'antu?"

"Yes?"

"You know I was sitting by Señor Romero?"

K'antu nodded and said, "Mm-hmm."

"I was listening to him. He talked a lot. He was arrogant and self-serving, which is what we should expect from him, right?"

K'antu assented with a dip of her head.

"But while I was listening to all the drivel, things must have crept in. Things he said through the rest of the bull. Details... I don't know why, but I have the feeling he said something important. Something that I was only half paying attention to."

K'antu gripped the sides of the tray.

"I don't remember exactly what he said. I just get the feeling something I heard might have been important. We will need to talk to him further. I... I hate to say it, but my aunt's timing is kind of bad. I won't be able to go grill Señor Romero by myself for a while."

"But we have time. We have plenty of time," K'antu said. "Let's go greet your aunt and Mario. The sooner we do that, the sooner you can get back to Señor Romero and find out what it is."

K'antu grabbed the tray of coffee and cookies. I followed her out the door, deep in thought and frowning. I was going to face Mario again, and I did not know precisely how to do it. I walked across the compound. K'antu was way ahead of me. The group of kids in the back rooms was sounding restless. Juan was yelling in a frustrated voice about something. I could hear Oliver trying to placate his friend. Before I reached the room, Juan came into the courtyard, and the group of teens was behind him. They all scattered, some rushing into the kitchen, others wandering around in the sunlight. Juan spotted me walking up.

"It is about time. What took you so long?" He yelled at both me and K'antu.

"Tamara." I heard my aunt's voice. I turned to see Antonio leading Laura and Mario to them. Elías was with them. Juan pushed his way past me and K'antu. He charged over to Elías and grabbed my cousin by the throat.

Chapter 20

K'antu screamed. Oliver and Mario struggled to pull him off. I was fed up with Juan. Without thinking, I grabbed a cookie, went, and smashed it on the side of Juan's face. Oddly, that was more effective than the two boys tugging at him. He let go of Elías, wiping savagely at the crumbs. He threw a punch at Elías, which landed squarely in the boy's stomach, and left the room.

We all stared at each other for a moment. Then Laura gave me a big hug while Elías collapsed onto a sofa. He doubled over and clutched his injured rib. He put his hand up to his throat. He was trying to say something, so K'antu bent over him. He murmured something to her and put his hand in the pocket of his jacket. She shook her head, and he took his hand back out.

Mario stood there, looking numb.

Laura was about to say something when Juan burst in the door again.

"Everyone out."

We all turned to him.

"Why?" Mario asked.

"Let's go. Out."

"What is going on, Juan?" K'antu asked.

"Come on. The police are here. They are arguing with the guards. We have to go before they let them in." Juan's eyes flickered but did not focus on any of us in particular.

Nobody said anything as we filed out of the room. When we were out, Juan raced past us and over to the cage. I was the last one out of the room, and as I exited, I saw a shadowy figure come down the covered walkway toward the little group. It was Taki. She was with Oliver. They both held *macanas* in their hands and *Tumis* in their belts.

"Taki, what are you doing here? And what are you doing with those spears?" I said.

"Juan called me. The weapons are with us just in case."

I looked at her. "What?"

"There is no time to explain, Tamara. Follow us."

Juan had opened Tomás Romero's prison and was in the process of tying the man's hands behind his back.

"Laura," Tomás began.

"No. You don't talk, old man." Juan counted who was with us by saying our names, "K'antu, Oliver, Taki, Tomás Romero, Señora Villanueva, Mario, Tamara, and Elías."

He spit the final name out, his hands clenched. But he controlled himself and continued, "All nine of us are going to leave. Taki will lead the way, and Oliver will be behind everyone to make sure no one has any bright ideas to leave the group."

"Where are we going?" I asked.

Juan lifted his hand. I stared at him, trying as hard as I could not flinch. He lowered it and lifted his chin before giving me an answer, "We have to get Tomás out of here before they take away our best bargaining chip. No more questions."

Taki led the way to the one side of the compound where I had never been. To my left was 'my' room. Directly behind was the office area and front door, and to my right was the kitchen. The tunnel I had been in twice was on the other side of the kitchen. Oliver prodded me to keep moving, so I turned back and kept going.

We went inside the building. It was dark and cool. It looked like it had once been a gathering place. It might have been nice back in the days of town meetings and local dances. It had brick red tile floors and ornate light fixtures hanging from the ceiling. There was one lone chair in the room near the door we were heading towards. The chair had three legs, which presumably was why it was still here and not in the courtyard like its mates.

Taki led them to the only other door in the room. She opened it and went in, the rest of us filing in after her. I heard faint voices of people calling. I thought I heard Lorena's voice, so I turned and was about to call out to the woman, but Oliver barked at me to hurry and pushed me, making me lose my balance.

"Hey, stop it." I turned my head but did not stop.

"Keep going," he responded.

The room we walked into was small. It had little alcoves with religious symbols built into each wall, and there was a row of three pews and an altar. Taki tugged on a small string on one of the floor tiles, and a door-sized trap door opened to a hole in the ground. She pulled a flashlight from the same belt that carried her knife and turned it on. Juan and Oliver also had flashlights, which they switched on with clicks that echoed hollowly through the room.

Taki disappeared down the hole, and the others followed. When it was my turn, I saw they were leading us down a flight of stairs. The staircase was dark and narrow. I did not want to go, but Oliver was breathing down the back of my neck. Reluctantly, I went. A hand reached back to grab onto mine – Mario's. It had to be his. He was directly in front of me.

"I am sorry, Mario," I whispered.

"Shh. It's okay. We'll talk later."

We continued down. Oliver closed the trap door quietly behind him.

At the bottom of the stairs was a tunnel-like the other one, except this one was shorter and narrower. We all had to bend to move forward, except Taki. I dragged my free hand along the wall to steady myself. It was damp, but it did not matter.

After about thirty feet, the tunnel curved and got wider and taller. Everyone was able to stand up straight, and I heard a few people sigh with relief before Juan's voice whispered for them to keep quiet. We walked for about fifteen minutes. When we got to the end of the tunnel, it became so narrow we had to crawl. But that only lasted a couple of feet, and soon we were out in the open air, at an oasis. The trees were thickly cropped. Juan directed us to a pond.

"Everyone, go sit over there."

We went to it, but I noticed K'antu sat far away from the water. I looked around and gripped Mario's hand tightly.

"Mario," I whispered, "this is -"

It looked like the same oasis Mario, and I had come to the first night we had gotten out of the compound. Someone had been here since. There was a small pile of bones, but other than that, no sign of the sacrificed animals. We all sat down, except for Juan, Taki, and Oliver, who remained standing.

"All right, the police came again, so someone must have called them." Juan was talking to himself.

"It had to have been someone in Patabamba," Taki said.

Juan pounded his fist on a *huarango* tree and uttered a muffled oath. The trunk of the *huarango* is short and thick – and unmovable.

"So now we are running because our neighbors have decided to give us up. So we have to figure out a new plan."

"You did not seem to have a good plan in the first place, Juan. What exactly was it you were going to accomplish by keeping Señor Romero prisoner?" Laura's calm voice was the only one to respond to Juan's declaration.

He turned to her, "Justice. But I guess I was being stupid. There is no justice for me or my people. What should we do now?"

I couldn't believe it. He was showing a rare moment of indecision.

"Let's go up to Urqu. The people there will help us. Or at least we will get to them before the police do. From there, we can negotiate," Taki suggested.

K'antu spoke, waving an impatient hand at her friend. "Urqu? No, Taki. The walk up there will take us an hour or two. And it's rough going."

"So?" Juan asked. "Do you have a better idea?"

"No, but I don't think everyone is in good enough shape to climb the mountain."

As a group, our eyes all came to rest on Tomás. He flushed. "That plan is ridiculous. We can run all you want. You could force us to walk through the mountains to the jungle on the other side, but the government of Lima will still not give you what you are asking for."

Juan got a dreamy look in his eyes. "To the jungle... Taki, haven't you always wanted to see the jungle? Oliver? Maybe Romero has a good idea there..."

He shot a look at the magistrate. "One way or the other, people will start talking. We are all fugitives now. The newspapers will come. They'll be all over this. Publicity will force people to pay attention to us."

"True," Taki said. She looked happy.

Juan pulled out a cigarette. Except for this time, it was not a tobacco one. K'antu went to Juan and smacked the drug out of his hand. It fell with a plop into the little pond. Juan grabbed her and turned her, so her back was against him. His left arm was around her throat, and he placed his *Tumi* to her face, making a little cut on her cheek.

Seeing red, I rushed over to Taki and pulled the *macana* out of the girl's hands, drew it back, and thrust it at Juan, trying to avoid hitting K'antu. But my aim was off. I was aiming for his heart. But it merely grazed him on his side. He pushed K'antu away from him and bent over, putting his hand to his side. Laura ran to catch K'antu before she tipped into the pond. The weapon fell halfway into the murky water and was about to slide in. Taki ran to retrieve it. She grabbed it and came toward me, but Mario stepped between us. He grabbed both of Taki's arms. They struggled. I came up and pried the *macana* out of Taki's hands. I turned it around so the blade was facing down, and the handle could be used as a club and drew my arm back.

"Stop it, all of you." Laura's voice carried far in the thin, still air. "We are not fighting a battle between ourselves. Juan, you are injured, so this is over. You can go down to the clinic in Manchay and have your wound sewn up, and Tomás and I will clean up the rest of the mess that you've gotten all of us into."

"No." Juan panted. He was clutching his side. A dark stain appeared on his shirt. "You will all start walking."

He called to Elías.

Elías, quietly sitting by the water's edge, had been trying his best to avoid getting in the middle of the fray. But his reprieve was over.

"Elías, you will carry the supplies."

"Supplies?" Laura asked, "What supplies?"

He ignored her and kept talking to Elías. "Go behind those trees and bring the bag of spears."

Elías looked at Juan nervously. Juan advanced on him, so he got up and went to do what Juan asked him to do. He came back with a long, black canvass bag. He staggered under the weight of it.

"Put it down here," Juan said, indicating the patch of ground right in front of him.

Elías did as he was told.

Juan unzipped the bag. He put a hand in, and the others could hear the clatter of the wooden sticks inside.

"Good. I think they are all here. Zip it back up, Elías, and carry it with you. You will go right after Taki and everyone else after that. Let's go, everyone."

There was no actual path to climb, just a bunch of rocks leading higher and higher. I looked up, still breathless after the skirmish, and saw smooth dunes looming above me. It might be easier to climb once we cleared the rocks, but I knew from experience that going up a sand pile was no piece of cake either.

No one was making any effort to start walking. Juan was about to lose control of himself.

Then Oliver said, "Everyone move."

I turned to look at him. Everyone else did too. He had an AKM rifle pointed directly at me.

"Oliver, what the hell?" K'antu said.

"Move," he replied.

We moved. The going was slow over the rocks. I glanced back several times. Oliver had stayed where he was, waiting for everyone to clear the rocks.

"Can't we run?" I muttered to Mario.

"That gun has a range of over a thousand feet, Tamara. He'd pick us all off. Keep moving," Mario said.

"Where did he get that gun anyway?" I wondered, "And why do they bother with *macanas* and *Tumis* if they've got guns?"

"That rifle is not easy to handle if you don't know what you are doing. It is probably old too. I would guess these guys found it in one of their father's stash of stuff." Mario said.

I glanced at him. "If they don't know how to use them –".

"Then they are more dangerous than if they did. So take it easy," he responded. "Keep walking."

Ahead, I saw Elías struggle to carry the bag of spears. I was about to shout to Juan to let Elías drop the bag when Elías got his foot stuck between a rock and the ground and fell. I raced past Tomás and Laura and grabbed Elías, trying to help him. Someone pushed me gently aside and got Elías up and sitting on a rock – Mario.

"I am fine," Elías said, looking gray and sweaty. He looked at Juan nervously. "Let's keep going."

"No. This is ridiculous," I said, raising my voice. "We are already having a hard time climbing. Why does he need to be the one carrying all those spears?"

Juan laughed, "Why indeed? No reason. I want him to suffer. And to look ridiculous, the way he made my family look. Keep climbing."

"Don't be so cruel, Juan," I said to his back.

He turned. He looked at me. Then he went to Elías, who was still sitting on the rock recovering. Juan put his hand on Elías's shoulder. Elías seemed to sink into the rock under the weight of Juan's hand.

"Cruel? I am cruel? What about him?" he pulled out his knife and shoved it under Elías's chin. "This... person... got... my brother... killed."

K'antu and Taki both gasped. I saw drops of blood fall from Elías's chin. *Tumis* had a curved blade, so they made lined cuts, not small points.

"Tell them, Elías," Juan said.

But Elías was straining to breathe under the pressure of Juan's hand.

So Juan continued, "The night Eduardo and I went to Romero's house, I found papers - documents that showed an amount of aid money had come in, and the same amount going into someone's bank account - Romero's bank account! I was about to take those papers when Romero," he stopped and spit at Romero, catching the older man in the eye. Tomás wiped at his face, "caught Eduardo and me there. He threw us out and told us that he'd call the police the next time he caught us, Elías," he pulled savagely at the other boy's shirt, "was supposed to be the lookout. He was supposed to tell us when Romero was coming back so we could be out of there in time."

"But -" Elías started to say. He pointed to the bandage by his ribs.

"Shut up. Tomás found us rooting through his house, and he knew we had found information that would ruin him. That's why he let us go. But he came back for us – he got his revenge by killing Eduardo. Now my brother is dead, and I don't have those papers. So shut up and carry that bag before I cut you into pieces like those animals back there." He waved the *Tumi* around and jerked his head back toward the oasis.

"That is a ridiculous story." Tomás' voice rang out.

Both Juan and Elías glared at him.

"We need to get going," Oliver's voice was anxious.

"We will settle this later," Juan said. "Let's go."

Elías got up slowly and started to pick up the bag. I went to him and grabbed one end of it, ready to help him carry it. He looked at me with tears in his eyes. Mario came also. He took my hands off the bag and took it himself.

Juan saw what we were doing. "No. Elías will carry the bag alone."

"I will help him. It's no big deal," Mario said. But Juan came toward him, slashing the air with the knife. Mario backed away.

As we walked, Elías fell several times. Mario and I helped him. The others kept walking. I remembered Joaquín's description of K'antu's kitchen – Eduardo lying there in a pool of blood – and two perpendicular lines scratched into what the Chief Inspector assumed was the beginning of a K. What if it had been a T for Tomás or an E for my cousin's name? Or it could have been the start of an R. Rodolfo did have drugs with Eduardo's name on them after all... A dying man's hand probably wouldn't have produced a perfect letter. I looked at Tomás. He had sweat dripping down his face. He looked pitiful. Did he look like a murderer? What about Elías?

We kept walking. At one point, we stopped. Juan was looking wan, and his face was pinched.

"Is your wound hurting?" I asked him, hoping he'd say yes.

He smirked. "You enjoy my pain, Tamara?"

K'antu came to us with a cloth and looked like she wanted to administer first aid to Juan. Both he and I gave her dirty looks. She backed away.

"I do. It would make me happy if it matched mine. Or surpassed it."

"Don't be arrogant. Your pain is nothing compared to mine."

"Of course, Juan. You are always right."

"We finally agree on something." The side of his t-shirt, his impromptu bandage, was black with dried blood. It was probably sticking to his wound and would be painful to pull off. He breathed as deeply as it looked like was possible. I smiled, showing my teeth. I felt guilty. He was right. If we were talking about all kinds of pain, his had been worse throughout his life. He was trying in his weird way to make life better. But people were in his way. He had been livid at Elías' failings. How had he felt about his brother's? I frowned.

"Why didn't you tell us about the documents before, Juan?"

"It was none of your business, Tamara. I had my plans –"

"You had nothing. And now you have even less," I said and walked away.

"Get up, everyone. Keep moving," he shouted, looking to punish everyone for the things I had said probably. Since Oliver still had his AKM, we all obeyed.

When we finally came up to the tiny village of Urqu, women came out to the edge of town to see who was approaching. Juan went on ahead to talk to them. About twenty minutes later, our party of nine was guided into the largest house and told to sit on a pair of sofas and a few scattered armchairs. The furniture matched, but it was all old. Their tan upholstery, covered with a barely distinguishable design of large pink and white flowers on green stems, was faded and stained.

After a while, one of the women gave us cool Chicha *Morada* to drink. Despite my distaste for it, I gulped it. It had been an arduous trek. After everyone had drunk, Juan and Oliver went outside with some of the men. Taki tried to join them but was rebuffed, so she sulked on a sofa . K'antu stared into space.

A couple of moments later, Juan came back in with a wooden chair and rope.

"Come here, Romero," he called to the magistrate, who had been sitting between Laura and Taki.

"I refuse to sit in that chair. I will stay here," Romero said.

Juan went to him and grabbed him by the collar. He forced him to stand. He called Oliver to follow him with the chair and headed to the stairway.

"Don't get any ideas," Oliver told the rest of them, "I gave my rifle to the men outside. They think you are all with Romero, so they won't hesitate to shoot you if you try to leave."

He disappeared upstairs behind Juan and their prisoner. I flinched as sounds of muffled voices and someone being hit repeatedly came from the second floor. After about ten minutes, Juan and Oliver came back. Juan was wiping his hands on the side of his jeans.

"Was that necessary, Juan?" I said in a weary voice.

"Seriously, I am sick and tired of your mouth, Tamara." He grabbed me. Mario rushed to extricate me from Juan's grasp, but Oliver held onto him, and the two of them struggled while Juan dragged me up the stairs.

The second floor was made of a great room at the head of the stairway, followed by a short hallway and two back rooms. Señor Romero was sitting on the chair in the great room. His hands and feet were tied to the chair. He was bleeding from his nose and several cuts on his face. His breathing was labored, but his eyes were open. They widened when he saw me.

Juan pushed me, and I fell. I lay there, the wind knocked out of me. He knelt over me; his knee pressed against my back. I could smell him, a heady mixture of sweat, cologne, and smoke. He was breathing through his mouth. I felt the sharp blade of a knife run up and down my back. I shivered.

"What? Nothing to say now, Tamara? Why couldn't it have

been this way all along? Why can't you stop running your damn mouth? Now I am going to have to -"

Oliver called to Juan from the first floor. Juan stopped talking. In the silence that ensued, I heard the sound of a helicopter. Juan dug the blade into my back enough to cut the fabric and a couple of layers of my skin.

"Don't move, or I will come back and kill you." He got up and disappeared down the stairs.

I did as he said and stayed right where I was on the ground. The small cut he had made burned, but I did nothing to try to relieve the pain. It wasn't as if I hadn't endured other injuries recently. I tried as hard as I could to will the helicopter land somewhere near the town and save me from Juan. I was trying not to think of what was going on downstairs with my Aunt Laura and Mario when I heard a voice.

"Tamara," it was the magistrate.

Ignoring him, I continued concentrating on mentally calling for help. But a moment later, I heard him call my name again.

"Tamara, come untie me."

I couldn't believe it. "Really? You want me to untie you? No way. Go to hell."

"We can still make our deal..." His voice was weak, and his breath still labored.

"Shut up," I told him, borrowing Juan's favorite phrase.

We were both silent for a moment. I closed my eyes. It was uncomfortable, but I did not have the energy, physical or mental, to get up or move positions, never mind I had been told not to move. I did not hear the helicopter anymore. Where did it go?

Sometimes situations like these are so stressful the mind

opens up to something completely different. I remembered a detail from when he was rambling on in the cage. The information that I knew was important.

"Señor?" The term of respect seemed ridiculous, but I used it anyway.

"What?"

"When you were in the cage, you said something about Lorena Guerra. What was it?"

"So now you'd like to listen to me?"

"Please."

"Fine. I said that I had no idea she had been helping –"

The lights went out. Someone cried out on the first floor. I put my hands on the floor and pulled myself to my knees. My body swayed back and forth. There was a weird vacuum of quiet, and then the air around me was sucked out of the room. The ground rumbled like a million trucks were bearing down on me. It began slowly and then exploded into the room. The house rocked as if something huge had collided with it. Things – probably pieces of the roof – fell on my head.

"Oh my God. Earthquake. Again." I closed my eyes and sat on my butt. I would not scream this time. The end was near. I knew it had been too good to be true that I had survived last year. This time I would not be so lucky. I breathed shallowly in the falling debris and waited for death to take me.

Chapter 21

There were sounds of other people screaming and running exactly like last year. But these sounds were different. They seemed closer. And instead of shouting *at* me, they were shouting *to* me. To me. Calling me. Calling for me. The house kept moving. But I was still alive. Except I was on the second floor. Not a good place to be.

I forced myself to stand. The floor shook. I lost my balance and sat down heavily.

"Tamara." Someone was close. I recognized the voice. It was Tomás Romero. He was calling to me. Hope had come and gone so quickly I had not realized it was there – until it was gone again. It had only been him – the voices – it was only the magistrate. No one was coming to rescue me. I looked toward space where Tomás and the chair had been before the lights went off. I saw their outlines. There was a weird greenish light coming into the house from the windows, same as last year, faint but enough to see shadows. No one had believed me about the green glow. It was like a sinister science fiction plot. The glow was real. I found myself thinking about how unfair it was that no one had taken me seriously. My thoughts floated around.

"Tamara, please. Untie me. We have to get out of here," Romero said, jerking me back to reality.

I shook my head but shuffled toward him. "I will untie you, Señor Romero, but it is useless. We are going to die. There is nothing we can do to stop that. It is -"

"Tamara," he shouted again as the shaking became more intense, "you are panicking. I know how you feel. But you have to snap out of it. We can survive. We will. But you have to help me. Please."

His plea ended in a kind of strangled scream. I stopped cold. Something fell with a loud crash right where Señor Romero was, and then I heard crumbling sounds. I couldn't see him anymore. Coughing from all the dust, I got down on my hands and knees and crawled over to him, fumbling around in the debris. It seemed like he was a lot farther away. Where was he? Oh God, he was under the rubble. The house still shook.

"Señor Romero?" I called. There was no answer. The crumbling sounds got louder. My heart lurched. I stood halfway up and moved behind the pile. My eyes strained in the low light, but I saw him. His prostrate body was lying at a weird angle. "Don't worry, sir. I will untie you, and then we will go downstairs. Everything is going to be all right."

But he did not answer me. A gasping sob escaped my lips. I should have untied him sooner. I had been in that defeated daze for too long. I should have gone to him right away. I should have gotten him out of here. I should have...

But it was not too late. I grappled with the ropes around his wrists, and after what seemed like an eternity, got them untied. He flopped face down on the floor. I crawled around the chair to him.

"Señor Romero. Wake up. You are free. We need to go."

He was unresponsive. I slapped his face. "Señor Romero. I am sorry. I should have untied you earlier. I am sorry."

I shook him. I screamed at him. He did not respond. I put my head down by his chest. I cried, sobbed, shook him, but he did not move. He was not breathing.

The crumbling got louder underneath the crackling and rumbling. I began to hear something else - voices. People called my name. Or did they? I cast one last anguished look at my companion and scooted closer to the stairway. The voices called me again. I was about to shout when there was another tremendous crash behind me.

I opened my mouth to scream, but nothing came out. The horror of the moment froze in time. I clawed, cat-like, at the floor, trying to regain a sense of security. The boards had come loose, so I was able to grab ahold of one that was half off. I screamed. Over and over. Until someone grabbed onto my leg and pulled hard. Mario. He was saying something to me, but I could not hear. He continued to talk, he shouted at me. I shook my head and continued to cling to the floor. He pulled me harder, and finally, I had enough faith in him to let go.

"We will get you out of here, Tamara. But we have to hurry," he leaned over and shouted in my ear.

Turning my head, I looked back one last time at the mountain of rubble. The body of Tomás Romero was a dark nightmare. I got up on my hands and knees and went to Mario.

"Señor Romero... he... he is crushed. The house ... fell," I sobbed.

"Come on. Someone else will get him." He was at the top of the stairs. Laura was behind him, holding on to his shirt. K'antu was behind her, Taki came next, and then Elías and Oliver. I was passed from one person in the human chain to the other. None of them lost physical contact with each other, and as soon as I passed, Mario followed and then the rest of them until we were all at the bottom of the stairs.

We all ran outside and dispersed into the chaos. I yelled into the murky air, screaming about Romero, shouting at no one, in particular, they had to get Tomás out of the house. I tried to get someone's attention – anyone. But no one listened. Soon I stopped moving and stood watching for a second as other people rushed here and there, like ants, except the people were panicking. Laura came by and tried to pull me farther away from the house. So I screamed at her about Tomás. Laura screamed back that Juan and the owners of the house were also still inside. Elías was right behind her, and when he heard about Juan, he started running toward the house.

I called to him. "Elías, stop. You can't go in there. It is too dangerous."

But Elías was not listening. He kept moving toward the house. I ran after him. Behind me, Laura and Mario also-ran. The ground listed back and forth, and I lost my balance. I stumbled but did not fall.

I was about to catch up with Elías when the building seemed to sigh, and adobe bricks started flying in the air from the crumbling second floor. I screamed and ran faster toward him but was pulled back. Someone pushed me to the ground. Something fell on top of me. Debris rained down. I was going to die after all.

And then, as suddenly as it had begun, it stopped. Mario rolled off me, and we lay there, alternately panting and coughing up brick dust. The only sound was the wailing of a woman somewhere in the distance.

I wanted to melt into the ground and disappear. But Mario pulled me to a sitting position. We looked at each other. A moment later, Elías came out of the house. He was dragging someone – it was Juan. Both had blood all over them. Juan seemed to be unconscious – or worse.

Suddenly there was a shout from somewhere to my left. I looked up and saw a shadowy figure lifting a large stick above their shoulder. But it was not a large stick. It was Oliver, and he had the rifle pointed directly at Elías. He was going to shoot. Time went in slow motion. Sound was in a vacuum. Wild, my senses sharp, I assessed the situation. I did not have time to run and stop Oliver from shooting my cousin.

"Mario!" I called. But he was also far away from the armed boy.

The ground had stopped shaking, but debris was everywhere. I crawled over pieces of brick and the remains of a broken plastic chair. A few yards away, Taki and K'antu stood like statues. I grabbed at Taki.

"Where is it?" I shouted to her. "Where is your *macana*?"

Taki ignored me, so I searched in the rubble. I could not find the *macana*, so I frisked Taki, grabbed the *Tumi*, and stood. Offering up a little prayer to my Quechua ancestors, I ran as fast as I could, took aim, and threw the *Tumi*. I heard a dull thud and saw the figure of Oliver fall. As soon as he fell, the others picked their way over to me amongst the destruction. I had run, and it was only with luck that I had not tripped over anything. Fate, or something else. Had I just killed someone?

Taki knelt next to Oliver, screaming, "You killed him. He's dead. My brother…"

"I had to do something. He was going to shoot Elías."

"I'm not dead, Taki. The bitch got me in the leg. Help me stop the bleeding."

Taki turned his body. "He is alive. Thank God."

"He doesn't deserve to be," I said.

"Go away, Tamara," Taki ordered.

I turned. K'antu was by Elías and Juan.

Someone turned their flashlight app on the two boys, both of whom lay on the ground with their eyes closed.

I knelt and touched Elías on the shoulder. He opened his eyes. Laura knelt beside Juan and felt his pulse.

K'antu was by her lover, "He's breathing."

She started crying. Two women and a man appeared as if out of nowhere. They picked Juan up and took him away. K'antu followed them. I barely noticed. I was concentrating on my cousin.

"Elías's pulse is sporadic, Tamara. He needs help. I will go and call Manchay. Maybe they can send the helicopter back," Laura said. She had turned her attention to Elías after the others had taken Juan away.

She walked away. Elías had closed his eyes again. But now he opened them and looked at me.

"Eduardo?" He said.

"No, Elías, it is Tamara. Eduardo is... well... Laura went to get help. I think Oliver shot you." My chest heaved. "I tried to stop him..."

"Don't cry." His eyelids fluttered. "Did your best... like always..."

That made me cry harder, "Elías, you are going to be fine. You must be. They are coming now. They will take you to the hospital."

"Tamara?"

"Yes, *primo*?"

"Cut... this cut... it was Tomás... when I was watching."

"I figured that out, *primo*. Don't worry about anything. Stay with me."

I felt around his body, but I was no nurse. I had no idea what to do. Despite that, I continued inspecting him. I desperately wanted to do something – anything. Suddenly I felt something smooth under him and pulled it out. There was blood on it, so I wiped at it with my sleeve and peered closer. It was a glass swan-like the one in his workshop. Why did he have it with him here? My eyes welled up at the sight of it – such beauty amid pain and death. Death – I looked down at my cousin. His eyes were rolling to the back of his head.

"Elías," I cried.

But he said nothing. I stood and screamed for help. Mario touched my arm. I had forgotten he was nearby. He put his arm around me. I stuffed the swan in my pocket before he could ask me what I was holding and looked back at Elías. He was still. I turned and saw Laura off in the distance. She had a phone to her ear.

"*Primo*, say something. Please." I got back on my knees.

Elías moaned. He opened his eyes and closed them again. Then his body jerked, and a stream of blood dripped out of his mouth.

I screamed at Mario to go get help. He ran off.

Moments later, the sound of the helicopter's blades whirring in the air came closer and closer. Suddenly someone was beside me. It was K'antu.

"I am leaving, Tamara."

"What?" I looked at her. I could not process what she was saying. My cousin was dying.

"Juan is not dead. And we cannot be here when that helicopter arrives. We are going higher into the mountains, and we are taking Taki and Oliver. We will find family members up there who will help us. I wanted - I needed to say goodbye to you."

I half stood and clutched at my friend's shirt, "No, K'antu. Things will be all right. Things will change now. Tomás is dead. Eduardo's killer is dead. Don't leave me. I stayed for you; you have to stay with me. My cousin is hurt badly. Stay. Help me."

"Tamara, I am sorry about Elías, I am, but I have to go. The magistrate's death does not help me. It makes things worse. I am sorry. I am. I know you stayed for me, did everything to help me. But I must go. I hope one day I will see you again, *amiga*. In the meantime, take care of your cousin" K'antu looked at Elías. A multitude of emotions came and went on her face.

"Please, K'antu," I begged, crying.

"I am sorry, Tamara."

She kissed me on the cheek and disappeared into the dark. I stood looking after her, feeling numb. After all, I had gone through. My hair rushed upwards. The air around me whooshed in circles. The helicopter had reappeared. A light beamed down, and Laura came back. I squinted, turning my head up and following the path of the chopper. It landed in a mostly flat area on the far side of the buildings.

"They will be here momentarily, Tamara, and this nightmare will be over."

"I don't think this nightmare will ever be over, *Tía*," I said, not caring who "they" were.

I knelt again and held Elías's hand. It was cold and limp, but I kept ahold of it, running my thumb up and down his knuckles. It did not take long for three men to make their way toward us. Laura croaked out orders, and I got up so the two of them could minister to Elías. They took a few moments to examine him and then put him on a stretcher, heading back toward the helicopter.

Another man came up. It was Joaquin. He looked at me with his camel eyes, and I stared into them. He put his hand on my shoulder and told Laura to take Mario and me to the helicopter while he rounded up the others.

"Good luck with that," I thought to myself. K'antu, my friend, my ally, was gone. And I did not want to ever see her again.

Laura took us to the clearing. She stopped briefly to talk to a couple of the women of Urqu, assuring them help would be on the way soon. If I hadn't been so shell-shocked, I would have let out a bray of laughter at that promise. I had had enough of earthquakes and tragedy and lack of progress to last me a lifetime. I wanted to go home.

My aunt joined us again, and we climbed the ladder into the helicopter's cabin. I was about to sit down when I heard someone say something. It was Lorena.

"Lorena," my aunt exclaimed, "what are you doing here?"

"I came to make sure everyone was okay," She looked from Laura to Mario to me. "Where is Tomás?"

I started crying again. Through my tears, I saw Mario fidget with a loose string on the chair he was sitting in. Laura breathed loudly.

"Tomás did not make it, Lorena," Laura said.

"I am sorry. I… I was too late. I could not save him," I said, crying harder.

Some emotion flitted over Lorena's face, but I could not tell what it was.

Shouting noises came from outside. Then Joaquin burst in and said, "She is gone."

"What?" Lorena said, standing up.

"K'antu... she is gone. She went into the mountains. That is all the townspeople would tell me."

Lorena stared darkly at me. "Do you know where they went?"

"No."

"You are sure about that?"

"I am sure."

Lorena narrowed her eyes. She put her hand up and gestured at Joaquin.

Joaquin took something out of his pocket. Metal clinked. He came up to me. I felt something slip around my wrist. I looked down. He had handcuffed me to the post that attached the armrest to the chair I was sitting in.

"What are you doing?" I protested.

"Tamara Villanueva, you are under arrest for vandalizing the Barranquilla School of Manchay and for assisting a fugitive to escape. Please say nothing until you can talk to your lawyer," Joaquin said.

My aunt jumped out of her chair, "Joaquin, what the hell are you doing? You know perfectly well -"

But Lorena interrupted her, "Laura, sit down. Since Tomás is dead, I am now the acting magistrate of Manchay, and it is I who have ordered her arrest. If she had not done everything she did, we could have had both K'antu and Juan in custody, and our dear magistrate would still be alive and well. You can try to help your niece when we reach Manchay."

I stared at Laura. She nodded curtly at me, perhaps trying to reassure me. I wasn't sure. I looked over at Mario, who was staring at me, his eyes dark and his mouth twitching with some dark emotion. There was nothing for me to do but lean back in my seat and wait.

Chapter 22

Manchay. I hated it. I sat in the well-lit cell by the receptionist's desk at the town hall, which doubled as the jail. When we had landed back in town, Laura had gone home, assuring me she would be on the phone with her lawyers as soon as she opened her front door.

Joaquin had driven me here. When we arrived, he had led me to a row of connected metal and plastic chairs in the lobby and cuffed me to the one I sat on while he went to the reception desk and spoke to the woman behind it. The lady looked familiar. I had stared at the woman until recollection hit. It was the same person who had been in the front room of People Help when I went to find Mario. Her name was Señora Ramos.

Soon he led me to a little room. He indicated I should go inside, and when I did, he shut and locked the door. I sat on the wood chair and put my hands on the table. The room started shaking. I almost fainted. I grabbed at the table in front of me, hands wide, nails clawing into the wood. The shaking did not last more than a few seconds. It was an aftershock from last night's earthquake. When it stopped and my blood pressure went down, I looked around. There were no cracks on the walls. I stood and looked out the window facing the town square. Nothing outside seemed out of the ordinary. People were rushing to work, and everything appeared normal.

Thinking about how normal everything looked made me wonder: what would have happened differently in Urqu if the earthquake had not hit? What would Juan have done with Romero? Would he have killed him? I felt sad at the death of the magistrate.

Was my sympathy misplaced? Maybe it was not so much sadness for him as an extreme reaction to all of the emotional and physical turmoil I had been through in the last week. I thought about how Juan had accused the dead man of killing Eduardo. Had Romero been such a good politician – convincing everybody of his innocence while at the same time stealing large amounts of money and then killing to cover it up? If it were true, it would be the most convenient answer. At least, it would work for me. If he were the killer, I could learn to live with the fact that I had saved him yesterday. But was he the guilty one? I wished I had been listening more closely to him when he was in the cage. I was still convinced I missed something. Why was he so surprised Lorena was helping the earthquake survivors? He had not finished his sentence, but that must have been what he was about to say.

I got up and started walking in circles again. After a while, the key turned in the lock, and the door opened. Lorena walked into the room.

"Hello, Tamara."

"What do you want?" I was in no mood to talk to her.

"Please sit down." Lorena indicated the same upright wood chair I had just vacated.

"I don't want to. Tell me why you are here."

Lorena peered at me through her glasses. Her eyes looked enormous. Then she sat down on the other chair. "Fine. I thought you should know that we were unsuccessful in our search for K'antu and the others. They have effectively disappeared. So not only does that put the nail in K'antu's coffin, but it also makes things worse for you."

"What? How? What do you mean?"

"Unfortunately," she peered at me, "you are the only one available to prosecute for all of the mess you and your cronies have created."

"Cronies? I am not associated with them, at least, I am – was K'antu's friend, but nothing more. I am not the guilty one. Surely now that Tomás Romero is dead, the police can search his house better than we did and find something... or search Juan's house. He is the one who has run away after all."

"All of that has been done. There is nothing. There are rumors Elías had some kind of proof, probably fabricated, but no one can prove it. So we will continue to look for K'antu and the rest of them but finding her won't be easy. You, however, are right here, and you most definitely are guilty – of vandalism and conspiring with terrorists."

My eyes welled up.

"You," Lorena continued, "will have to stay here and face charges."

"You don't understand. Juan drugged me. I would never have vandalized -"

But Lorena stood before I could go on. She shook her head sadly. "If you had stayed in town and out of the business of trying to cover up for K'antu, none of this would have happened. Your aunt should be here shortly with a lawyer. I will have food brought in to you."

"Don't bother."

Lorena smiled grimly and left the room. I was so angry my vision clouded. My hands shook so badly I had to stuff them in the pockets of my jacket to calm down. I felt something in one pocket. I put my fingers around it and pulled it out.

Blinking several times, I focused on what I had in my hands. It was the glass swan I had found under Elías. I had forgotten it was there. Remembering how it had found its way to my pocket, suddenly, all the frustration of the last few weeks came rushing up inside of me. Now, everything that had gone wrong with me in Perú flashed in my eyes and seemed to be reflected in the small crystal figurine – starting with last year's earthquake; Eduardo's murder, my failed attempts to help K'antu, Juan's abuse, K'antu's desertion of me, along with all the minor tremors, the deaths, the suspicion, the uncertainty – and me being dragged into all of it. With a cry, I lifted my arm and threw the swan hard, flinging it toward the wall. It made impact and shattered. Shards of glass flew in the air. I covered my face with my arms. When all of the pieces had clattered and clinked to the floor, I peered out over my forearms—what a mess.

There were sharp pieces of glass all over the floor and on the table. I looked toward the door, but no one came running, so they must not have heard. I would have to remain unmoving until Laura got there since anywhere I stepped would be over broken glass. I had nothing to clean the mess with. Instead, I spent a few seconds gingerly feeling around my body, making sure there were no pieces of glass on me.

There were a couple of them. I cut my finger on a splinter of glass I picked out of my hair. I dropped it on the table, then wrapped my finger tightly using the bottom of my t-shirt. I stared at the largest pile of glass that had fallen close to the wall opposite me.

While focused on the pile, my eye caught a vision of something white. There was something there in the fragments.

I got up and stepped gingerly around the table and closer to the wall, crackling glass under my feet. I bent down and touched the white thing. It was paper. I pried it away from the glass and picked it up, being careful not to cut myself. It had been folded so many times it took me several moments to flatten it out. When I finally got it, I started reading. My eyes opened wide, and my hands began to shake. I looked toward the door. I folded the paper back and stuffed it into my shirt.

I was still shaking when Lorena opened the door again. Four people exclaimed at the mess, and Lorena's arms went out to prevent the other three people behind her from entering.

"Tamara, what on earth happened there?" I heard my aunt say.

"Someone, please go call the custodian. No one should come in here until all of this has been cleaned up," Lorena said, her eyes looking sharply at the mess by the wall. The only thing still recognizable was the swan's head, now separated forever from its graceful neck, somehow still intact. Lorena looked at it and then turned slowly to stare at me.

"Don't be ridiculous, Lorena. No one is going in there at all. Tamara, come out of there – carefully. We can talk in one of the offices."

"Laura," Lorena began.

But Laura stepped in. "My niece is not a hardened criminal, Lorena. She will come out of this cell, and I will take custody of her in the office down the hall. In the meantime, you can have all of this cleaned up."

Laura took me by the hand and led me to the office. Rodolfo was with her, and the other person, a lawyer I assumed, following us. She opened the door to a small room. This one had a desk and two chairs, which were also wood, but with cushions - a step up from the cell. The lawyer disappeared for a moment and came back with another chair.

He sat down and talked for a while about a possible defense for me. He was cautiously optimistic but emphasized the serious-ness of the charges against me and the fact that they had surveillance video showing me vandalizing the school. He warned me with Juan gone, the judge would be eager to make an example of me and reluctant to let me, an American, off easy. Laura discussed getting the people in Patabamba to talk about Juan's history of violence and the probability that he did, indeed, drug me and incite me to do the things I did.

I did not listen to any of it. I was reeling from the information that was on the paper – and from how close it had come to disap-pearing altogether. If I hadn't been with Elías. If he hadn't given me the swan. If they had taken it from me when I was arrested. If I hadn't shattered it in a fit of rage. If I hadn't seen the paper…

The lawyer had stopped lecturing me and sat writing and murmuring to Laura. I looked at Rodolfo. "What was he doing here anyway?" I thought uneasily to myself. I started to sweat.

As if he had read my thoughts, he leaned forward and said in a low voice, "Tamara, when you were in my car the other day, did you find anything?"

"No, Señor, I did not." I could not, under any circumstances, let him guess I was lying. I was becoming a decent liar. "Was there something I should have found?"

"No, I… I thought I had lost my… my wallet in the passenger seat. But if you say you did not find it…"

"I'm sorry, no."

He searched my face but appeared satisfied with my answer and turned toward the other adults, leaving me to my thoughts. I relaxed and ruminated about what I should do with the information I had now. I knew of only one person I felt I could trust one hundred percent.

"*Tía*, I need to talk to Mario."

My aunt turned to me in surprise. "*Cariño*, we have a lot of work to do here. Lorena is pressing serious charges against you. I hardly think this is the time to talk to him."

I waved the hand that did not have cuts on it around in the air, "Yes, I know. And I trust the two of you to do the best you can. But you can't do any of that here in this room, can you? I need to talk to Mario. Please."

The lawyer shook his head, thinking me foolish, but agreed

he would get to work at his office. He left, promising Laura a report later that afternoon. Laura turned to me.

"Why Mario, Tamara?"

"I... I owe him an apology." It wasn't entirely a lie. I did have to tell him I was sorry for thinking he could have killed Eduardo. Of course, I did not believe he had, especially now. I had been upset. Looking at Laura, I let a few tears drop from my eyes – not difficult to do after so much stress.

"Please *Tía*, please Señor Alvarez. I know he is mad at me, but I want to see a friendly face..."

Laura looked at Rodolfo, who smiled and relented. "Fine. I will go get him, and I will talk to Lorena to see if she will let him see you or not."

They stood and turned to leave.

I grabbed my aunt's arm. "*Tía*, Mario might be reluctant to come. Please tell him what I have to tell him is important."

Laura looked at me. I had an idea of what I looked like. I had dark circles under my eyes. My hair was tousled, and my skin was dull – good for looking pitiful. Laura gently pulled another piece of glass from my curls.

"I will tell him."

I sighed, relieved.

Three hours passed. I spent the time back in the same room I had made the mess in. Some brave soul had cleaned it all up. When the door opened, I jumped up, but it was not Mario. I slumped back down on the chair.

Lorena came and stood over me.

"Tamara, where did you get the swan you broke?"

I thought quickly. Should I tell the truth? I decided against it. "K'antu gave it to me."

"And was there any particular reason why you broke it?"

I looked into Lorena's eyes. "I was upset. I am sorry for the mess."

Lorena sat down on the other chair. "Was there..."

I waited, looking questioningly at the woman.

"Was there anything... unusual about the swan? I... I mean, why did K'antu give it to you?"

"I think my cousin knew it was my favorite piece of his. I had admired it the other day in his workshop. I believe he passed it to K'antu to give to me as a gift. I wish I had not broken it." It didn't take much for me to look sad. I was. I shouldn't have broken it. On the other hand, if I hadn't, I might never have found the paper.

My hands, clasped together, started sweating. There were bandages on the cuts. They would fall off if I kept sweating. I widened my eyes and tried to look like I was telling the truth.

"I should never have gotten so angry. Now I have lost a precious memento from my cousin, who is now gone," I said, allowing a tear to drop from my eye. I looked through my eyelashes at Lorena.

"A memento? That's all it was?"

I stared. "Yes, why?"

"Nothing, nothing I meant it was a foolish thing to do, throwing it like that." Lorena pat my hand absentmindedly. I slowly but firmly inched my hand out away from her thin, dry hand. My skin crawled at her touch, but I couldn't afford to directly antagonize her. I needed the woman to agree to let me talk to Mario.

"Lorena, I understand you must do your job. I know you have to show an example and punish me for what I did. I ask for one favor. Let me talk to Mario. Please. You see, I... well this is so embarrassing, but I have fallen in love with him, but I made him angry with my... my behavior. So now all I want to do is apologize to him. Please." I put my head down in her arms and cried. Once again, it wasn't difficult.

Lorena stood and walked around the table. She put her hand on my shoulder and said, "Well, of course, it is totally against protocol, but for two young lovers, why not? It could not harm anything. Yes, yes, I will allow this visit. When he gets here, I will send him in."

"Thank you." I lifted my head and smiled.

Lorena feigned a smile of generosity and turned to leave. Before she shut the door, she looked back, "Tamara, you are sure there is not anything you need to tell me about Elías... anything unusual he might have said or done before he, well, before he passed away?"

I made a show of frowning and looking thoughtful, "Unusual? What do you mean?"

"Never mind." Lorena left.

It was dark before the door opened again. A few hours earlier, I had been served a basic lunch of rice and butter beans with a glass of pineapple juice. I had only picked at the food. Most of my time had been spent planning my time with Mario. I knew I would have to be quick – and discreet.

When the door opened, and Mario came in, my heart beat faster. He looked tired but exceedingly handsome. What he did not look was happy to see me. His straight, patrician nose seemed to be pointing down, emphasizing the sober, serious line of his mouth. He stepped in and stood just inside of the room by the doorway.

"I won't bite, Rodolfo's son. You can come in and close the door." My lighthearted attempt at humor did not go over well.

"I can't close the door, Tamara. They told me not to."

That would make this even more difficult. I peered around him but did not see anyone directly behind him. I thought quickly and came close to him, making eye contact.

"Mario, I am sorry. Why won't you forgive me?"

"Tamara, I know we were in a difficult situation, but I'm not a monster. And I am not a murderer either. Even if you believe I could be," he said stiffly.

"No, Mario. I don't think you are a monster. I never should have said you could be the murderer. I was under a lot of stress, but I understand why you are still upset with me. It was unforgivable, what I said. But I have been through such a hard time..." I started to babble, recapping everything I had been through. I rambled on and on, going into great detail.

His eyes glazed over, and he took a breath like he was about to stop me, so I grabbed him and stood up on my toes, kissing him several times and throwing out several words of affection loud enough for anyone in the hallway to hear.

"Mario," I said, "I love you, please forgive me."

I kissed him again, pulling him closer, and he responded briefly. I opened my eyes and saw two parallel lines appear between his eyebrows. He was about to pull away from me, so I grabbed his hand. I spoke even louder as I moved his hand.

"Mario, you won't abandon me now, will you? I need you. You will help me through this, won't you?" I emphasized the word "help". I continued to guide his hand, taking his fingers and shoving them into my bra. His eyes widened. But seconds later, he had the folded piece of paper in his hand. I closed his palm and gripped it with my hand, shaking our fists up and down and looking at him so he wouldn't say anything about what he had found.

"You will help me, won't you, Mario?" I repeated, "I don't know what to do. It is so hard to trust anyone after everything Juan did to me."

I let go of his hand and waited, my eyes wide and my heart pounding. What if he said something to call attention to the fact I had given him something? Or what if once he left, he told someone what I had done before he read the paper? But he kept his fist closed and pumped it an inch or two in the air, only for me to see. Then he put his hand in his pocket and left it there, winking at me.

"I love you too, Tamara," he said quietly as Lorena came in.

"All right, break it up, you two. This is not the time or the place for all that. Mario, it is time you left."

I was staring at Mario. His final declaration had taken me by surprise. I was talking for the benefit of anyone listening and had not expected him to say anything back.

He took his hands out of his pockets to grab mine. He had left the paper in his pocket. I felt my knees buckle with relief. Or was it because of the look he was giving me... "I will not leave you to

282

go through this alone, Tamara. Give me time. I will be back when I know what to do. I just need some time."

And with that, he turned and left. I understood what he was saying. Lorena followed him and snapped the lock into place, leaving me alone in the room. I collapsed back into the chair. My effort had exhausted me. But it was done. Now it was out of my hands. I was certain Mario would read the paper when he was alone and in a safe place. I knew once he read it, he would be smart enough to keep it safe, maybe make multiple copies of it. And I was confident he would get it to the proper authorities. The question of whether my declaration of love for him was genuine didn't even go through my mind. I knew I did.

But that would have to wait. The paper was my ticket out of jail. I had vandalized the school, for sure, but I was fairly certain once the information I had found in the swan became public, it would no longer be significant enough to keep me here. Because what I had found proved someone had an even stronger motive to kill Eduardo than K'antu did.

The paper that Elías had hidden in the swan was a document showing the movement of money, a great deal of money, from People, Help to someone's private account. Eduardo must have found it and given it to Elías to hide, which he had. I stared at the door. I knew now why Lorena had been working so hard to focus attention on me and lock me away. The signature on the paper was hers.

Chapter 23

A tapestry of light and dappled shade spilled through the trees and fell on the floor by my feet. The soft tones of Eva Ayllon played in the background. The temperature was a beautiful seventy-seven degrees Fahrenheit. I sat stiffly in a white wicker seat with light blue cushions. It was wider than an ordinary chair but not wide enough for two people. I had my eyes closed.

There were three other people there with me. Mario's face was dark with some emotion. His father Rodolfo sat with a bottle of *quebranta* Pisco in front of him. It was Laura's house brand. I noticed she had been surprised at his empty hands when he arrived. Usually, he brought his own Pisco, and she did the same when she went to his house – their little joke that the other did not have any "good" Pisco lying around.

Laura, of course, was there as well, her hair caught up in a chignon, streaks of gray fanning out around her head. She had some paperwork artfully arranged in front of her, but she did not look at it. Instead, she chewed on pecans from a glass bowl by the documents.

After I had given him the paper, Mario had read it, made several copies of it, and given a copy each to Joaquin, Laura, and Rodolfo. He forwarded another copy to his attorneys in Lima. They had arrested Lorena the next day after I had spent the night in a small cell on a plastic mattress resembling the one I had poked at in Taki's room at the magistrate's house. I hadn't slept much.

The bad news was that a detailed search of her accounts had only turned up a little more than five percent of the money so far. The good news: police had come down from Lima. They had gone through Eduardo and K'antu's house more carefully and found matches to fibers from Lorena's clothes and hair – both in the house and mixed with some of the blood samples they had taken the night he had died. The perpendicular lines in blood found at the scene must have been an attempt by Eduardo to write Lorena's name. An L, not a K.

Laura's phone rang. She picked it up and listened for a while. When she turned it off, she said, "Joaquin has charged Lorena with murder."

"That's good," I said, "because she confessed?"

"No," Laura looked thoughtful, "but he says he has enough evidence anyway."

"I should have known it was her earlier," I said.

"What do you mean, Tamara?" Rodolfo asked.

"Well, for one thing, she was the only person who could move freely between Manchay and Patabamba. And she always wanted to know everything. And then, when Juan forced us to go to Tomás' house, I should have questioned her more about why she was there. It... it was like she knew we would be going there, and she needed to make sure we did not find anything."

"There was nothing to find anyway, was there?" Rodolfo asked.

"That's what she told us, but maybe there was," I said. "If Señor Romero had anything incriminating in his house, then she would have kept it from us. She controlled what we saw there pretty closely."

"I wonder how she knew we would be there at that exact time," Mario said.

"She had bugged Juan's car and tapped into his phone to be able to track him," Laura said. "She must have known he would eventually show up at Romero's house again looking for more evidence – especially since the paper Eduardo had found was missing. Lorena did not know where it was, and Juan must have suspected the killer had destroyed it..."

"What about the money, Tía? Will they find it?" I asked.

Laura shook her head, "This morning, I spoke to several people, including the main branch of People Help, their lawyers, and the police from Lima. It looks like they will recover a portion of the money, but not all of it. Both Tomás and Lorena were stealing money from People Help. Tomás' accounts show he stole some, but not nearly the amount missing. I think he was skimming little bits off. Lorena took most of it, but her accounts are clean. The money must have been moved somewhere else."

I tapped my fingers on the arm of my chair, "Why were the Lima police able to find evidence at K'antu's house, but the police here in Manchay missed it?"

"Well, *cariño*, the police here are not as advanced –" Laura began. Then she saw the look on my face. She stopped and said, "No, no more excuses. You are right. They should have found it. I... I did hear from Joaquin that Lorena and Tomás had both pressured him to not look for any evidence which pointed away from K'antu."

Seeing that my aunt had just checked herself, had started by defending her friend and finished by taking a good look at her beliefs, and concluded they were wrong, made me feel good. Never had I admired her more than at that moment. I smiled at Laura. She smiled back.

"I – we – will work to make sure things like this do not happen again here in Manchay, won't we, Rodolfo?" Laura said.

"Indeed. Your aunt and I, Tamara, are going to work closely with the new magistrate, whoever that will be, from now on. There will be more police oversight. And, I have decided that People Help is not the right organization to help Manchay. We will be asking them to withdraw, and I have contacts in the U.S. who will be sending me a representative from another organization. Instead of giving money to our government, they train local people to build homes that will resist earthquakes. The training they provide will create jobs as well as making Manchay's buildings safer. This, I believe, is what the people need."

I saw Mario looking at his father with admiration. Rodolfo noticed too and blushed slightly. "I am going to be a better father – and employer – from now on, Mario. It felt good to help Elías, poor boy, but I must do more. And Tamara..."

"Yes?"

"I know you found that bag of drugs."

I jumped and looked guilty.

"I had found them in Elías' workshop. I was trying to figure out what to do with them. I do not think they were Eduardo's. Juan probably put his name on them for a reason of his own."

I wondered about Juan. And K'antu. And if I were ever going to see them again. One of them I would miss.

One of Laura's workers approached our little group. He greeted everyone and asked Laura questions about the latest round of grapes. Then he stood there wringing his hands as if he wanted to ask something else.

"Yes, Domingo, what is it?" Laura asked him, not unkindly.

"Is there any news about K'antu?" the man asked.

K'antu. Hearing someone else speak her name reminded me I was angry with her. She had acted selfishly. But then again, what was she supposed to do? After all, no one had found a way to help her, and she had no idea I would find the paper. I would have to forgive her. Eventually, life is weird. You love. People leave. You are angry but miss them with every heartbeat. You wish they would come back so you could be angry with them in person. Or that you could be a better person and love them.

Rodolfo answered the man, "No, Domingo, unfortunately, there has not been any news."

K'antu and the other three had disappeared into the mountains. They had probably heard all the news through the grapevine. So far, they had not come out of hiding, even though everyone knew they were innocent.

Laura turned to her employee. "I am so sorry, Domingo. I know everyone must be so worried. But rest assured, now that Lorena is behind bars, K'antu is not in danger anymore."

"Do not worry, Domingo, everything will turn out well in the end," Rodolfo added.

There they were again, full of casual, baseless optimism. But I forgave them. This time they were right.

"Yes, I believe you, Señor," Domingo said, bowing to me, "and Señorita, may I say I am so happy you are all right and out of jail."

"Thank you, Señor," I smiled.

He bowed again and went back to the vines.

My aunt said, "Domingo has articulated exactly how I feel. Tamara, it is so good to have you sitting here. I can tell you now I should have been more worried about you when you went up to Patabamba. I am sorry to say I was too trusting of everyone."

She dabbed at her eyes. Rodolfo handed her a handkerchief. "I … I have known these people all my life, after all. At least, I thought I knew them. I never believed anyone would hurt you, cariño. I thought because I treat my workers well, everything was all right. But I guess in my blind way, I have been a part of the problem. I wonder if K'antu will ever be able to forgive me…"

I went and knelt in front of her, "Of course she will. I know I was angry you didn't see what they did, but K'antu never was. She knew, better than you or I did, that sometimes it is hard to acknowledge things that are right in front of you. She will forgive you. I am sure she already has. Wherever she is."

"Well said, Tamara, but enough of that talk for now. Tamara, have a seat. Laura, you are perfect the way you are. We all make mistakes." Rodolfo poured a shot of Laura's Pisco for everyone. "This isn't bad stuff, Laura, but kids, if anyone asks, you did not hear me saying that."

My aunt and Rodolfo laughed. Mario saw I was still serious.

"Tamara?"

"I'm just thinking –"

"Well, don't," he grinned, "it gets you into trouble."

"Very funny. But how can I stop?" I asked.

"I can think of a few ways," He began.

"Mario!" My aunt and his father exclaimed at the same time.

This time we all laughed. But before letting it go for good, I went over everything that had happened: Eduardo found proof Lorena was siphoning money away from People Help. Juan knew he had found something, but instead of giving it to his brother, who was becoming increasingly volatile, he gave it to his lover, my cousin Elías, who hid it in the swan and kept it safe until I found it and smashed it. I rebuked my cousin gently in my mind. If he were listening, he should know he had been foolish. What if no one had ever smashed the swan? But I had, and I suppose I should be happy with that.

Mario grabbed my hand and squeezed. "You can stop thinking about it now, Tamara."

It was as if he knew what I was thinking.

"But there is the small detail that I did destroy the school," I said.

Laura was about to say something, but Rodolfo spoke first, "You do not have to worry about the damage, Tamara. I have donated enough money to them so they can repair it all."

"You did?" I said happily. "I –"

He put up his hand, "Let me finish. I have given them money, but not as much as I have donated to this new organization so that they can begin work – first and foremost – on the school across the street. And I will personally oversee the rebuilding of that school, which will include a new gym, auditorium, and pool - plus the stocking of new computers and other supplies. Once the school is rebuilt and the kids are back, I will also make sure they keep their word to train the men and women of Manchay in the jobs they want and need to rebuild the town and continue working into the future with their new skills."

"Rodolfo," Laura exclaimed.

"That is wonderful." I finished for her.

"Wow, Dad, that's terrific," Mario said.

Rodolfo turned to him and smiled. "Dad?"

Mario squirmed.

"It is wonderful," I said, "I am exonerated, and Manchay will be rebuilt. But Elías. I should have helped him, and I should have helped Señor Romero. I won't be able to forget –"

Laura and Rodolfo both made exclamations disclaiming my guilty feelings. But it was Mario who said, "You could not have saved either one of them. They died as a result of a force more powerful than you."

"It's true, Tamarita. We all like to think we have control of our lives, but in the end, Mother Nature and a higher power are the ones who guide our destinies," Laura said, hugging me.

I thought about that. Control. How much humans want it, work for it, fight for it, and believe they have it.

Mario's voice intruded into my philosophical thoughts. "You threw me at the town hall yesterday, Tamara. Don't get me wrong, I had a lot of fun, but it was confusing."

I relaxed and laughed. We were good again. That was going to help me get through so much of the trauma I had suffered. "I had to pass you that paper without anyone knowing. I knew you would do the right thing with it – I just needed a foolproof way to give it to you."

The adults smiled indulgently at me. I sighed. The next morning, I would be on my way back home to Chicago. Rodolfo was sending Mario back to Spain, but soon he would be coming to Chicago.

"Let us toast to the future," Laura said, raising her glass of Pisco. We all raised our glasses and drank.

I choked on mine, and they all laughed at me. I wiped my mouth with a napkin and looked up at the hills. In my imagination, I saw K'antu's shadow running carefree over the rolling dunes and heard the zing of a *macana* echoing through the rocky peaks of the Andes Mountains.

Epilogue

The woman sat behind a large, mahogany desk. She was old. Today she looked older still. Her reading glasses fell off her nose and bounced on her wrinkled chest. She shivered and closed her cardigan, buttoning it to the top.

"Winter is still here." She said to her companion.

"Indeed."

"Tamara is back with Laura?"

"Yes."

"She will be going back to the States? She won't be staying to look for K'antu?"

"I hear she leaves tomorrow."

She nodded and dismissed Tamara from her mind, "So word is there was a sighting on the coast?"

Joaquin leaned back in his chair and blew out a puff of smoke from his cigar.

"Yes. A young woman looking like K'antu was spotted near Caral."

The woman looked thoughtful. "Elías only had the one paper – isn't that right?"

Joaquin leaned forward. "It is."

"Then I think a trip to Caral is in order." She looked at him with narrowed eyes, "But this time, make sure you get what she took, and she doesn't escape – I don't care how you do it."

He stubbed out his cigar, nodded, and stood up to go.

Glossary

Ají - a pepper grown in Perú
Ají de gallina - chicken in a yellow pepper and peanut sauce
Artesanales - souvenir shops / craft shops
Ayllo -intertwined ropes with two or three stones at the end, used to swing or throw at enemies
Bodega - wine shop or warehouse; in this case part of the name of the Villanueva property
Butifarra - a typical Peruvian sandwich of ham and salsa
Criolla - an onion sauce with vinegar and ají
Cancha - dried, salted corn kernels
Cariño - a term of endearment, as in "darling"
Ceviche - raw fish marinated in lemon juice, topped with onions and rocoto, and served with cancha and sweet potato
Chicha morada - a drink made of purple corn infused with pineapple, cinnamon, and cloves
Chupe de camarones - Peruvian shrimp chowder

Colibrí - hummingbird
Doña Pepa - a vanilla flavored cookie covered with chocolate and round colored sprinkles
Huaraca - a sling
Huarango tree - a desert tree with a long tap root
Loma - an area of lush vegetation watered only by fog
Macana - a star-headed spear
Margaritas - a vanilla flavored cookie shaped like daisies
Marver - a steel work top used in glass blowing
Muro - wall
Nazca Lines - large rock designs on the desert floor - many so large they cannot be seen in entirety except from an airplane
Pacay - a cotton candy-like fruit in a pea pod casing
Paco - a dried form of cocaine paste
Picarones - pumpkin doughnuts with honey sauce
Pisco - a brandy made of grapes made in Perú
Primo / prima - cousin
Quebranta - a type of grape used to make fine brandies
Rocoto - a red, spicy pepper
Santa Rosa de Lima - the first person from any of the Americas to have been canonized as a saint
Shotgun house - houses with all the rooms on one side and a long hallway leading from the front door to the back door on the other side
Sublime - a chocolate bar with peanuts or almonds, made with real cane sugar - good for alleviating altitude sickness
Temblor - tremor, or in some cases, earthquake
Tequeño - the only Peruvian food that uses a tortilla, rolled up with various meat fillings, and served with avocado cream sauce

the Nazca people - a pre-Incan people of the coast of Perú
Tía - aunt
Tumi - an Incan ceremonial knife with a half-moon blade and carved handle
Verguenza - shame

Tremor on the Pyramid: Tamara's Peruvian Adventures
CHAPTER 1

"What's wrong, Piero?" I asked. I was back in Peru. Unbelievable after everything that had happened the last two times, I was here, but here I was. I didn't know this kid very well, but it seemed like Piero was always moody. Something about being an orphan and a rough upbringing. This time was different, though. This time he seemed nervous and a little scared.

"I have to go find Hugo." Hugo was an archaeology student like Piero and his best friend.

"Ok, let's go find him," I said. We were both leaning on a wall of the Central Pyramid. I stood, wiping sand off my back. "Maybe he's at the circular altar."

"Yeah," he perked up a little, "Ok, let's go."

The circular altar was up a set of ten stairs on the western side of one of the sprawling pyramids that led to a low circular wall. Inside of that, on the ground, was what used to be a hearth connected to underground ventilation ducts. The circle was about fifteen feet in diameter, with a doorway space built for only one person at a time to enter. It was open-air and probably always had been. Archaeologists knew that 5000 years ago, the people of the area had spent their time growing crops, making nets for fishing, and peacefully trading with other tribes in the vast area that was now broken down into Ecuador, Bolivia, and Perú. There was no evidence of weaponry or warfare in Caral that had been a surprising mystery to scientists.

As we got closer, dark shadows on the ground made me look up sharply.

Vultures were circling in the blue, almost cloudless sky.

"That's weird. Must be a dead animal in there." I said.

Piero looked even more worried. He made his way more quickly to the altar, got to the low walled entrance, and stopped short. A moment later, his face pale and his body racked with shaking, he stumbled over to dry heave down the stairs of the pyramid.

"Piero," I cried, "What happened?"

But he was bent over hacking, so I went to look for myself. Soon I was puking along with him. What he had seen in the Pyramid of the Circular Altar was the body of Hugo – his face still recognizable although its features were twisted in an expression of sheer horror. Blood covered the entire interior of the Circular Altar. The rest of Hugo's body had been completely skinned.

ABOUT THE AUTHOR

SURVIVING AN 8.1 STRENGTH EARTHQUAKE ATTRACTED A LOT OF ATTENTION. DUE TO LACK OF WILL TO REPEAT THE HORRORS OVER AND OVER, CRISTINA DECIDED TO WRITE ABOUT IT SO PEOPLE COULD JUST READ WHAT HAPPENED. THAT STORY CAN BE FOUND IN NEVER SHAKEN: TALES OF SURVIVAL.

OVER THE YEARS, AND BECAUSE SHE HAD ALWAYS WANTED TO WRITE A MYSTERY, THE STORY MORPHED INTO A YOUNG ADULT MYSTERY LOOSELY BASED ON HER EXPERIENCES BUT WITH MORE ACTION, ADVENTURE, AND MURDER: TREMOR IN THE HILLS. THE TREMOR SERIES ARE ALL BASED IN PERU, SOUTH AMERICA, WHERE THE EARTHQUAKE HAPPENED. LOOK FOR THE SECOND BOOK: TREMOR ON THE PYRAMID COMING SOON. CRISTINA HAS BEEN TO PERU 20+ TIMES AND HAS A LOVE/HATE RELATIONSHIP WITH THE COUNTRY.

SHE IS FLUENT IN SPANISH, LOVES DOGS, DANCING, TRAVELING, AND MEETING PEOPLE FROM ALL OVER THE WORLD. HER IDEAL JOB BESIDES AUTHOR IS TEACHING ENGLISH AS A SECOND LANGUAGE.

CRISTINA MATTA
TREMOR IN THE HILLS

Cristina Matta

SURVIVING AN 8.1 STRENGTH
EARTHQUAKE ATTRACTED A LOT OF
ATTENTION AND HER STORY CAN BE
FOUND IN
NEVER SHAKEN: TALES OF
SURVIVAL.

CRISTINA IS AVAILABLE
FOR BOOK CLUBS AND SPEAKING
ENGAGEMENTS.

CONTACT HER AT HER WEBSITE
WWW.TREMORINTHEHILLS.COM

CRISTINA MATTA
TREMOR IN THE HILLS

WWW.TREMORINTHEHILLS.COM